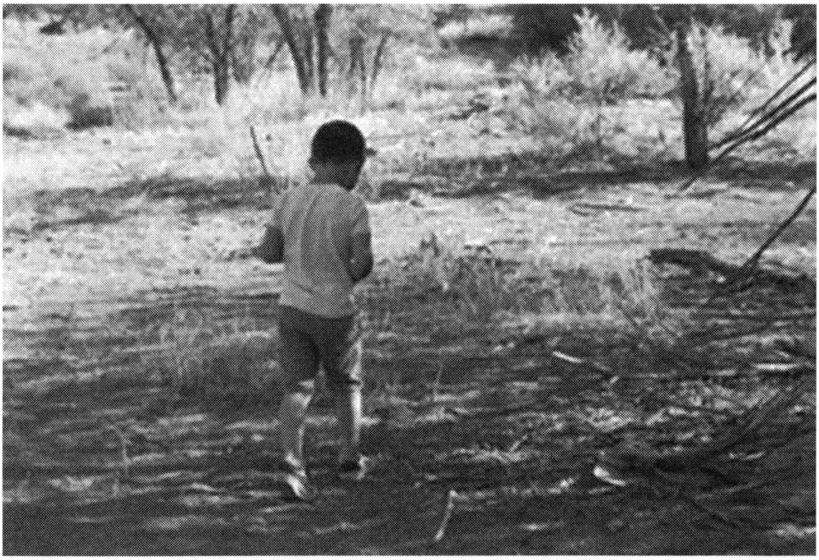

Setting down their packs and a very annoyed Jesus, they sat and caught their breath. It was time to reconnoiter. Far to the southeast, lightning was snapping against a bank of dark clouds. To the southwest, the sinking sun came and went as cloud fragments scuttled across it. Sifting the drought-fried dust through her fingers, Camilia narrowed her eyes at her husband. "So. You killed him, didn't you?"

Eduardo's mouth dropped open, then closed as he regarded his wife with adoring amusement. "Oh, Cam! Of course not! We should have, but you can't kill an ICE agent. We just gathered him up, lugged him to his car, and stuffed him in. Then I drove him a couple miles down the road toward Duz and Carmen's place and left him in his car while Nancy picked up the furniture, wiped up the blood and so-on."

Relieved but puzzled, Camilia said, "Why did you do that? Drive him away, I mean?"

"*Quién sabe?*" Eduardo shrugged. "It just seemed right. We thought if we got him away from there ... if he wakes up behind the wheel of his car, maybe he'll think he ran off the road and cracked his head. Maybe get him out of Nancy's, he'll forget what actually happened."

Camilia shuddered, looking back toward the road, and pulled her little son to her. "We can't go back. And we can't take Jesus."

This novel is a work of fiction. None of the characters herein are intended to be portrayals of any real person, living or dead, nor are any real events and places portrayed. All are products of the author's imagination and are used simply to tell a good story.

Also By This Author

All the Bad Stuff Comes in Threes

Baby Skulls and Fowl Odors

The Climbing Dog Affair

After the End: The Sumbally Fallacy

HIDDEN TREASURE
or
WHERE IS JESUS?

Karen Weinant Gallob

Karen W. Gallob

Earth Star Publications

Map Illustration by Rita Clagett
Photography by Brian Matus
Cover Design by Ann Ulrich Miller
Model for little Jesus: Tyson Juarez

*For Nancy,
I hope you enjoy this book!!
Love, Aunty Karen*

HIDDEN TREASURE
(or)
WHERE IS JESUS?

Karen Weinant Gallob

Earth Star Publications
P.O. Box 267
Eckert, CO 81418
www.earthstarpublications.com

FIRST EDITION

October 2018

Copyright © 2018 by Karen Weinant Gallob
All Rights Reserved

This book may not be reproduced in whole, or in part, by digital or mechanical, or by any other means, without the express written consent of the author. For information, address Earth Star Publications (www.earthstarpublications.com), e-mail: *starbeacon@gmail.com*

ISBN 978-0-944851-57-9

Printed in the United States of America

This book is dedicated to

Juan Ramon and Maricela,
Cassandra, Alexis, and Maria

As well as our other neighbors and friends,
those who courageously overcome prejudice,
danger, and capricious legal obstacles,
hoping to gain freedom and safety in America
for themselves and their children.

Ramon and Maricela's story is gripping,
but it is private. The story you are about to read
in these pages is fiction, true only in so far as fiction
inevitably contains its own inherent truths.
Those truths, I think, you will recognize as you read.

I would not creep along the coast, but steer
Out in mid-sea, by guidance of the stars.
— George Elliott, *Middlemarch*, 1871

Main Characters

You didn't think there would be just a few, did you? This is a typical, interwoven, rural community, after all!

Sheriff Pat Garrett — Darn those bad guys! The sheriff would much rather focus on beautiful Jenny, but what must be done, must be done, and he is good at it.

Deputy Leigh McCracken — This fiery redhead with freckles on her freckles doesn't let anyone mess with the mojo of her boss, Sheriff Garrett.

Antonio (Toño) Jorge Romero Suré — He probably did the right thing, but now he has to take the consequences.

Jesus — Toño's little brother: where is he?

Eduardo — Toño's dad, who claims to have left the past behind.

Camilia — Toño's mom, who shows us that we don't always know our neighbor.

Nancy Jane Barnswallowper — A woman of strong principles and many guns.

Alma Weinant — How can we know what's in that mysterious old mind?

Gus Westberg — This old boy embodies a surprising history.

Tess Westberg — She would do anything for her dear husband, Gus.

Gordy Smith — Grandson to Gus and Tess, he plays Fortnite; he loves his granny's home cookin', and he has a lot of heart.

Paul Frickleson — It's not just his theft of water that makes everyone he meets hate him.

Katelyn Corbit — Toño's girlfriend, a tall, willowy blonde who will inherit much more now that her sister is dead.

Jenny Threewinds — The sheriff's fiancée, she knows how to look under the surface of a suspect's psyche.

Lew Harris — His memory might be going, causing him to mix up a fact or two, but the compassion at his core will be there forever.

Lucky — Lew's dog. Kind of. He's not so easy to spot, but you might see him if you take a close look at the map.

Roy Plover — A mean S.O.B. Greedy, too.

Frankie Belle Corbit — She's ready to turn over a new leaf and head for Vegas.

Mickey Rippe — He meant no harm. All he did was love Frankie Belle and recognize the truth about his wicked daughter.

Nola Rippe — Mickey's daughter, who will never be nominated for mother of the year.

Syd and Spook — Nola's kids.

Jim Patchit — This rumble-voiced old chap seems to have found love at last.

Percy Bush — Really? Is that his name?

Supporting Cast

Edith (pronounced A-*deet*) **Ovieda**—secretary and all-around person, she holds the sheriff's office together.

Detective Hobbs—May be packing donuts instead of a six-pack, but this guy is fast on his feet when necessary.

Deputy Louie—Uses her skills as mother of many to excellent advantage.

Deputy Red—Good lookin' guy; McCracken's main squeeze.

Tiffany Gallenas—Single mom, paramedic, always in the thick of things.

Larry—Tiffany's youngest, his kindness sometimes forces Tiffany to make tough choices. Part of teen squad.

Pewter—Larry's girlfriend, part of teen squad.

Cesar—Astute part of the teen squad.

Duz, Carmen, and Gritty—Alma's family

Doc and Annabelle Clary—Local veterinarian and wife.

And so-on ... So, let's get started.

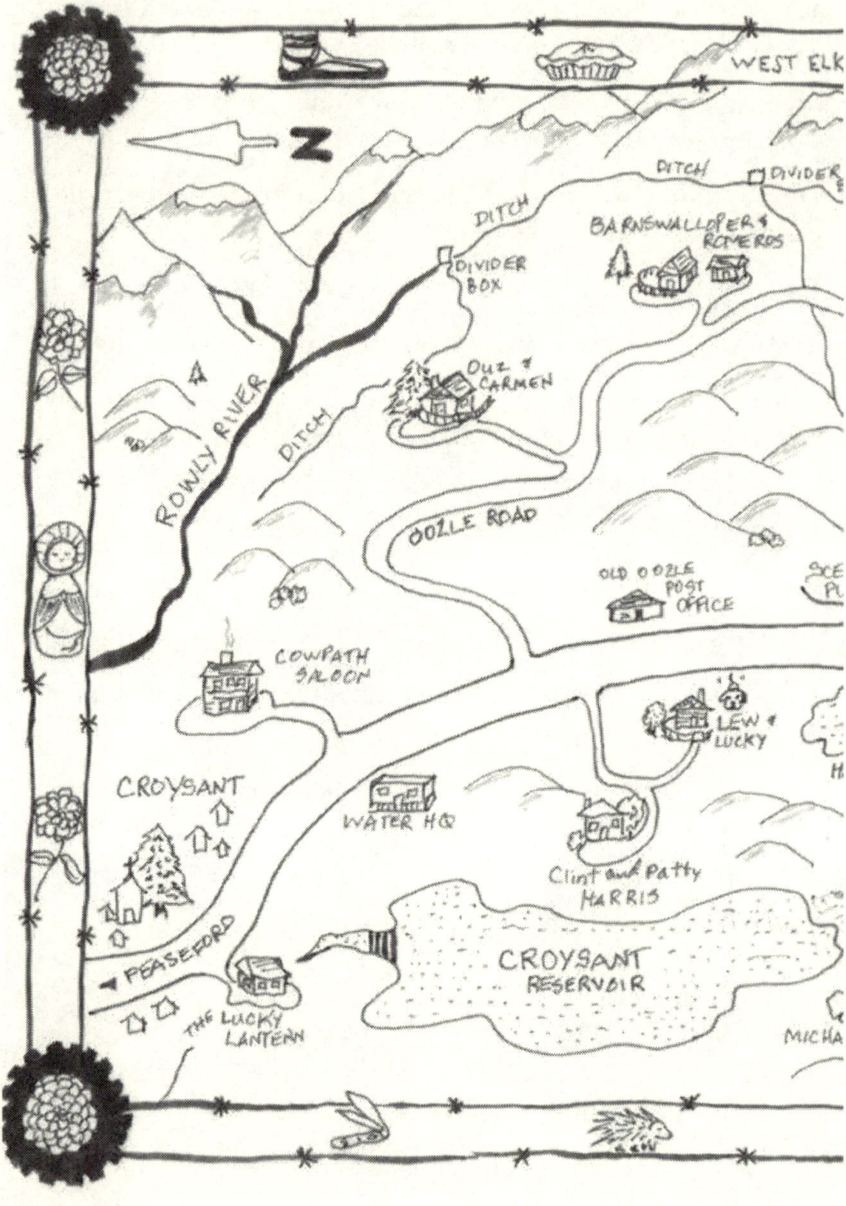
WEST ELK
DITCH
DIVIDER
BARNSWALLOPERS & ROMEROS
DITCH
DIVIDER BOX
OUZ & CARMEN
ROWLY RIVER
DITCH
OOZLE ROAD
OLD OOZLE POST OFFICE
COWPATH SALOON
LEW & LUCKY
CROYSANT
WATER HQ
Clint and Patty HARRIS
PEASEFORD
THE LUCKY LANTERN
CROYSANT RESERVOIR

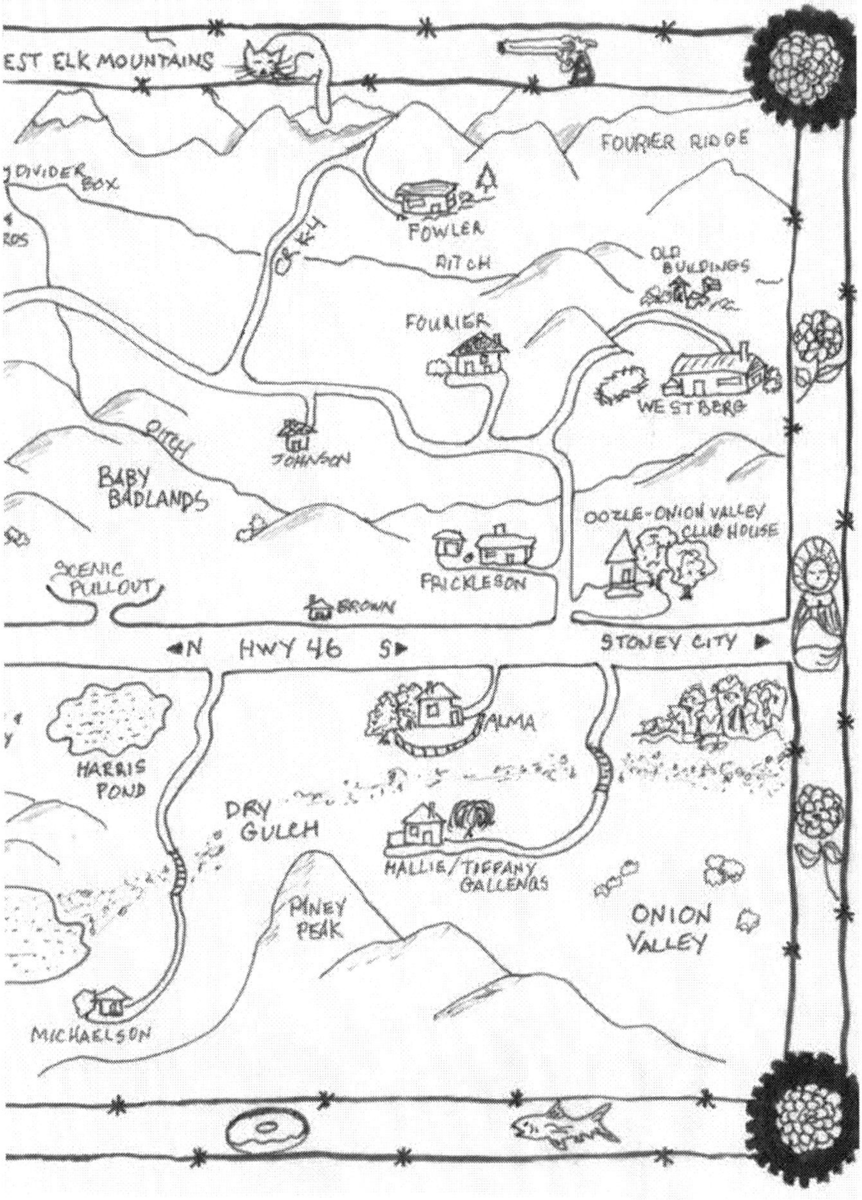

EST ELK MOUNTAINS
FOURIER RIDGE
DIVIDER BOX
CR K-4
FOWLER
DITCH
OLD BUILDINGS
FOURIER
WESTBERG
JOHNSON
DITCH
BABY BADLANDS
OOZLE-ONION VALLEY CLUB HOUSE
FRICKLESON
SCENIC PULLOUT
BROWN
◄N HWY 46 S►
STONEY CITY ►
ALMA
HARRIS POND
DRY GULCH
HALLIE/TIFFANY GALLENAS
PINEY PEAK
ONION VALLEY
MICHAELSON

1

The Romeros Escape

Antonio Jorge Romero Suré loved to run. If he hadn't been so scared, this would have been the best part of his day. The evening air was cool; huge, bruised storm clouds closed in on the southeast, sending remnants over the glittering western sun. Darkness would come early, but right now it was still light enough to force him off the road to jog where he would be unseen, dropping into the curves of the hills, winding his way through sage and rabbit brush. With each footfall he cursed. "The dirty bastard. The dirty, sneaky bastard."

His family had been anxious for a long time, worried about the arrival of an ICE agent. As it was, Immigration and Customs Enforcement had sent someone even worse, even more sinister than they had feared. His eyes were hard behind dark glasses. A thick, brush mustache covered his upper lip, but the rest of his face was shaved clean. He appeared to be bald until you noticed a heavy pony tail dropping out of his duck-billed hat in the back. The pony tail was dark, but the eyebrows were faded blond, his face pale. The hat said ICE, and the uniform jacket also said ICE, followed by the threatening label, POLICE. He looked mean. Toño thought, 'Joe Arpaio.' This guy, too, had a stocky build, a bullish neck that suggested strong muscles under the uniform. There was something just wrong about him. Crooked. Then the guy said, "Look, you wet-backs. We can make this easy. A thousand bucks fixes it. I can easy make this trouble go away—

just a thousand bucks."

At this, Toño gritted his teeth and thought, "Well, yeah, duh. There you go. This guy is as crooked as a scrub oak." He could see that his parents were also gauging the situation. Their family documents weren't in order. He himself wasn't yet DACA. He wasn't sure what his folks did to navigate legal requirements. At this point, their boss, Nancy Jane Barnswallowper, just looked furious, ready to fight. His mom was clutching Jesus closer to her leg, but Toño said, "Yeah, sure. Why not? I'll get it."

The agent's hand hovered near the pocket of his uniform coat, like he maybe had a gun there, and his face was a smirk. Toño could see Nancy Jane's eyes going to the corner of the kitchen, where she always kept one of her .22's propped by the door. Nancy loved guns; they were all over the house, and that one, Toño knew, was loaded. Eduardo and Camilia had pulled Jesus with them into a defensive stance behind the kitchen table. Eduardo looked as if he was debating throwing one of the chairs, but Toño felt his own brain running clear and cool. He hadn't spent hours in shop classes and sports for nothing. Holding up an admonishing hand, he said, "Just take it easy, everybody. I'll get the money."

Edging across the kitchen, his eye on the ICE man, he pointed to the shelf above the sink, nodding and appeasing. "Our safe," he said. "Our savings are in this little safe." He'd made that safe in shop class, and he was proud of it. He and Mr. Plummer had been heads together on the design for weeks. It was rock solid; it wouldn't be an easy safe to crack. Turning now, he even managed a smile as he said, "Of course, you'll need to have the key to get this open." With that he raised his arms and, using everything he had, thinking about a good, fast ball over first base, thinking about that, the pitch that made the groupie girls tag behind him at school—with all that strength, he threw the safe. It hit his target, right above the ICE agent's left eye, and the man crumpled.

Jesus began to wail and Camilia knelt beside him. "Shh, shh, *esta bien, mijo*. Hush now." Nancy Jane grabbed her rifle in one swoop, then pushed past the table to kneel by the flattened agent. Looking up, she said, "Son of a bitch is still alive, just kookoo.

Hidden Treasure (or) Where is Jesus?

You people better get out of here for now, while I figure what to do."

Eduardo grunted. "Camilia, get the packs." This, Toño now realized, was what brought the seriousness of the situation home to him. For as long as he could remember, his folks had thought of themselves as American. They called themselves Cammy and Ed, not Camilia and Eduardo. Now he stood by the door in a daze, hearing his dad call his mom 'Camilia,' watching Nancy Jane bring out a cargo of guns and ammunition. His mother was putting the packs they had prepared on the table, saying, "Hush, now, Suso, hush, honey," and when his little brother continued to fuss, she snapped, "Jesus, you be quiet now," leaning heavily on the Spanish pronunciation of the name, *'hay-soos.'*

It was one thing to lob the safe; it was another thing to know what he should do next. Toño stood speechless, eyes half-focused on the big tattoo on his father's heavy biceps, trying to think. The tattoo was for his mother, a camellia, the delicate pink petals portrayed as shading to black toward the center. Within the forest of green leaves surrounding the flower was a pair of huaraches. They symbolized his mother's heritage. The tattoo was so well done that you could tell the huarache soles were traditional, made of tire rubber. Although it wasn't visible right now, he knew his mother also honored his father's heritage with a tattoo. On her back, on the shoulder, were three sassy, grinning chihuahuas, each wearing a large sombrero and a serape, all enclosed in a big, red heart. Each sombrero had a name on it: Eduardo, Antonio, and Jesus. His mama's men. Those tattoos were there because of love and family. Would some cop turn it around now and find some way to claim they were a gang brand?

Camellias, their petals fragile and short-lived, symbolize mortality. Toño shivered. Some form of reality was trying to reach him. Nancy Jane was pushing a pistol toward him, saying, "… and you take this one, kid."

"Uh, no, I don't think … "

"Take it, Toño. You might need it." This from his father. The words struck Toño as odd. There was something missing from the voice, something that had always been there before, something light and normal and hopeful. Toño put his hand out for the gun, meeting his father's eyes.

"We'll follow the original plan," Eduardo said. "You lose yourself, Antonio, until you know for sure it's safe. Then find us. See what's needed." He stepped across the room and put his hand on Toño's shoulder. "I know you, son. I know you'll use your head."

Suddenly the room was quiet. Jesus, no longer whimpering, looked from face to worried face, dark eyes huge. Eduardo spoke again. "We need to get going. Where is it, Toño?"

Toño knew at once that he meant the ticket. "It's in a little Jesus figure thing, over at Alma's."

"Alma's!" Eduardo was surprised, then he grinned, pleased. "Of course, Alma's. You *diablos pequeños!* It's very safe there! So. You go now, *mi hijo – sé valiente.*" He gave Toño a gentle, fatherly shove, and as the boy stumbled toward the door, he heard his father say, "You and Jesus start, too, Camilia."

"*Pero tu, papi?*"

Toño turned from the door to see his father gesture toward the still figure of the ICE agent. "I'll just help Ms. Barnswallower clean up this mess here. Wait by the south 40." Glancing up, he saw Toño hesitating at the door. "Get going, Toño. I mean it. Nothing else here concerns you." His voice was sharp. Toño looked away, then dropped down the rough board steps and slipped into the sultry air of the early August evening.

Where the hell was he supposed to be going? In his head, his dad's voice, annoyed, said, "Look, *muchacho*, if we told you where to hide, you wouldn't be hidden, would you? This isn't a game now!" Jogging just out of sight of the road, dodging brush, listening for vehicles, he thought, "No, not a game," and he felt scared and lonely. "How could they put so much responsibility on me? I'm really just a kid." The word 'game' reminded him that it was Thursday night, football night. He should be home, peacefully watching the pre-season Bronco game. The fact that something so simple had been torn from his life made him angry again, and the anger did him good. It washed over the other pain, the fear and the shock. He stopped, narrowed his eyes, clenched his fists, took stock of where he was, getting his bearings.

Hidden Treasure (or) Where is Jesus?

He was getting sick of dodging the brush, and had already torn his shirt crawling through one of the numerous barbed wire fences. He knew that Oozle Road was to his right; it exited Highway 46 at the community house, curved up toward the mountains, then circled back around, joining 46 again across from the Croysant Reservoir. As it made its way around the curve, lanes and driveways connected it to the local ranch houses. Pushing aside brush and making his way to the top of the nearest hill, he could see one of those ranch lanes winding through a stand of cottonwoods below him. He knew whose ranch that went to, and he couldn't imagine that ICE bastard starting there to look for him. It was just an old couple that owned it; they wouldn't even have to know he was there. He'd hide nearby until he could get his head straight.

Squaring his shoulders, he dropped down the hill to the ranch lane. This would beat fighting the sage and the uneven ground. Winds high above him moved the western clouds, covering and uncovering the sun, masking and unmasking the cluster of cottonwoods hugging the lane. He slipped into their dappled shadow. It was beautiful here. Toño thought about how everyone he knew who lived around here called this part of the world "God's Country." Once, his grandfather had been sick, and Toño made the long trip south with his mother to visit him. His mother told him they would be in a place called the Copper Canyon. It was long ago, and he was very small, but he remembered that there were still the fearful things, the visas and papers, to fuss over. He recalled some stranger coming by, saying something about counterfeit work costing a lot, and his dad handing the guy money. His dad tried to kid around, telling Toño, "We gotta get you and your mom back," but even then he could tell it was serious. Now, leaning against a cottonwood, he recalled Copper Canyon, recalled playing in the dust with other kids that Camilia told him were his cousins. Everyone there was as brown as his mom; they wore huaraches, like she did, and lots of them wore some kind of skirts. He thought he remembered that even some of the men wore some kind of short skirts. Maybe like the Scottish guys. Maybe they were kilts.

He had one memory that stood out, probably because

of how his mom acted when she called him over. He recalled that his mom was way weepy-throated. She said, "Take your *abuelo* some beer," and he had carried it to the old man; beer in a jar, it was. The grandfather wasn't husky like his dad, but frail, sinewy, and whisper-voiced. Even so, when he told Toño, "You sit and listen," Toño, who did not know his grandfather's language, understood and knew he must obey. The old man spoke, and someone … was it a cousin? Someone sat next to him and translated the ancient words. He told Toño about God. He said, "You know this is true. Our people do not lie. Here is how it was, grandson. You must know this. You must know this from me, before I leave you.

"God, the God you know as the father of *Sukristo*, that God worked with his big brother, who is the Devil. God and the Devil created the world together. When they created the people, God used pure clay for his creation, and he created us, the Raramuri. Meanwhile, the Devil mixed white ash with the clay he used, and he created the Chabochi. You understand, grandson? The Chabochi—all the others. You must understand that it was God who gave us life, who gave the Raramuri life, and who even now protects us, and that it was the Devil who gave life to the others, the Chabochi. The Devil protects them and loves them, just as God loves us. God and the Devil are brothers, so sometimes they disagree, maybe even fight, but together they make this world. This is true. I am Raramuri, and cannot lie. Now you are Raramuri, also, and will always speak the truth. You will tell this story, which is true."

Now that he thought about it, after all these years, Toño found this whole story to be really puzzling. Would his *abuelo*, if he were still alive, call this "God's Country" or the "Devil's Country" or what? Feeling grim, he started on up the road, not jogging now but trudging.

Leaving the shelter of the cottonwoods, he plodded up the next hill. At the top, the road curved, then led down a short driveway to the main ranch house, beyond which lay corrals and a pasture containing a dozen or so head of cattle. Toño knew the rest of the ranch's cattle would be up on high mountain pasture; these had been kept nearby for some reason, maybe to take to market. To his right, on the hilltop, was an area with several buildings. He turned and walked toward them. Maybe this was the original homestead, but it was clearly not inhabited now. Like all the old buildings around here, these were sinking back into the earth, time gradually reducing them to weathered boards and rubble.

An old, open-faced tin shed housed a usable tractor, an ancient Bronco, and a pile of dry straw. A rickety two-horse trailer sat in the middle of the lot, and north of it a log structure was in the process of caving in over a root cellar that had been given cement steps at one time. Shining his phone light into the door of the log structure, he could see plywood, broken glass, and drywall scattered willy-nilly on the floor as if dropped there by a tornado. The sun was almost down; lights were going on in the ranch house below him. The cloud bank to the southeast was ominously black, with splinters of lightning crackling across it. Sighing, he walked over to squat near the horse trailer and contemplate the ugly old log building in front of him. It must have been the original settler's home. It looked spooky. He couldn't resist another longing look at the white frame house at the foot of the hill, which now had many windows giving off a rosy, grandmotherly glow. Turning back to consider the settler home, he knew, but didn't want to know, that it might be a perfect hiding place. Was it locked? The last of the sun was sending a sharp reflection off the door window, and he shaded his eyes, trying to see. He hoped it was locked. He would just go sleep in the shed in the straw, which would be more vulnerable, but ... but he didn't want to be a chicken shit. His folks were counting on him. They expected him to hide, to be serious about the hiding.

In a few short strides he closed the distance from the trailer to the door of the old house and found, to his dismay, that it had no lock, although it had warped with the weather and required a hefty push to convince it to open. It opened with a grinding sound and a deposit of dirt from the ceiling above his head. He found himself staring into one large room, no inner walls, filled with old couches, washing machines, car parts, bed springs, tarps, glass shards, and just junk, in general. It crossed his mind that he had uncovered a treasure trove for the TV show, "American Pickers." Again, he turned on his phone light and made to step in and look around when a very large mouse ... no, a packrat ... shot across his foot. "Ugh," he grunted, shrinking back. "No way. Not tonight. I'll take the straw." He had just backed out onto the step, his hand on the door latch, when the whole area behind him lit up completely, a deadly crackle of lightning followed instantly by the eardrum smashing thunk of mountain thunder, close enough, loud enough to feel it had cracked his skull. Toño leaped into the center of the old settler house, the Chabochi house, and stood shaking as lightning lit up the room again and again, showing him broken windows, strange tongs and saws, cans of dried paint, a ladder half suspended from the ceiling, a floor of broken cement chunks, everything appearing and disappearing with each violent flash, while outside the Devil, the white man's God, spoke in roaring thuds, thundering against the logs, terrifying and angry.

2

Eduardo and Camilia Agree on a Plan

The issue was Jesus. They agreed that he must be hidden at once. They did not agree as to where he should be hidden.

Lugging two of the backpacks and her justifiably cranky three-year-old, Camilia had worked her way south on Oozle Road until she reached County Road K-4, by the Barnswallowper south 40, then she slipped into a cluster of tall sage and rabbit brush, the rabbit brush sporting its yellow late-summer flowers. She hunkered down, soothing Jesus and anxiously watching back the way she had come. It seemed an eternity. Finally Eduardo appeared. He was careless, she thought, trotting over the hill right on the road, in plain sight, his early years with the cartel maybe making him a little too macho. She sighed and stepped from her cover, making a soft sound, barely audible. "*Venga aquí.*" Seeing her, Eduardo nodded and grinned, slipping into the sage beside her.

"Papa!" Jesus burst out, but Camilia said, "Hush, Chucho." They picked up the packs and Eduardo hoisted Jesus, at first carrying him casually, using one hand to prop him against his hip, the kid dangling horizontally sideways, like a wriggling pup. Then, in response to Jesus's grunts, he brought him on up to be draped across his shoulder.

They headed west into the area Eduardo always called the Baby Badlands, a short expanse of rough terrain so rumpled with bare dobie hills and cut by intermittent arroyos that the nearby ranchers ignored them, deeming them fit for neither livestock nor legal crops, although it was known that illicit stills had been hidden there during prohibition, and now community gossip suggested that "someone else" was probably growing marijuana there under a well-hidden overhang or two. Within a few minutes the little family had reached a dry gulch well out of view of any road or habitation. Setting down their packs and an annoyed Jesus, they themselves sat and caught their breath. It was time to reconnoiter. Far to the southeast, lightning was snapping against a bank of dark clouds. To the southwest, the sinking sun came and went as cloud fragments scuttled across it. Sifting the drought-fried dust through her fingers, Camilia narrowed her eyes at her husband. "So. You killed him, didn't you?"

Eduardo's mouth dropped open, then closed as he regarded his wife with adoring amusement. "Oh, Cam! Of course not! We should have, but you can't do that. We just gathered him up, lugged him to his car, and stuffed him in. Then I drove him a couple miles down the road toward Duz and Carmen's place and left him in his car while Nancy picked up the furniture, wiped up the blood and so-on."

Relieved but puzzled, Camilia said, "Why did you do that? Drive him away, I mean?"

"*Quién sabe?*" Eduardo shrugged. "It just seemed right. We thought if we got him away from there ... if he wakes up behind the wheel of his car, maybe he'll think he ran off the road and cracked his head. Maybe get him out of Nancy's, he'll forget what actually happened."

Camilia shuddered, looking back toward the road, and pulled Jesus to her. "We can't go back."

Eduardo shook his head ruefully. "Not till we get it all straightened out again."

Looking grim, Camilia said, "So here I am, back in the desert with a little kid, just like when I came through with Toño. I hate this. But now we have to hide Jesus."

"We'll just take him to Lew Harris, like we agreed."

"You agreed, Eddie. I didn't agree to Lew Harris. We talked, and I told you Lew is crazy and I wanted Jesus somewhere else."

"Lew isn't crazy. He's just a little older, is all. And he's got that quirk." Eduardo stood, impatient.

"Right. Some quirk—he's a dotty old man that sees ghosts."

"No, he doesn't."

"Yes, he does. First he thought his dead wife was alive, going everywhere with him, and then he forgot her and started thinking he had a dog, but there isn't any dog there."

Eduardo smiled fondly, considering what Camilia had just said to be a good description of the rather endearing traits of his old friend. Camilia snapped, "Ed! He won't even know whether Chuy is real or not."

Chuckling, Eduardo responded, "It wouldn't matter. He takes better care of invisible Lucky than most people take care of their real dogs. He's got the kindest heart of about anybody I know."

Camilia was getting really angry. "Jesus is not a dog; he is a little boy. And he is a real boy. You need to get serious."

Sobering, Eduardo said, "Okay. Where do *you* want to hide him?"

"I ..." Camilia began, and felt herself deflate. She didn't want to hide her son anywhere. She just wanted him with her, and she had never been able to think clearly about the 'what if' question: what if they had to hide their baby? Her voice shaky and she murmured lamely, "Corbits'?"

Sitting down next to her and taking her chin in his palm, Eduardo said gently, "I'm afraid it will be one of the first places they'll look." He kissed her cheek. "And Corbits are older, too. As old as Lew. They've been good to us, and they would try really hard to keep Jesus safe, but it is asking too much. The thing is, the bastard isn't likely to look at Lew's."

When they argued, it helped to change the subject. Camilia lowered her head, said, "I can't believe that creep wanted money. He acted like we could buy him off."

11

"Yeah, he was crooked. I wonder ... looks like he could get money from us, then just keep up the blackmail. Maybe it's something he does a lot."

"He had us cornered," Camilia said. "I'm glad Toño threw that safe, but now I'm worried about him. Where do you suppose he went?"

"He may be in a hell of a fix if we can't get this all figured out." Eduardo was thoughtful, his face worried. "You know what was weird about the creep—he even handed me a business card. I didn't know government agents actually carried cards. Like he was on some kind of ego trip." Eduardo pulled the card from his pocket to show her. It read: Roy Plover, Special Agent. Immigration and Customs Enforcement.

Camilia poked at the card thoughtfully. "I don't think he could hurt us if we could get some papers in order. Toño could apply for DACA, and you had that friend who was good at ... at ... " She didn't want to say the words. 'Faking documents.'

Eduardo's head went into his hands. "DACA. Then they'd have us in all their records, and it wouldn't take them any time at all to figure out that we belong across the border. Maybe we do. The damn politicians keep changing the rules. I don't trust our government here anymore."

"Well, speaking of cards, don't forget that card I got from Flor, about the Denver lawyer." She unzipped a pocket in her backpack and pulled out a business card with a 'BL' logo surrounded by leaves, all in a pleasant rustic color. The print said: Bridger Law Offices, p.C., Specialists in Family Action for Immigration Law, this followed by an address in Denver, phone and fax numbers, and a website.

Eduardo took the card, turning it over and over in his fingers. All he said was, "Flor. Right."

"Yeah, Flor. She's my friend, like that damn Lew Harris is your friend. She knows stuff. And she says that lawyer, sometimes he will help without charging so much. Sometimes he doesn't charge anything when he sees you are poor."

Continuing to turn the card, Eduardo made a face. Jesus wiggled against Camilia's leg and emitted a tired snore. They both looked up, realizing that the sun was going and that dusk had changed the face of the terrain around them, filling it with deep shadows. Eduardo sighed. "Did Nancy Jane put guns in all these packs?"

"You know Nancy Jane. They'll all be loaded, too."

"Tell you what. Let me get Lew to hide Chucho just for a few days, and I'll let you see if you can reach this Bridger outfit."

"You'll let me?" Camilia was being sarcastic, one of the little mini-challenges about power that occur in marriages.

"Camilia! You know what I mean."

Now it was her turn to be silent. Finally, Eduardo said, "We gotta go—you know, I'm not sure that guy was completely unconscious by the time we stuffed him in the car. I think he was coming to. He held on to Toño's safe, clutched at it like he knew what he was doin'."

"So he has the safe?! With the money we were saving for Toño's college?"

"I had to let him have it. I was afraid if he felt me pulling it loose it would get him completely awake. I think Toño has the key, anyhow."

"I thought he said that the key was at Alma's."

"No, Toño meant that him and his buddies hid my lottery ticket at Alma's. We gotta go there now and be sure where it is, then we can leave it awhile. And we can call Lew from there." The look he gave Camilia was questioning.

Camilia stood and hefted her pack. "You know I can't call that lawyer. The ICE people could trace me if I use my phone."

Eduardo looked at her thoughtfully. "Yeah," he said. "I know. I guess we better ditch our phones."

3

Plover Finds Jesus

Roy Plover didn't knock. The night was dark as a witch's teat, so the old lady should be in bed and sound asleep. The door wasn't locked — doors never were in this Godforsaken country — and he barged into the house, crossing an entry area, then patting the walls of the living room for a light switch.

The switch triggered a bright overhead light which revealed antique wooden china cabinets, some bookshelves, and various shadow boxes, all laden with assorted knick-knacks. His eyes darted around, exploring the room with the experience of a person used to looking for items of value owned by other people. He knew he was looking for a Jesus figure. He'd gone in and out of consciousness after the safe whacked him and he had heard Toño say, "It's in a little Jesus figure thing, over at Alma's." Before he passed back out, he'd heard Eduardo say something in Spanish, and something about "safe." They had to have been referring to the key, the key to the safe. He knew he would need it; when he regained consciousness, he had struggled with the safe door and seen that it wasn't going to yield easily. Now, however, he felt a little ill, the surplus of figurines, mementos, and photos covering every spare surface made his aching head swim.

He had to start somewhere. Taking a tentative step toward the nearest cabinet, his eye caught a movement to his left. He wasn't alone. Alma was sitting right there, in a large recliner, staring up at him. Neither was more surprised than the other.

Hidden Treasure (or) Where is Jesus?

Plover spoke first. "What are you doing here?"

Alma's stare had become increasingly suspicious. "Well, I live here, young man. What are *you* doing here?" There was no alarm in her statement. Her voice was slow. It had a weighted quality, heavy with her long years of lived experience. She gave one a sense that not much would surprise her anymore.

Trying to get his wits about him, Plover watched Alma's hands grope at the front of her nightie, and he realized that she was searching for her medic alert button. Shit. Not now. He didn't need her to call someone now. He started talking, anxious to distract her from her search for the button. "Alma," he said. "It's okay. I'm just a government agent. You know, like the F.B.I." He held out a Roy Plover business card to her. Taking the card stopped her hand from the search. He continued to gabble. "We are ... we're looking for something. Somebody told us it was here—something a bad guy hid here. I thought you'd be asleep in your bedroom, and I didn't want to bother you ... uh, not wake you. I just thought I'd check for it, then I could leave quiet and all. Not disturb you."

Alma was thoughtfully patting the arm of the big recliner. "Duz gave me this chair."

Looking at the chair, Plover tried to make the connection. He would rather have liked to knock the old gal in the head and get on with his search, but he restrained himself, considering consequences. "Uh ... nice chair."

"Yes, you're right. Far too expensive. But everything this day and age is too expensive. And I like this for sleeping. But Gritty is like you. She says I belong in bed."

Alma gave a soft harumph. "My daughter, you know. Gritty. Big fusser."

Plover searched for a response, but Alma wasn't done. "Duz and Carmen. They may be frivolous, but at least they are thoughtful." Plover tried again to enter the conversation, but she had fixed him with an icy glare. "Not like you, young man. Nobody should be sneaking into an old lady's house in the middle of the night without knocking. Duz would never do that—I raised him right. He's a good son. Didn't your mother teach you any manners? Maybe it's you who is the bad guy."

"Look, lady, I just ... I'm sorry. But did somebody hide ... I need to know. Did somebody hide something here? A bad guy, maybe a kid, like a delinquent, did he hide something ...?" He finished lamely.

"Just think. You could have woke up the baby. At first the poor little tyke was too tired to sleep. Little Jesus." She gave it the Spanish pronunciation: 'hay-soos.' "I love babies. But we had to do a lot of cuddling to get him to drift off. Haven't you ever been too tired to sleep?"

Plover didn't actually feel tired. It was just that his head above his left eye had begun to give gigantic, vessel-breaking throbs. He couldn't take much more of this. The old girl was rambling. Had to be dementia. Turning away from Alma, he looked shakily around the room again. From behind him he heard Alma say, "You're actually the only bad guy to show up here. The boys that came, they're my friends. They come all the time. What they hid, they put in the Jesus. And you leave it alone. It's not your business."

Just then Plover's eyes, roaming across the excess of assorted bric-a-brac everywhere, caught on a dusty Christmas creche toward the back of one of the noble, old-fashioned cabinets. Sure enough, Jesus was sitting there on his mother's knee, arms out, smiling beatifically at one and all. "Ah." Plover grunted with relief, but as he reached out to pick up the holy figurine, a loud, male voice filled the room.

"Yes, Alma, what is it? Can we help?"

Replying in an offended tone, Alma said, "There is a strange man right here in my house, going through my things. I think he is a bad guy. You need to call Duz. Tell him to bring his gun."

She'd pushed the damn life alert button. Plover snatched up Jesus and made for the door.

4

Toño Weathers the Storm

The storm kept him in the center of the eerie room. Time stopped. Lightning flashes became motionless, an unrelenting constant. The rhythm of his heartbeat rocked his whole body, and his skin crackled as thunder forced its invasion of the living world. He couldn't breathe. Then, just as abruptly as it started, it was gone. Progressing westward, it morphed into something fit for a newscaster, a distant weather phenomenon, rattling down the thirsty valley and carelessly scattering a few spare and stingy drops of water behind it.

Toño expelled his breath and flexed his stiff fingers. Without lightning the room was pitch black. Worried about running down his phone battery, he reached for his Swiss army tool. His dad teased him when he bought it, but he loved the low price he got and all the stuff he could mess with on the thing. In addition to a penlight, it had a knife, bottle opener, pliers, screw driver, and saw blade, all in just three nonintrusive inches to be carried in a handy scabbard on his belt. "Ay, *chico duro*," his dad had said. "You think the buck you shoot gonna be so tiny you can skin it out with that thing?" Recalling, he tried to smile again at the joke, but his lips had gone stiff in his face. Instead, he fumbled at the tool, released the tiny light, and turned it on. It didn't show much. He snorted. Of course, his dad had been right, as usual.

He thought he recalled the family putting in better lights as they prepared their packs. The room felt filthy to him; he didn't want to set his pack down in the dirt, mouse droppings, and whatever other unseen, gross, possibly liquid, thing might be on the floor, so he stood, held the pack, and grappled with it in the dark, patting and trying to feel what they had crammed into the various pockets. The strenuous search helped calm him, and he remembered which zipper they had opened to pack the LED light. Trying not to drop stuff, he dug it out, and as he did his hand brushed plastic. Ah ha! An idea! They'd pushed plastic trash bags in any remaining spaces, thinking they might serve as survival gear, like makeshift raincoats, for example. Well, too late for that now, but how about this? Poking around, he got a couple of the sacks out. He put his backpack in one. Now he felt safe to set it on the creepy floor. Next he shone the LED light around the room. A ragged, grayish couch frumped in the middle facing him and the door. Yeah, that would be right. He wanted his face to the door and his back to ... well, to the wall, like a mafia kingpin expecting betrayal by the mob. Whatever. At least he knew he wanted to see whoever or whatever might try to come in that door.

Spreading garbage bags over the couch, he tucked them in. There. That should protect his sorry ass from Chabochi ash or whatever else might be on that thing. Sinking tiredly onto the couch, his backpack beside him, he started to cast his light around the room when he heard the unmistakable sound of an approaching vehicle.

Once more he must freeze, his light off, staring helplessly into the dark. The thing came closer, probably not a truck, maybe an ATV. He tensed, gripping the light, ready to shine it in someone's eyes. Then the thing seemed to top the hill and go past the complex of old buildings where he was hiding, continuing down the lane, the sound fading as it went in the direction of the ranch house. Frantically he tried to reason as he listened for the sound of a returning motor. If it was that ICE agent, planning to talk to the old couple that lived there, at least they didn't know about Toño. Plus it was late for old people, he thought. He peeked at his phone. Yeah, already close to 10:00. And he knew the Westbergs; they were old and lived alone, but they had a big family. It was probably one of their kids or grandkids, staying overnight. He stared into the dark and listened, straining to hear. The old building snuffled and muttered, and a breeze left behind by the storm tormented a loose piece of tin on the nearby shed roof—clackety clack, clackety clack.

The day had taken its toll on him. Finally, he couldn't sustain it. He leaned against his backpack and slept.

He dreamed about Jesus. As usual, the little *pícaro* had all of the blankets and most of the space in the bed they shared. Toño grumbled and extended his hand to give the kid a "move over" push, and his hand encountered fur. Warm fur. Very plushy warm fur. A lot of it. Toño screamed, remembered where he was, choked it back, pulled up his knees, then realized that the fur had shifted contentedly and was purring. "Jesus," Toño gasped, English pronunciation. "Jesus! Where did you come from? What time is it, anyhow?"

It was 2 a.m.; whatever that vehicle had been doing must be long since done. All was quiet; even the banging tin had ceased. Toño was sore and stiff. He shone his light on the cat, a large, short-haired gray animal who looked as if he'd found heaven by unexpectedly encountering a human in his private space. He stretched, wiped his nose on Toño's leg—a gesture of friendship—then curled up, his purr fading into the distance as he went back to sleep.

Somehow the cat made it better. He wasn't so alone now, not so alien. He was just sitting with another creature in a junky old building, and it wasn't long till morning. In the morning he'd think what to do, how to find his family, find out what their plan was. They would probably even praise him for his quick wits in throwing the safe, giving everyone time to get away. He stretched, careful not to disturb the cat, and felt in his pocket to reassure himself that the keys to the little safe were still there. The whole thing was starting to seem seriously unreal. Had he really thrown that safe?

The cold night air was seeping throughout the old building, and he shivered. Their family didn't have sleeping bags; his dad said they couldn't afford them. Instead, his mom had made them each a serape. He pawed in the main compartment of his pack and extracted the tightly jammed-in garment with some difficulty. He put it on, then felt in the outer backpack pocket for the gun Nancy Jane had shoved at him. Getting it out, he laid it nearby. Again, his dad was proved right. He felt safer.

He dug around to see what else might be in there, and his fingers encountered something unfamiliar, a sack of something that hadn't been there when the family prepared the packs. Pulling the squashed sack free, he knew at once. The fragrance was unmistakable. Camilia had been making *churros* for supper, and somehow, in all the shock and chaos, she'd been able to put a sack of fresh *churros* in his pack. He clutched the paper bag, absorbing the sugary fragrance. His mother had sent *churros!*

For the first time, tears made their way hesitantly through the down that darkened the soft cheek, a shadow of fuzz that spoke of hope for the strength of whiskers yet to come.

5

Roy Plover Finds a Surprise

The Oozle-Onion Valley Community Clubhouse sat at the intersection of Highway 46 and Oozle Road, not far from Alma's. It had a large parking area, and Roy Plover had chosen to park there, thinking his car would be less conspicuous than if he parked at Alma's. Just across Oozle Road from the clubhouse was the rickety modular home of Paul Frickleson, the least popular man in the valley. Frickleson had been called a water thief and worse by more than one local tongue. Water was more valuable than gold in this thirsty valley, and Frickleson was known to enhance his share by sneaking to headgates and divider boxes to adjust the flow, increasing what would go to his own property. People in the valley disliked and avoided him, but Gus Westberg came close to hating him. Gus was the president of the Oozle Ditch Company. He was old and tired, and every time Frickleson made a crooked move it was up to Gus to rectify it. The man had even messed with the main headgate up at Big Slide Rock. Gus had been forced to make calls to the water commissioner, hold special meetings with share holders to get things straightened out, and confront the man himself on several occasions. The whole thing damn near wore Gus to the bone. Frickleson had become more than a nuisance. He had become, in Gus's words to his wife, Tess, "A dirty, trashy, thieving, marijuana-growing hippie that no one should have to put up with for a neighbor. If he comes around here again, I'm gonna kill him."

"Oh, Gus, for pete's sake."

"Well ..." Gus looked sheepish.

None of this concerned Roy Plover. What did concern him was the Jesus figure, which he held carefully, as it was clearly hollow and probably contained the safe key. He didn't want the key to fall out as he walked in the dark. Once he reached the top of the incline that was Alma'a driveway, he paused and tried to shake the key into his hand. Nothing came out. Behind him, car lights approached on 46. Already? Crap, that medic alert worked fast. Or maybe it was just a random car. He stuffed the figurine in his pocket and stepped off the road. Not wanting to be seen, he crouched behind a feral apple tree growing west of the bar ditch, near the fence. Sure enough, the car turned in at Alma's before it reached him. Well, that settled one thing; he couldn't go back to look again at the old lady's. He stood and untangled himself from a stray apple branch that the tree had released into the wind that was coming up before the storm, then attempted to clear his pants of thistles.

Back on the road, he held his aching head and pushed himself into a jog. The jarring motion shot pain across his temple, but he wanted to get to his car where he could turn on the lights and inspect the figurine with more care. He suspected that the kids had taped the key inside so it wouldn't fall out easily.

With relief, he reached the parking lot. His car wasn't locked — people just didn't lock things in this godforsaken valley, so why should he? Without further ado, he yanked open the door.

Sitting in the driver's seat, looking enraged, was the last person he ever expected to see, and that person had a gun trained directly at his chest.

6

Duz and Carmen Visit Alma

His mother was definitely getting worse. It worried him, and it annoyed him. In fact, when the medic alert people called him, Duz was far more concerned about the degeneration of his mother's mind than he was worried that there might actually be a man in her house. The service asked, as they had arranged when they were hired, whether he wanted them to place a call to 911 this time. No, not this time. This would not be the first hallucination his mother had reported. There was his deceased father, old friends, occasionally Gary Cooper, and she often chatted with Mamie Eisenhower. He hated to bother people for nothing, especially not the police, who were miles away. He was fairly certain that she didn't need rescued. She just needed comforted and tucked back in.

As did he. He dragged his tired, heavy legs out of the bed, put his feet on the little rag throw rug Carmen had woven, and stared at the wall. He wasn't any spring chicken himself. Sympathetic, Carmen reached over to rub his back. "Next time it's your sister's turn."

"I know." He groaned it.

"Doesn't help this time, I guess. How about I go with you?"

"Ah, shit, Carmen. I hate for you to lose sleep over the old gal, too." She ignored the words and tuned in on the hope in his tone. Thrusting her own legs off the side of the bed, she said,

"Why don't I make us some coffee? She'll be all right for a few more minutes, won't she?"

By the time they arrived at Alma's, the storm had passed over and made its way far into the lower valley. They took off their shoes, slipped in the back door, felt their way through the kitchen, and ascertained that Alma was asleep in the big chair, her snore reassuringly burbly. Stealthily, they turned back, headed for freedom, when Duz caught his little toe on the runner of the old wooden rocker. Why was that thing moved out from its usual place in the dark corner of this dark room, anyhow? He suppressed a roar of pain, bending over to nurse the injured appendage while Carmen patted at him desperately, whispering, "Oh, honey! Oh, ouch, honey!" And, of course, all of this ruckus brought Alma around.

"What are you two doing here?" This in a bewildered, sleep-fogged voice. Carmen, gathering her wits and surrendering the original intrigue, made for the light switch.

Duz sat on the old rocker and rubbed at his throbbing toe with a certain amount of resentment. "You called us, remember? You pushed your button and told them there was a man in your house. So, was there?"

Alma was thoroughly disgusted. "Of course there was, or I wouldn't have called, but that was hours ago. He's gone now. You're late, as usual, Douglas Ulysses." Now, Duz was over sixty, and for sixty years his mother had painted her methodical, careful son as being "always late." He could never move fast enough nor arrive soon enough to keep up with his impatient, hard working, and rather slap-dash mother. He'd given up long ago and the slur no longer bothered him; he let it attach to her, not himself.

Giving his toe a final rub, he merely said, "So, who was the man? What was he like?"

Scowling, Alma tried to remember. "Well, he wanted Jesus. You know, he found little Jesus."

Carmen and Duz caught each other's eyes. Now what was this? This was new. Alma had never been a church goer. Had she been visited by some thoughtlessly late evening proselytizer?

Probing, Carmen queried, "Uh, what do you mean? How did he find little, uh, little Jesus?"

Alma herself realized that this was odd. She knew that her reasoning and memory were gradually leaving her; how much of her mind could she still rely on? She wasn't sure just what she did mean. After trying to puzzle it out, she said, "Well, I guess it was Lew."

"Lew? Lew Harris? What would he be doing here this time of night?"

Alma was indignant. "Well, it wasn't this time of night. You're the ones who are late. Lew was here much earlier."

Duz sighed. "Okay, I get it. We were late. But what did Lew want?"

"I told you already. He wanted Jesus. We visited a while, and talked about what to call him. He's American, so we thought maybe to just call him Jesus. You know, what with his folks and all. Their problems. Probably calling him Jesus might help him. So then, Lew took him."

Duz shifted in the abusive chair and Carmen sank onto the couch. They both contemplated Alma, Duz chewing on his knuckles. Finally, he thought of something. "But Mom, you told the people at medic alert that it was a strange man here, going through your things. You said, 'a strange man,' and I know some people think Lew is strange, but you've known him forever. We thought you meant somebody you didn't know, like a stranger." Duz found himself slowing his speech and raising his voice, trying to get through to his own mother, and he felt sad.

His question had distressed her. She raised pale, blue-veined hands to her head, holding it as if it would help steady her thinking. Duz, contrite, said, "It's okay, Mom. Don't let it worry you." The big rancher reached over to take her hand. "You probably just had a bad dream." But Alma freed her hand and spoke with sudden conviction.

"No, Duz, I remember now. It was a stranger who came here. A bad guy. That's why I pushed the button."

Both Duz and Carmen leaned forward. "Soooo ... there really was somebody in here? Somebody you didn't know? Why was he here? What did he want?"

25

Now Alma's voice was firm. "Oh, like I told you. He wanted Jesus. My Jesus was not his business. Doreen gave me that Jesus years ago. But I think he took Jesus, anyhow." With that, Alma sighed and leaned back. "I am so disappointed, but nothing can be done now. It's too late, and he's gone. You better just get on home and quit bothering me. I know you like to visit, but it's late, and I need some sleep."

7

Lew Stops by the Cowpath

Jenny Threewinds, Sheriff Pat Garrett's girlfriend, could tell that Lew Harris was having a great evening. His cheeks were pink, his adrenaline high. He bounced into the Cowpath with a peppy "How ya doin', Jen?" She felt she'd been doing pretty well until Lew popped in. Cliff Atcheson had been drinking on a stool in the back with Hillbilly Lily, the cowgirl poet. They seemed to have a thing going, but fortunately they left just before Lew came in. Old Jim Patchit was also on his way out, having snagged a twelve pack of soda. He told Jenny that it was to take over for the Romero kids tomorrow, and Jenny read into that the unspoken part: the Romero kids and his newfound love, Nancy Jane Barnswallowper. He asked Jenny to "put it on my tab." Now, nobody really had a tab at the Cowpath except for old Patch, who seemed to just assume this was the way of the world. Jenny kept a pad of paper by the cash register and Patch came in at the first of every month, regular as the rising sun, to settle up. It was always a pittance. No harm done. With these last stragglers gone, she could have tidied up and relaxed for the half hour before closing, then gone on home, but clearly that was not meant to be. Now she'd have a session of humoring dotty old Lew. Damn.

She didn't fuss about it; that wasn't her nature. No, she wiped her hands on a bar towel, leaned against the front counter, and said, "I'm doin' pretty good, Lew. How 'bout yourself?"

"Not so bad! Not so bad!" Lew pulled up a chair opposite Jenny and sat. "Just had a good visit with Alma. She was trying to figure out why those Mexicans name their kids Jesus and then pronounce it 'hay-soos.'" Jenny opened her mouth, then closed it. This was looking like it could be a long half hour. Lew continued, "Alma and me both think 'hay-soos' is a pretty good name, but why not just call the kid Jesus? Do they figure it's too holy?"

Well, how do you get into this topic, or how do you get out of it? Trapped, Jenny ventured, "Well, Lew, 'hay-soos' is how they pronounce Jesus in Spanish. And I think ... well, I think ..." She had to summarize. "I think it has to do with Spanish history, maybe the inquisition and all. Naming your baby 'Jesus' is an honor in Spain, I think. And Portugal, too. And I have a friend named Christian. You know, Christ and Christian? That's kind of the same, isn't it?" She was starting to get into this. Now that she thought about it, it wasn't a bad topic. She began wiping salt and pepper shakers with the bar towel. "And 'Christine.' Isn't that like 'little Christ' or something? Maybe in Italian?" She finished the sentence with a flourish.

Lew looked puzzled. "Well, I guess that's okay for Spain and Portugal. Or Italy. They're a whole ocean away from us, across the Atlantic and all, aren't they? They are actually foreigners. But all that doesn't explain Mexico. They're right next door to America; you'd think they might learn the right pronunciation after awhile."

This earned Lew a moment of silence and a very long look. "Well. Yeah. Well, Lew, isn't it a little late to be visiting Alma?"

"It is, it is," Lew agreed cheerfully. "But I had to pick up the kid. Kind of a baby, really, that she had there."

"So." Jenny scrutinized his face. "So. Where ... where is this kid? Why was it at Alma's?"

"Well, of course I can't tell you, Jenny. You're a little too close to the sheriff as it is, and this is all kind of hush hush. That's why I left him in the car."

"Lew, you left a baby alone out there in your car?"

"Well, no, Jenny, of course not. I left Lucky with him. He's asleep, and Lucky'll make sure nobody bothers him."

Hidden Treasure (or) Where is Jesus?

Jenny felt herself relax. This was just Lew being Lew—an imaginary dog guarding an imaginary kid, and probably even an imaginary visit with Alma. She smiled kindly at the lonely old man and set down her towel. "Oh, I see, Lew. That makes sense. So, we're just about to close." She looked meaningfully at her watch, which said there was at least twenty minutes left, but whatever. "Was there something you needed, a cup of coffee or something? I could let you have it free, 'cause what's left in the pot I'm just gonna throw out anyhow."

"Nah, that's okay." Lew slapped his knee and stood. "Shoot, I didn't mean to keep you so long, Jen. Everything else is closed, and I need some food for the kid. You got anything you could send me?"

This was a new one. Would he be willing to take imaginary food for his imaginary companions? No, probably not. This wasn't a grocery store, but how could she turn down the innocent old geezer. "Uh, just give me a minute, okay, Lew? How much food you need, anyhow?"

"Tomorrow, maybe. Maybe couple days, till I can shop. I ain't got much around the house right now except buck steak and spuds and coffee. Lucky and me, we like that steak, but I think kids nowadays are more picky."

"How old is this ... uh ... this baby?"

"Maybe three, I think. Got good teeth—won't need a bottle."

In the end, Jenny found a few of the little boxes of cold cereal they offered on the breakfast menu, some apples, a banana, a package of wieners and some buns, and a half dozen individual cartons of milk and juice. Weirdly, she found herself thinking that if the kid didn't like wieners Lucky would probably eat them. Hanging out with Lew did stuff like that to your brain. She was tempted to follow Lew to his car just to reassure herself that the so-called child was as invisible as Lucky. But get serious. Where would Alma get a child, and why would she send it with Lew Harris if she did?

As it was, Lew doddered out and she started closing down in the back, swiping at the bar stools with her towel and dousing the lights, glancing once out the window facing the parking lot. Lew was still there. He seemed to be looking for something, but then he got into his car and drove off. She smiled to herself, an indulgent smile. Lucky had probably slipped out of the car and Lew had to call him back. Dear, invisible Lucky would surely mind Lew and come right back. Otherwise, from what she could see in the dark, the car was empty. No little stray kid.

Meanwhile, Duz and Carmen Weinant made their way home from Alma's. As they pulled out of the driveway, Carmen twisted to look back. "Honey, do you think she'll be okay?"

"Yeah, I don't see why not."

"But what if there really was a man? What if he's lurking outside her house right now, waiting to attack her when we leave?"

"He'll be sorry." Duz chuckled, pleased with his own joke.

"Seriously, honey. She worries me."

"Okay, seriously. She worries me, too, but not because of some phantom man. I just worry about getting enough CNA help to keep up with her if her brain gets any more mushy."

"We could put her in a nursing home."

"That would be the end of her."

A thoughtful silence. They were curving up Oozle Road. Two big bucks made a leisurely crossing in front of them, and Duz made lip-smacking sounds. He did this to tease Carmen, who always wanted him to "just once" comment on the beauty of the deer, not their potential as dinner. She didn't take the bait, but instead said, "So where do you think all that Jesus stuff was coming from?"

Duz shrugged, turning into their lane, imagining their warm bed. "I dunno. Maybe just her being so old, thinking about dying, wondering about God and heaven and stuff."

Carmen was doubtful. "Well, it doesn't sound like your mom. She was never a real religious woman." Duz had pulled up to the yard gate, where he let her out, and as she walked to the door Carmen said to herself, "And I wonder who moved that big rocker out of the corner so Duzzy would jam his toe into it? It would be way too heavy for Alma to move."

8

Nola Rippe Takes Care of Her Kids

The scuttlebutt in the community had two themes with respect to Nola Rippe. The first was that she was the best damned irrigator in the valley, and if you were lucky enough to hire her you wouldn't be seeing big, open, dry patches anywhere in your fields come haying season. Nola was one woman who knew how to wield a shovel. The second theme was that she was the worst damned mother in the valley. Bar none. It was a wonder her kids were still alive. People suspected drugs, but if so, she was sneaky. Child Protection Services had come up dry a couple of times, and nervous neighbors were left fuming, at a loss for how to help the "poor little devils," as some referred to them. Who was the father, anyhow? They speculated that it could be Frickleson. Birds of a feather, after all. They didn't like him, either, and they figured both Frickleson and Rippe had 'Meth' as their middle names.

At any rate, it was sympathy for the kids that put Tiffany Gallenas into the position of agreeing to babysit them; anything would be better for them than being dragged around or ignored by their mother. Of course, at first Tiffany resisted. As a young woman on the go, the last thing she needed around her house was a couple of little kids. She was a single mom who had finally succeeded in getting two of her kids out of the nest, with just one left to go, and it had taken all her energy to feed, clothe, and keep a lid on her own brood. Their one stroke of luck had been when they inherited her aunt Hallie Flute's place, just over the hill from Alma. Hallie had been Alma's best friend. Getting her place meant that Tiffany and her family weren't homeless.

When Nola Rippe first asked Tiffany if she'd watch the kids while Nola irrigated, just for the summer, Tiffany had turned her down flat, explaining that she not only had their own place to run, but that she was a paramedic, on call most of the time, with frequent unpredictable emergency runs. Nola shrugged. "No worries if you get called out. The kids are very mature—they won't cause trouble. They can just stay in your house."

Tiffany stared at the kids. What were they, three and four? At best, five? Just then Larry, her high school kid, spoke up. "How much you payin'?"

Larry did need a summer job, but shouldn't it be him using those sinewy teenage muscles to irrigate, and Nola keeping track of her own kids? Nola, however, replied, "Oh, I can pay you good, better than minimum wage."

Where would that money be coming from? Irrigating was minimum wage. Tiffany interjected, "Larry, you …" but her son said quickly, "It'd be okay, mom. Pewt would help—she loves kids."

Yeah, right. Pewt, as Larry called her. Short for Pewter, and currently Larry's main squeeze. Again, Tiffany started to object, then she saw the direction of her son's gaze. He was looking at the two hopeful, snot-encrusted little faces turned toward them, and he was clearly distressed. Damn kid. Some kids took in stray pups, but no. Not Larry! He had to get hung up on Nola Rippe's desperate little ragamuffins. Tiffany sighed, and capitulated.

They'd done their job pretty well, Larry and Pewter. She backed them up, but they held up their end, which made her proud. The little ones had issues—who wouldn't, with a mother like that?—but at least while they were here they had clean clothes and clean faces, and they were happy to tumble and play. The only problem was that Nola often took advantage, not showing up to claim them on time, leaving the Gallenas family in charge far into the evening. Tonight was one of those nights. Tiffany had been out on a hospital run; it was ten o'clock and she was just getting back. Larry and Pewter had made plans to go to the Potato Days melodrama, and now they were stranded here, waiting for the delinquent mother.

Pewter said, "Tiff, that woman can't still be irrigating. It's hours past dark. There's corn pudding."

A glance at the stove clarified the last garbled statement; the teens had been cooking, and there was still food in the casserole. Good. Tiffany was hungry. She ate directly from the baking dish, scraping the bottom to get at the tasty crust, her favorite part. Larry was grinning. "Hey, Ma, the pig would have loved that."

Licking the spoon, Tiffany sassed back. "Yeah, yeah, well, he didn't get a chance, did he? I don't suppose she called."

"Course not. She doesn't give a shit about them."

"They're asleep?"

"All bathed and 'jammied up and snoozing away."

"Well, I can watch them if you kids want to … want to …"

Pewter snorted. "No point. The play's been over forever. I wanted to see old cocky Ginger screw up her lines. She was really strutting over getting the part of the heroine."

Larry shrugged. "She'd just giggle. Anyhow, so what we gonna do?"

At this point, an extended exchange developed between Larry and Pewter, cycling through the words, "Whadda you wanna do I don't know whadda you wanna do?" repeated with no apparent intended move toward closure. Tiffany poured herself coffee and went into the spare room, which was piled high with junk, but in Luke's old bed in the corner were two sleeping kids. Like any sleeping babies, they looked angelic, curled together, and it broke Tiffany's heart to think it would be Nola Rippe who picked them up.

And pick them up she did—finally. Pewter had gone home, deciding that she and Larry needed their beauty sleep and would meet tomorrow. Larry slouched on the couch, looking glum, and when he heard the sound of the 4-wheeler, he announced, "Well, here comes the old Ripper now. Jesus, she's late. Maybe we oughta just keep the kids."

Tiffany was too drained to argue with Nola Rippe about some kind of custody of her kids, much less to care for them if they stayed. Ignoring Larry, she went to the door and watched

Nola park her ATV where they had agreed she could leave it. Then she went back to help Larry get the kids. He was shaking them gently. "Come on, Syd. Spook. Your mom's here."

Both kids' eyes popped open. Tiffany could feel them tense, and Spook, who was just three, made a whining sound, the beginning of a wail. Nola had followed them into the room. With faked good humor, she said, "Come on, you little shits. Rise and shine. You can sleep at home." Yanking them both out of the bed, she added, "Hurry up. I got stuff to do."

They padded after her in their bare feet, flinching when they crossed the gravel driveway. Larry and Tiffany watched the husky woman stuff the kids into the back seat of her junky car. Larry said, "She probably couldn't find their seat belts even if she did try to buckle 'em. I hate her."

Tiffany swallowed her reproof. She was going to say, "We don't hate people, Larry," but then realized she couldn't honestly say it. Sighing, she responded, "Me, too. I hate her, too."

Nola drove like a demon down the long, gravel road that led from the Gallenas's place to Highway 46. Thrown around the back seat, Syd and Spook struggled for purchase. They began to push each other, hitting, screaming, and crying. A large cardboard box, loose among the junk, tumbled out and whacked Spook on the nose, and the screaming intensified. Driving with one hand, Nola turned to the back, hitting at random and shouting, "Shut up, you little shits. I've had enough of a day. I don't need this." Wheeling over the bridge across Dry Gulch, they rounded the curve and shot out onto the highway. As the car turned sharply, the kids were thrown violently against the door, causing them to yowl in pain.

By the time they passed Alma's, Nola was grinding her teeth in rage. Duz Weinant's truck was parked there, and she thought, "Pompous ass," then gunned her car, causing its ancient frame to shudder with the exertion. Nola said under her breath, "I don't know what the fuck I'm gonna do. I can't think. They gotta shut up." Impulsively, she drove into the scenic pullout just opposite Harris Pond and squealed to a stop. Scrabbling over the seat, she grabbed each of the kids by the pajama front and slapped them, hard. "Now do you hear me, you little shits? SHUT UP! If you don't clamp it down, and I mean right *now*, I'm gonna dump you at the next driveway. Then we'll see how smart you little assholes are. You can just find your own way home, can't you, and I'll have peace and quiet. You hear me? I mean it." She slapped them again for good measure; Syd ducked and the second slap missed. Nola's hand flew past, hooking her little finger violently on the seat back. Yelping in pain, she hissed, "See what you did? See what you did? You damn near broke my finger!" Scrambling back to the front, she jammed the car into gear and, sucking on her finger, shot onto the highway.

Syd got the message, but Spook, only three, had entered an alternate reality set in pain and fear. There was nothing rational or hopeful left in that world. In Spook's mind, the deafening scream that filled the car came from somewhere else, a universal screamer that must voice sorrow when it happens, and Spook was merely a bystander in the turmoil. Meanwhile, they were approaching the Harris's driveway and Nola was slowing the car, pulling over.

At five, Syd saw it happening and understood. "I'm quiet, Mama!" Syd's yelling a counterpoint to Spook's screams. "It ain't me! It's Spook! It's Spook! I'm quiet!"

Grim faced, Nola stopped the car, bailed out, and yanked open the back door. "Get out! Get the hell out, both of you screaming little shits. You two have made my life hell for long enough. You just get out and go see if somebody else can stand you." Dragging them out, she slammed the door and got back in the car. Syd made a grab for the door handle, but Nola gunned the vehicle, knocking her child to the ground. She muttered to herself as she shot into Croysant, "Maybe the coyotes will eat the little bastards."

9
Toño Hides Among Chabochi

In the muzzy state between dream and wakefulness, Toño's thoughts drifted to his father. Eduardo was the second son, and had been rebellious. He was just 15, Toño's age now, when he ran away from his father's ranch, lured and threatened into working for Barrio Azteca. For three years he smuggled drugs for the cartel. It was dangerous business. Toño wanted to hear about those years, but his dad only harped on one refrain when Toño asked: "Just forget the cartels. Stay away from them. Stay out of trouble." Toño heard this, and believed it, but he also heard an underlying note of pride in his father's voice. Eduardo had faced danger and overcome it. He mentioned the rattlesnakes lurking in the greasewood along the border. When he said 'greasewood' Camilia would interrupt with, "Hah! It is chicowood. If you eat its leaves, you won't go hungry in the desert."

"Oh, yeah, hah yourself," Eduardo shot back. "You might not go hungry, but you'd only stay alive if *víbora de cascabel* doesn't grab you first." If Jesus was on his lap, Eduardo would give him a tiny pinch, making a whirring sound with his tongue. Jesus would jump, and they would all laugh. Then Eduardo would become quiet and sober. "No, it's only funny if you're here and safe. There were human snakes, too, cartel bosses and border patrol people. Some of them would kill you if they could. They'd put your head where your neck couldn't find it." The family would become quiet then, contemplating the dangers, but Toño knew that his father's strength came from successfully overcoming those dangers. Eduardo had crossed the border numerous times back then. He told them that when he decided to leave the cartel once and for all, he had managed to disappear into itinerant work in America. Toño admired his dad. He knew how to deal with crooked systems as well as survive harsh surroundings.

Awake now, Toño pushed the cat off his chest. "I could do that. If he could do it, I could do it." Standing and stretching in the weak morning light from the dirty windows, Toño was filled with resolve. He was also curious. He wanted to know what had happened after he left. What had they done with the ICE man? Maybe he was dead by now. Would that mean that Toño was wanted for murder? That would give him all the more reason to stay undercover. The first thing to do, he decided, would be to slip back over to Nancy Jane's, hide cautiously nearby, and watch the house. He wouldn't go near if the sheriff was there, but after he knew more, he could formulate a next step.

The cat gave two hops, lit on a tattered chair back, then scrabbled out a broken window, its hind feet scratching against the wall for leverage. As for Toño, he preferred to use the warped door. Dragging it open, he made his way to a gnarled apple tree nearby to relieve himself, then went to the standpipe he'd spotted last night. Yes! It was good for fresh water. Washing his hands and splashing his face, he stretched again, refreshed. It was nice and early. The sun had barely crested the eastern mountains. He was enjoying being private, alone with his thoughts. He could do this thing! The old tree had apples. He was out of *churros*, but his backpack had granola bars. Apples with those would be a great way to start the day. It would beat greasewood leaves and lurking snakes. Chuckling to himself, he jumped to catch a lower branch and swing into the tree. Then, as his father might have said, all hell broke loose.

Somehow, he'd thought that the Westbergs, being an old couple, would have a quiet, peaceful place. They should shut up, like old people were supposed to do, and hang out in their sleepy old ranch house, puttering at their boring old business, while he tended to his own problems here at the settler buildings. Instead, it was just the crack of dawn and the whole place was suddenly swarming with activity.

Two trucks entered the lane, their dust engulfing him as he clung to the tree branch, which suddenly felt very conspicuous. One truck pulled a horse trailer that rattled and banged across the cattle guard, then lurched and rocked precariously as it encountered the ruts and potholes in the lane. Toño eased to the ground and plastered himself against the tree trunk. Had they noticed him?

They pulled into the yard at the ranch house, and, as if from clown cars, packs of people piled out of the trucks. Toño realized that sound was carrying clear as a bell across the 75 yards or so between himself and where they were disembarking. A voice was saying, "I'll go with Mark to git him. I don't think there's any way to keep that damn bull in. Let's just take him on to Riversmet and auction him off."

Another voice replied, "Dad wants to give him a chance. He throws good calves."

"Anything he throws will be a fence-bustin' asshole." That comment seemed to be made with a snort of good will. Toño scooted in tighter to the trunk of the tree. The voices from the ranch house yard continued.

"So that's a good idea. Let Jeanne and me go to Fourier's and get the old bastard. We can put him in the stockade a couple days, give him a chance to cool his jets. Why'd he head over to Fourier's, anyhow? They don't run cattle. That dude shouldn't have anything in heat."

"Oh, you know Garfield. He's an old-settler slash cowboy wannabe. He bought a couple heifers at the sale, and they must be bulling."

"Doc said it was a bad move. He was out to check 'em out yesterday, and told Gar he'd play hell gettin' any weight on 'em. They're poorly, just skin and bones, loused up, one's lame ..."

"Also probably bred up now that old Fritz is over there visiting. Ha, Mom, Garfield, your cuz."

"Yeah, maybe bred. Anyhow, Gar's more distant than a cousin, and he's a nice man. Just wasn't raised here. He probably bought the heifers 'cause he felt sorry for 'em. Too bad him and Honey can't have kids." Toño thought the last speaker must be the old lady, Tess, and he was convinced when she continued, "Look, kids, there's cinnamon rolls and coffee inside. Get some before you hitch up. Then we need to get after those flies. Cows is fightin' 'em bad. Jack, don't forget to set out the ear tags if you take your trailer with the calf."

And so it went, their voices fading as they entered the ranch house. Toño peered around the tree trunk. He felt tortured. He wanted cinnamon rolls, too. Probably old Tess had baked them herself, fresh, and they'd be great. Even more, he wanted the camaraderie of working with the cattle. He always helped with the cattle at home, when he wasn't in school. Cowpunchers were the best team players in the world. They'd yell and cuss, but everyone did their job, and the kidding around made you feel good. He knew he could fit right in if he could just go down and help. He'd be part of the group. He didn't want to be up here, slinking and hiding. If he wasn't a possible murderer, he might be able to think of some way to just show up and help out.

Well, at least they should be preoccupied for a while, stuffing themselves with rolls and coffee. He'd try again for the apples, then maybe slip away, cross the yard and get behind the shed, into the brush. He made a grab for the lowest branch and pulled up, flipping himself onto it. Right at the end hung an apple bonanza. He scooted along to get close enough to reach them when he realized he'd made a false assumption. The Westbergs weren't staying inside. They were bringing the rolls and coffee with them, and still talking up a storm. Someone said, "Well, Jack, you set out the fly tags and Jeanne and I'll take dad's trailer for the bull then. You gonna take the calf to Doc right now?"

"I want to go."

"Don't you have to irrigate, Gordy?"

"Look, Uncle Jack, I need to know what Doc says about that calf. I was there when the branch fell and the damn thing didn't break its back."

"It's early for Doc, anyhow."

The conversation went around and around. Somebody left the yard and started walking across the field, headed directly toward where Toño perched. A pickup turned around by the house, then drove up the lane toward him. Toño dropped from the tree so fast that the branch tried to come with him and cracked. His knees hit the ground, several apples following him down. He made a scoop for the apples, got three to stuff in his pocket, and without looking around, scuttled to the warped door, rammed it open, fell in and jammed it shut behind him, dragging it all the way. He shot across the broken floor, tripping and stumbling over debris as he went, and made it to the north window, a jagged piece of broken, fly-stained glass that remained in the original frame.

He could still see the figure advancing from the ranch house. It was an irrigator lugging a shovel over his shoulder, and with a dog running around, checking things out over a wide area. It must be okay—the irrigator didn't seem to be looking with any special interest at where the branch had made the cracking sound. Better yet, Toño suddenly realized he knew him. It was Gordy Smith, Westbergs' grandson, a kid Toño's age. Gordy was from Denver, but he spent summers with Gus and Tess Westberg and sometimes hung out with Toño and the other high school kids in this area. Toño suppressed a powerful urge just to leave the building, head over to Gordy, and say "Hi." That's what seemed natural. He liked Gordy. But what then? How could he possibly explain himself?

At that point the urge was squelched as he heard the pickup pull into the yard outside. Picking his way back past bed springs, discarded car parts, and an incongruous 25-pound body building weight, he stood by the dirt-covered window of the old door and watched as the woman bailed out and took a position at the front of the rusty old horse trailer, prepared to guide the man as he backed toward the hitch. Toño knew this couple, too. The guy was Mark, a Westberg son, and the woman was Jeanne, his wife. They were friends with his folks. He yearned to go chat with them as they worked. At one point, the trailer hitch balked, the ball turning instead of tightening, and they had to locate a wrench to hold it in place. He could have helped with that. They were yelling at each other all the while, the friendly bickering that ranch couples do as they cope with the cranky resistance of nature and tired old machinery. Neither even glanced his way. When they got the thing hitched up they climbed back in the pickup and rattled off down the dusty lane, leaving him feeling … well, weird. He was looking out from a world no one was even aware of. He was invisible, a person without a place, and, somehow, a person no one seemed to care about.

For a while, Toño moved between the various windows, watching the omnipresent family. Gordy was apparently done irrigating and was trudging back across the pasture toward the ranch house. People were bustling around there, and it was clear that the intention was to work the cattle at the corrals north of the house. Old Gus and Tess got on a four-wheeler, and Gordy reappeared, following them on a tractor, all headed toward the corrals. Several of the family walked up the lane toward Toño, and he realized they planned to bring the cattle past his hideout, having gathered them from a nearby southern pasture. People were placing themselves at places along the route where the cattle might be expected to stray. It felt as if there were Westbergs everywhere. Toño was trapped.

He went listlessly to the old garbage-bag covered couch where he'd spent the night, at a loss. He didn't think he could sneak past them without being seen; the cattle would whoof at him if he made it far enough to hunker in the brush. Most ranchers were hunters, and they would spot anything that was unusual moving around their place. Surrounded by the busy, purposeful family, Toño felt pointless. Even if he could slip out unseen, where would he go, and why? Nancy Jane's place no longer seemed the right place to be, either. What if he made his way to the Copper Canyon, in Mexico? He had no idea how or why he would do that. He didn't really know any Mexicans; neither his dad's nor his mom's family had ever been to America to visit. The family friends here were just like them, kind of just American. His folks knew how to deal with border crossing risks, but that wasn't him. The events of the previous twelve hours had wrenched apart his understanding of the world. Sure, he'd helped when his folks prepared for an ICE agent, but that had been a fairytale to him. ICE agents were myths, like ogres and cyborgs, not real. He was just a typical, sheltered American kid.

He'd been on American soil since he was less than a year old. The only place he'd ever known as home until two years ago was the Corbit ranch. Then, when the fire destroyed the Corbit main ranch house and Mr. and Mrs. Corbit decided to retire, the Romeros moved to Nancy Jane's, and that felt like home now. It was a cool place to live, because everyone knew Nancy Jane was a corker. She cussed around the place and hollered at Toño to "hurry and bring that damn barb wire" and stuff like that, but her heart was as big as the mountains. Better yet, Jim Patchit, the old bachelor with the climbing dog, seemed to have discovered something he liked up at the Barnswallowper place. He was always there, "helping out." When she was out of Nancy's hearing, Camilia teased that Jim had either taken a shine to Nancy herself, or to Camilia's cooking. Toño suspected both. His mom was a fantastic cook, and old Jim spent a lot of time rubbing his full belly appreciatively after one of her meals, meanwhile eyeing Nancy's leathery person, her clothes stained with ranch dirt and sweat. It seemed he had just realized that he had finally found his kind of gals, and all that remained to be done was to convince the women in question. He teased Jesus and played at making objections to Nancy's slipping greasy venison scraps to Buddy, his dog, all the while remaining immovable in the chair that seemed to have become his place at the table. Toño wondered if old Patch knew yet about the ICE agent, and what he was doing now, anyhow.

The worst part about this thing, he decided, was his phone. He was supposed to have ditched it already because his folks had told him the ICE agents could trace it. His girlfriend was Katelyn Corbit, Mr. and Mrs. Corbit's niece. He wished he could call her, just to visit. He could tell her what had happened. She was like Hermione Granger in Harry Potter. She'd have good ideas about what to do. He fingered his phone and knew he couldn't call. He sighed. Maybe that's what he should do next — get out of here and ditch his phone. The problem was, he could still hear Westbergs hollering around outside. They were all over out there; he couldn't get past them.

He explored his backpack again, ate his apples and some granola bars. The Westberg bustle went on and on. They put fly

Hidden Treasure (or) Where is Jesus?

tags in the cattle's ears. One cow got away, jumping the fence into a neighbor's pasture. Everyone yelled and chased her. They caught horses and rounded her back up, returning her to the herd. They drove the herd back up the lane. Gordy and Jack took the injured calf to the vet. Everyone else decided to fix fences. Tess and a daughter went into the house to make apple pie. The bull arrived, having posed difficulty at Fourier's. He hadn't wanted to load into the old trailer, and when they got him in he broke it, going out the front. They fixed that, got him back in, brought him home, and unloaded him into the stockade. He broke the stockade, jumped the boards, and headed north. They fixed the stockade and returned him to his prison. Every time Toño thought he might slip away, some member of that family seemed to be walking or riding past. He finally decided to wait until dark — surely they'd leave by then.

Settling in, he assessed his surroundings. The old place was kind of interesting. Clearly, long ago, it had been someone's home; it had had several rooms. About a fourth had flowered wall paper. One corner had pictures cut from old magazines and glued to the walls, sailors and pin-up girls. Another had a cut-out of a chubby little man and woman holding hands. The man had a black cap that looked kind of like a modern duck-billed ranch hat, and the woman had a tall, white hat that seemed to have wings, almost like a nun's hat. Their shoes were odd, with tipped-up toes. Some kind of foreign costume, he guessed. Part of the floor in this building was still covered with an ancient carpet, now gray, its borders once gay with green and black decorations.

At some point, times had changed for this home, and someone had knocked out the inner walls, turning the place into the kind of shop that would be useful on a ranch. There was a forge at the center, with tools hooked along its edge. Along the walls on one side were heavy wooden work cabinets with tools still on them. Toño fingered them, the vises, grinders, planers and saws, and speculated on how he would use them. There was a heavy bucket of bolts, and a loose pile of gaskets. On the wall above that cabinet was a chart of tap and drill sizes, giving the equivalents in decimals. Next to that was a 1967 calendar showing a toddler on a beach, a dog tugging at her swimsuit, her skin red except for the white under the suit. It advertised "Solarcaine for Sunburn Pain."

After its life as a shop, the building seemed to have been transformed into a storage shed. There were things from every era in its existence, right up to today. An ancient inner tube, from the days when flat tires were repaired on the road, hung on one wall. It had been patched at least four times. There was a wringer washer, a large maple-wood record player covered in mouse cards, torn tarps and hopelessly ragged, cotton-filled sleeping bags, a deflated basketball, a box of Legos with a spider building her web across the top, and two wooden pallets on which were stacked sacks of protein pellets ready to feed to cattle, maybe even today. Poking around, Toño mumbled to himself, "Ha. Home Sweet Home."

The Westberg cattle were now being driven back up the lane to the southern pasture, so Toño settled in with a dusty stack of magazines from the eighties, *National Geographic* and *Popular Mechanics*. He was tired after his stressful night; he soon drifted off the sleep. When he woke up it was quiet outside. Ah, maybe now was the time! No such luck. There was the click of a shovel. Outside, Gordy was shoveling away on a stretch of irrigation ditch not more than 30 yards from Toño's building. Worse, outside his door, Toño spotted old Gus ensconced in a rickety, webbed lawn chair, patiently untangling and rolling baling twine. He realized that he was close enough to hear the old guy breathing out a toneless, whistled melody. Every now and then Gus would stop and take a generous swallow from one of the bottles of beer propped near his chair. Retreating to his garbage-bag covered couch, Toño looked around the room. It was starting to get very boring. His eye fell on a ladder near the bricked-in chimney. He realized that at the top of the ladder was a trapdoor-like opening that must lead to an attic area above the rafters.

Careful not to send noise into the yard, Toño went up the ladder, poking his head into the attic area. Not much there. A couple of boxes, an old leather chest. He went on up, crawling along the rafters, cautious about putting a foot down through the ceiling. One box had telephone directories and Montgomery Ward catalogs from long before Toño's time. The phone numbers in the books were given as two digits and a letter. John Warner was 11-K; Archie Smith was 27-M. He hadn't heard of them; he supposed they were long since dead. The Riversmet Hotel advertised showers and tub baths, with room rates at $2.00 and up. The mortuary touted "dignified personal services."

Toño turned to the other box. It had once been filled with newspapers, but now it provided mice with a nest of shredded paper. Toño poked at the paper and encountered a pile of naked, squeaking baby mice that twisted and squirmed back and forth around his hand, blindly seeking a mother. Yanking his hand back, Toño made his way to the leather chest.

It, too, had succumbed to the forces of time. Rodents had chewed through the tasty leather and insects had done their own work. The binding straps were no more. He lifted the lid to see fragments of cloth, a lacy baby's dress almost intact, a woolen stocking cap and matching knit sweater, both riddled with moth holes. He pulled out a child's tiny, tailored coat, defiled by animal urine, and held it away from himself in disgust. There was also a canvas bag. It, too, had suffered rodent attacks, but there were still books inside. Pulling them out, Toño realized it was two high school yearbooks. These interested him. He secured them in the canvas bag and teetered back across the edges of the rafters on his knees, which were aching from their trip across the hard edges of the boards.

Back on his couch, Toño fiddled with the yearbooks. They were from the fifties; one was Tess's and one had belonged to Gus, who had been senior class president. The old graybeard was a muscley-looking blond guy back then. In the pictures the boys all had clean-shaven faces and tidy, short hair cuts. The girls were in full skirts that came to their ankles, tiny scarves at their necks, their hair curled and pulled away from shining faces, all secured with barrettes and bands, no loose strands. Those groups of students pictured for chorus, pep club, student council and so-on all looked like aliens to Toño. There was no long hair, no variation in clothing, no Black faces, and for that matter, no one who seemed to dare to look brown like himself. The Future Farmers of America were all male, lounging against cars, sawing and hammering, busy as bees in each picture, whereas the Future

Homemakers of America were all female. There were a lot of them, sitting prim and poised, posed on bleachers, their hands folded in their laps and their modest, bobby-socked ankles held together.

Flipping to the back of Gus's book, Toño found dozens of autographs. None were obscene, like many in yearbooks today. Instead, most said some version of "Best of Luck to a Swell Guy." One said, "Best of luck to the best Kraut I know—ha ha." Tess's autographs were similar, urging "Best of Luck to a Real Swell Gal." Both yearbooks had loose papers stuffed in them: a booklet of rules for Colorado drivers, old school news bulletins, some copies of cheerleading rhymes. One of the most interesting to Toño was some kind of certificate from Gus's book. It was in German, about the size of a piece of notebook paper. It looked very official, with Gus's full name in a box at the top: Gustaf Gerhard Westberg. At the bottom was a signature of a German name, and some kind of red seal. Someone had handwritten a label at the top saying, "Dad's German Blood Certificate," and about halfway down, under some big, long German word, someone, probably the same person, had underlined the word *Mischlinge*, and above it written, "First Degree." The date on the certificate was 1940. Toño studied the thing for a while, wishing he knew German. He wondered if *Mischlinge* was a German word for Nazi. Gus had probably been a big, blond Nazi. Finally, concluding that he was getting nowhere, he replaced the mysterious certificate and prepared to put the yearbooks back in the bag. Just then he realized there was something else still in the bag, something stuck halfway in a hole near the bottom seam. Still repulsed by the squirming mice, he didn't want to put his hand down there, so he tipped the bag up and shook it vigorously.

A well-chewed little book fell out, a couple of its pages fluttering loosely across the floor. It was about seven by eight inches, and had a faded red cardboard cover. The cover had been laced together with something resembling shoelaces, but the strings now hung in shreds. The front was covered with flowers and declared itself to be "My Diary."

Carefully, Toño gathered up the loose pages, then looked inside the wrecked book. From what was left, he knew it had to have been old Tess Westberg's. He could visualize her, all those years ago, sitting on her bed, legs folded into her big, bulky skirt, and writing this stuff, things like, "I don't know if Betty likes me or Sue," and "I wish my mother would mind her own business. Billy came by again yesterday and she invited him in and gave him cookies!!! I was hid upstairs and wouldn't come down when she called. I can't stand that creep." "Sue says she is my friend but all she wants to do is be around Beverly. I heard Beverly telling her a joke that I can't repeat here. I must have blushed an hour. I mean Beverly H., not B ...." (Book torn here.) On another page, "I don't know what to think about God. Why did he make orphans in Italy?"

A few pages down, Toño came across, "I think Gus is the swellest guy in school. He always treats me polite. I wish Joyce would leave him alone." Toño thought, "Well, that figures," and started to fit the loose pages back in as best he could when he realized that one had been written furiously, using large, rough letters, all angrily underlined. "That baby **isn't** his. Joyce is spreading it all around that it is his, but he says it **couldn't be.** She is starting awful gossip. She is a slut, God forgive me for swearing. I don't know what to do!! What can I do? Joyce is going to force Gus to **marry her!!!!** He is so swell, he will try to help her even if he shouldn't. Should I go tell him I love him? **Oh, I would die!! What** ..."

And there it ended, the rest of the page gone. Wow! That was dramatic! Toño wanted to read more, but it was the last page. Wow, Tess really had a thing for Gus for sure, but he seemed hung up on the pregnant Joyce. Well, it must have come out all right, as it was a long time ago, and Tess and Gus were an old married couple now. Just the same, Toño couldn't help but wonder what happened to "that slut, Joyce" and her baby. Maybe the other guy did the right thing in the end and claimed the baby. Toño wondered if he'd ever find out. Probably not. Crap, he'd probably be in Mexico, wondering what hit him, before he could find out. Or in jail. For murder.

He took the books back up the ladder, then parked on the couch, feeling tired and confused. It was getting toward dark, and he could just now hear truck doors slamming as the Westbergs finally prepared to leave. He'd told himself that he would leave at dark, but the gray cat arrived and nestled against him. He didn't want to leave the cat alone. Being alone didn't seem right, even for a cat. Maybe tomorrow. Maybe the Westbergs had their work done now and it would be quiet out there tomorrow, and he could leave in daylight. One more night in a *Chabochi* house would probably be okay. It wouldn't have scared his dad.

10

Tess Westberg Searches for her Knife

For getting on to sixty years now, Tess Westberg's left hand had led a secret life of its own. First, the left thumb would creep over to the base of the third finger and assure itself that the ring was there and intact, as it should be. Then the whole hand would make a quiet, unheralded trip to the left jeans pocket to locate the knife. The hand never sent a signal to the rest of its organic world, that is, to Tess's busy brain, unless it found something amiss. Once, the ring band had worn through. The hand informed Tess, and the ring was taken to the jeweler for repair, where it remained a whole week. The thumb became so anxious about the bare skin left behind that Tess had to rummage in her jewelry box to find a substitute until the wedding ring was returned to its proper place, whole.

Hurrying to Gus's office, Tess told him the problem. Then she uprooted Gordy from his game and told him, too. "Your great-grandpa's knife, Gordy. He gave it to me for graduation. He never gave me much just from himself, and I was so proud; I vowed I'd never lose it. I have to find it!"

Today it was a different story. Several of Tess's family members had been here all day, eating, working cattle, and in general romping about the place, leaving Tess happy, contented, and tired by evening. Gordy went to his room with his phone set on a gaming program; Gus headed for his office; and Tess put the last of the dishes in the cupboard. The left hand, freed briefly, made its journey to her pocket. This was when the five-bell alarm resounded in Tess's head. There was nothing in the pocket—no coins, no slips of reminder paper, no special rocks, and no knife—nothing but a nickel-sized hole, sneakily making its overdue appearance in the pocket of the worn jeans.

Hurrying to Gus's office, Tess told him the problem. Then she uprooted Gordy from his game and told him, too. "Your great-grandpa's knife, Gordy. He gave it to me for graduation. He never gave me much just from himself, and I was so proud; I vowed I'd never lose it. I have to find it!"

Gordy didn't much care. He was right in the middle of trying to achieve the next level, and he'd never known his great-grandpa anyhow. Gus was desperate to get his bookwork lined out and pay a couple of those bills before bedtime. They both tried to comfort Tess, but they were both relieved when she decided to go alone to get out before dark and retrace her steps around the ranch that day. They left her to it, wishing her luck.

She decided to start at the corrals where they'd checked the cows and put the fly tags in their ears. Old #64 had jumped the corral fence down there, and everyone had been running around like crazy, trying to head her off and get her back with the herd. Tess remembered jumping the ditch just above the culvert, and she had a dim, subconscious memory of something happening with the pocket then; perhaps it had flopped against her thigh. Perhaps it dumped its contents when she jumped. Anxious, she started to hurry, adrenaline oiling her stiff old joints. There usually wasn't much water in the ditch this time of year, especially not with the drought, but the storm in the mountains last night had sent more down. The ditch water level had increased and if she'd lost her dad's pocketknife in the actual water, it might get washed into the culvert and she'd never find it.

She approached the ditch at the place where she thought she'd jumped, a few feet above the culvert, and her worst fears were realized. Apparently it had rained more in the high country last night than she thought. The water was high. In fact, it almost acted as if the culvert was blocked. What was blocking it? There wasn't that much brush along this part of the ditch. It was a good-sized pipe, meant to carry the water under the road that led to the upper pastures. Gus would be so annoyed." One more damn thing," he'd say to Gordy. He wasn't a guy who laughed stuff off.

Patiently, Tess began to scour the area where she'd jumped, then to work her way downstream. No knife or pocket contents, but something caught her eye at the entrance to the culvert. Curious, she gave up the knife search for the moment and made her way on down to investigate. The object at the head of the culvert was a head.

Tess was not the kind of woman to scream. The first thing she did was to calmly assure herself that the head was attached to a body. It was; the body was wedged into the culvert feet first. Any further details about the body were obscured by the pipe. The water was trying to get past it, and Tess's first thought was, "Well, that explains the blockage." The head was on its side, and flies were busy working it over where the water hadn't submerged it. This explained Tess's second thought, which was, "This guy needs an ear tag."

Securing herself so she wouldn't slip in the rocks and mud on the ditch bank, Tess reached down and took hold of the head by a handful of hair. The hair came off. Saying "ugh," she reached into the water with both hands. She wanted to get the head turned so she could see the face. Struggling, she finally got it turned and got a good look. It was then, for the first time, that she recoiled and suppressed a scream.

Tess may have been old, but she had descended from fierce settler stock, and when she wanted to she could make things happen. She wanted to now. She rushed out of the ditch and hunted along the bank until she found a large, heavy flat rock. Taking it to the culvert, she put it over the head and pressed down, pushing it back and forth, grinding the head as deeply as she could into the water and mud. Dribbles of blood escaped from under the rock and ran on down into the culvert. She did her best to shift the shoulders of the corpse, trying to let the water flow past. Then she got more rocks and piled them on the head. Climbing up to the road that crossed the culvert, she looked down at what she'd done. Nothing seemed to be visible. Not unless you were looking there, trying to find something. She walked up the ditch, found a pool, and washed off as well as she could.

Back at the house, she found Gordy still in his room and Gus in the parlor, watching the news. Slipping upstairs, she changed clothes, then joined Gus on the couch. He acknowledged her presence with a grunt. Finally, at the commercial, he asked, "Well, did you find it?"

She had regained her composure, but she was suddenly totally exhausted. "Yeah, I found it. It was in the ditch." She stared with unusual interest at the Xarelto commercial, long and weighty with warnings. Her left hand, unbidden, made an unsuccessful trip to her pocket, coming out empty.

11
Nancy Jane Barnswallowper Worries

Here's the thing. Nancy Jane Barnswallowper had spent most of her life alone. Hers was one of those convoluted mountain families that didn't make much sense in real time. Tiffany Gallenas and Nancy Jane both had Flute blood. Tiffany would have been a cousin to Nancy Jane's mother, but because the original family was large and had produced a lot of kids over a protracted period of time, Tiffany was much younger than Nancy Jane. They just called themselves cousins. Nancy Jane's grandpa, Jeb Flute, had been Tiffany's uncle. Hallie Flute, now deceased, who had been Alma's best friend, was Tiffany's aunt, but Nancy Jane's great-aunt. Oh, well, you'd need pencil and paper to work it all out, but you get the picture. That's how small country communities work, all intermingled. Everyone is somehow a relative, a friend, or perhaps even an enemy from earlier times.

Speaking of these old, interwoven communities, you need to know that they quietly store knowledge in their shared subconscious, stories that are there but have never been spoken. Everyone knows these things, and they have passed judgment, then they have moved on, nothing more being said about what happened. Nancy Jane's situation was like that. Her mother, Thelma Flute, had married Red Barnswallowper, given birth to Nancy Jane, then died before her daughter reached school age. The official diagnosis was an unexpected embolism, but Red was a drinker with a bad temper; Thelma was a wife with bruises; and the community knew there had been blood on the cement steps leading into the Barnswallowper house and a lump on Thelma's head when she was placed in the ambulance and taken to the hospital to die.

The community knew, but no one went to the authorities because Great-Aunt Hallie Flute stepped up to take little Nancy Jane in and raise her. Community consensus was that the little girl would be better off with gentle, practical old Hallie than kicking around in the system, and that Red would soon drink himself to death anyhow. Which he did. And good riddance.

He died when Nancy Jane was fourteen and had achieved that certain age of teenage rebellion, so Hallie suggested that her great-niece might be happier moving back over to the Barnswallowper place and getting it up and running again. After all, Hallie had taught her how to hunt varmints and wild game and how to protect herself with those guns, too. She taught her how to green up a place with her water allotments, how to deal with a wood stove, and how to keep her clothes more or less clean. She hadn't given her much appreciation for book learning, but did take time to teach her how to add up the ranch accounts, figure what she'd earned from her livestock sales, and decide what she still had left to spend on fences and feed. So it was that young Nancy Jane moved back to the old homestead on Oozle Road and lived there in relative solitude, seclusion, and contentment for many, many years. Then along came the Romeros.

In the beginning, Eduardo's job was only supposed to be temporary, but Nancy Jane was pushing 60 now; of course, she wouldn't admit it, but the ranch work seemed to be harder these days, her bones stiffer, her reactions slower, and Eduardo watched her. He knew how to be there when she needed him, whether it was to drag a newborn calf out of the mud or to buck bales of hay into the truck bed. Since Camilia had arrived, the house had brightened: colors, sunlight and the spicy fragrances of good cooking filled the rooms. A hollow place in her life that Nancy Jane hadn't even been aware of was filled. And then there were Toño and Jesus. Nancy Jane had never had a kid, much less a grandkid, so she didn't realize that her estimation of those two was merely what grandmothers feel for their grandkids. To put it plainly, she wasn't objective in her assessments. All over the world there are kids like Toño and Jesus: exceptionally witty and intelligent, strikingly good looking, and fated for amazing success in a difficult world. To locate the many kids like that, just ask their grandmothers! Grandmothers would die — or kill — for these kids, and Nancy Jane had unwittingly fallen into the category of grandmother to those two boys.

Well, to get on with it. Nowadays there was also someone else hanging around Nancy Jane's house. That Patch! What a pest! Always there, chopping wood, repairing the kitchen screens, helping Eduardo with the starter on the four-wheeler. When she thought of him, Nancy Jane grumbled to herself, "The old bastard. What the hell does he want from me, anyhow?" But she knew the sound of his vintage '64 Dodge truck, a vehicle whose continuing mobility alarmed the neighbors, and she knew when to expect that sound on the dusty gravel of her driveway. She'd come to count on it. The approach of that truck, with Buddy perched like royalty on the front seat beside his master, had come to be part of the way things should be, these days.

Today, however, after her adjustment to all these people having come into her life, Nancy Jane was suddenly plunged back into solitude, and she wasn't sure she could handle it. The first night and the first day after the Romeros fled the house felt like infinity. Where had they gone for refuge? Were they okay? Worse yet, Patch didn't show up like he was supposed to. Of course, she assured herself she didn't need the old geezer or miss him, but where was he, anyhow? Had word already spread about last night? Was he trying to steer clear of her for some reason? Did he only come to see them when Camilia was cooking?

There was extra work because Eduardo and Toño weren't there. Half-heartedly, she tackled it. It still didn't take her mind off the problem of the ICE agent. Of course, she kept her gun close by, knowing there could be more of those government sons-of-bitches, and they could pop up any time. It made her jumpy — she would open a few gates in the irrigation pipe, moving the water flow down the line, then she'd scan the hills nearby for human movement. It was like being tormented by no-see-'ems, those tiny stinging gnats that sneak up, swarm over you, biting and making life hell. F...ing cops. If she ever got a bead on one, she knew she could deal with him, just like she'd dealt with that loser last night.

She dug angrily at the ditches and cussed that other bastard, Frickleson, who she suspected was stealing water again. She wished she knew how to use a computer; she would look up ICE agents, maybe learn if more were coming, but she'd never touched a computer in her life. Her thoughts returned to last night. For what must have been the thousandth time she squinted into the surrounding hills and tried to reassure herself that what she had done was all she could do right now for her family. Yes, her family.

12
Neddie and Tess Share Tidbits

Neddie Corbit didn't even like potatoes. There was getting to be more entries every year, and she and Tess had to taste every darned one of them and read the recipe to boot before they made their decision and awarded the prizes. She was getting old. It was too much anymore, and this year Tess was no help. She and Tess usually chit-chatted away as they tasted, compared opinions, shared gossip, but this year Tess was quiet as a sick cat. She wouldn't say 'boo.' Neddie suspected health issues. Tess and Gus were younger than her and Freddy, but even so they were getting up there, enough to be in line for the stuff that could come at you: bad guts, stiff bones, even cancer.

At first, Neddie tried sharing gossip about herself, mostly old stuff; that was easiest, and might draw Tess out and get her to share her own worries. She led off with her favorite topic. "Been two years already since the fire. Can't hardly believe it, can you?"

Tess, walking in from the little community center kitchen with a warm potato pie said, "mmmf," and set the dish on a pad. Undaunted, Neddie continued.

"You know, the neighbors came so fast that day, and then the fire department. They were able to save a lot of our things." Neddie chortled. "Old Maggie, though. You remember how she threw the dishes out the window? She got so excited, and she thought she was saving them." Neddie looked at Tess for appreciation of the old joke. Tess smiled back wanly, so Neddie continued. "Yeah, I'm still picking up pieces of glass from where those plates hit the ground. She was flying them like frisbees."

Tess said something that sounded like, "Everybody's got problems," and turned to go back into the kitchen.

Neddie's eyes followed her, then she shrugged and mumbled to herself, "Well, that would be right." She moved the contest entries around, making sure the cold potato dishes were in one place, the hot soups and casseroles in another, and breads and donuts on another table. They always tasted the hot dishes first, before they cooled. Tess had them badly mixed up this year.

Returning to the room with a pot of soup, Tess seemed to make an effort at small talk. "Well, this is the last one. I think we can start tasting." This was followed by, "Your Mission furniture was destroyed in that fire, wasn't it?"

Glad her friend was talking, Neddie responded, "Yes, yes it was. It was too heavy and awkward to get out. That stuff is worth a pretty penny, too. Fred and I didn't care, though, since we made 'er out with our lives. And people grabbed old photos and papers from Fred's office. You know Romero's baby, Jesus? They even got out with his birth certificate. I was glad; Romeros had trusted us to keep it. That should help Cammie once this government figures out what it's going to do about wetbacks." She took a plastic spoon and made her first taste. She and Tess had a code that helped speed things up on judging day. If they pointed the spoon bowl toward the dish, that meant 'delicious.' The bowl pointed away and the handle pointed to it meant 'ugh.' A partially turned spoon meant, 'Maybe—we'll need to taste again.' Today there were many entries, so they were anxious to move things along. Neddie pointed the handle toward her first dish. She didn't like the olives that were rafting around in the soup. Tess was tasting a casserole, but Neddie could have sworn there were tears in her eyes. She'd have to try a different tack.

"Well, anyhow, Tess. That fire is old news. How are you and Gus doing these days? Everything all right over at your place?"

Tess looked up sharply, and Neddie could see her eyes shutter. "Oh, yeah. Everything's fine." Quickly she turned to the recipe in her hand. Different topic. "They really shouldn't use frozen hash browns, you know. This tastes good, but this contest is about real potatoes."

Before Neddie could comment on the definition of real potatoes, Kelly Gallowup, the town clerk, wandered in, sipping coffee. Neddie's heart sank. Kelly loved to chat, but they really shouldn't be doing their judging with someone else in the room, especially not Kelly. She was related to everyone in town, and she gossiped a lot. Neddie and Tess liked to compare their assessment of the dishes, but they couldn't do it with Kelly here. This was going to hold things up. Neddie checked her watch.

Kelly relaxed against a cabinet and said, "So, how's it goin', ladies?" She loved these old women. They represented a historical era she wished she hadn't missed. They were a real part of the festival itself, which had started when the town still had a clothing emporium, two gas stations, a building that housed phone operators, a station for farmers to deliver their fresh milk and cream, a pharmacy, a high school, and a post office. It was a booming metropolis. It had since lost all but the post office. It had managed to generate a farm supply store. The school was now a Montessori, grades one through six, and crowded with newcomers. Instead of the other enterprises there was now a restaurant with a bar, a bed and breakfast, and a shop that offered tourists the urban concept of what the West should be. Oh, yeah, there was also the church on the corner which had soldiered on through good times and bad.

Well, at any rate, those were the days. Kelly yearned for them. She had a concealed carry permit, and kept her gun close. It seemed she encountered so many weirdos these days in her work as the town clerk. There were hippies and atheists, sex fiends and dope dealers who regularly dropped into her office; at least, that is what they looked like to her. Back in the old days people knew what morals were. The weirdos would have been in jail. Unfortunately, the jail from those old times, which sat just up the street from here, was falling down, sinking back into the dobie hillside that had supported it. Kelly wished they'd restore the thing and throw the creepy elements that hung around town into it. She'd be glad to help round them up.

Responding to the friendly Kelly in a voice that she hoped

was courteous but not welcoming, Neddie said, "Oh, we're doing just fine, Kelly. We still have a lot of entries to go through, though." This was a pointed hint. Tess, on the other hand, seemed oblivious to their guest. She was poking among the various dishes, sliding them around, mumbling to herself.

"I wonder where it went? Where could it be?"

Frowning, Neddie asked, "Where could what be, Tess?" Kelly, interested, added, "Are you missing something?" to which Tess shook her head.

"Oh, no, no, I'm just a little ... tired today." Her left hand came out of the pocket of her long, quilted skirt. The hand was empty and annoyed. "I didn't sleep well last night. You know how that is."

Instantly sympathetic, Neddie said, "Oh, I surely do. I surely do." Kelly, who was no spring chicken herself, added, "That's right. That three a.m. tossing and turning. Why, just the other night ..."

Neddie interrupted with, "But Tess, were you missing something in particular?"

Tess stared at the table as if trying to find an answer, nervously rubbing the fingers of her left hand together. "No, I ... well, I ..." then she seemed to see a solution to her problem, something to say to the sympathetic, inquiring faces of the two women. "No, no, no. It's just silly. Usually Cammy Romero has an entry, and I ... well, I was looking forward to tasting it."

Suspicious and upset, Neddie said, "But maybe she does have something here. These don't have names." She didn't want Kelly to spread the word that the contest was somehow rigged, that they knew who had brought in which dishes. Tess spoke up.

"Oh, you're right. This is embarrassing. It's just that her food tastes like it really came from Mexico, so I recognize it. Last year she brought Mexican Skillet Potatoes with taco seasoning, pico de gallo, and sour cream and, and, and well, she's a good cook ... and ..." And, well, this wasn't going well. Tess felt herself babbling. She finished in a rush. "And I also lost my knife."

"Your knife? Here? What kind of knife?" Kelly had gone immediately into search mode. Knives, like guns, had a special value, good for defense. She pushed things around on the table,

Hidden Treasure (or) Where is Jesus?

re-adjusting the plastic signal spoons.

Both of the older women were now alarmed. Tess blurted, "No, Kelly, just my pocket knife. It wouldn't be here. I think I lost it by the corrals. But ... but ..."

"Did you look there?"

"I will. I did. Of course. It's just that it was from my father, and I'm used to having it handy. Like to cut a piece of this potato bread or something. It's just that us older people, we get habits. You're too young to understand. I just kind of expect it to be in my pocket, and when it's not, it ... I get distracted."

Neddie had now come up with a good solution to the Kelly problem. Standing at her elbow, she dished a bowl of soup. "Kelly, dear, I know you missed your breakfast, having to get here so early to open up and all, so you must be hungry, even though you have so much to do back in your office. Take this on in with you and eat while you work." By now, Kelly had the soup and Neddie had her elbow, steering her toward the door. "It's okay, dear. Don't worry about us. We just need to get going now, to get done." Kelly was in the hallway, and before she firmly closed the door, Neddie added, "That's a good soup. I already tasted it—lots of bacon, ham, potatoes, and cheese." With that, the door clicked shut and Neddie turned to her friend and sighed. "There, now. We are running out of time. We must get started tasting."

The women bent to their work: chicken-potato loaf; deep-dish potato pie; stuffed baked potatoes; an excessive number of potato salads; potato biscuits; potato bread; potato donuts; and a potato-nougat cake. Neddie was especially fond of sweet things, and she tried not to let that cloud her fair judgment. Tess had grown quiet, but they were both focused on examining the entries. Before she could worry again about her friend, Neddie's eyes lit on a soup recipe entitled, '*Kartoffelsuppe nach Bayrischer Art*,' which the entrant had helpfully translated as, 'Bavarian Potato Soup.' Unable to restrain herself, Neddie said, "Wow, look at this one! Some kind of foreign treat!"

Tess looked up, then seeing what Neddie was tasting she actually laughed. "Yeah, that's a dandy, isn't it? Reminds me of my old Gus and his German roots. What do you think of it?"

"Well, pretty good. Sausage and the works."

"Can you taste the nutmeg and paprika?"

Neddie sipped another spoonful, shook her head. "Not sure. It's good, though." She thought, 'Now, that's more like my old Tess.'

Tess said, "You know, I have to fight a prejudice I have. I like just plain food, you know, the old foods found around here. Some of these strike me as people trying to show off. Like this one. What are stupice tomatoes, anyhow? You'd have to go to Denver to find all the ingredients people use."

"Yeah. And then there's the ingredients you're supposed to weigh instead of measure." Neddie reached across the table to snag a recipe near some elaborate potato rolls. "Did you see this one? It calls for '60 grams of Parmegiano Reggiano, thinly grated,' and 'Italian speck.' What the hell is that?" Both women snorted, and Neddie added, "And where would you get it? Reminds me of the ones that keep calling for kosher this and that. This one calls for kosher salt. Where would you get that—and who the heck around here needs kosher, anyhow?"

Tess had looked up sharply. "Well, I ... I suppose somebody might." She hesitated, then added, "Whoever submitted the recipe is probably Jewish."

"Oh, sure, that's probably right. That makes sense. I just didn't consider it." She decided to change the subject. Something about the kosher thing seemed to have stirred Tess up again. Rubbing her stomach and eyeing the food-laden tables, Neddie said, "I didn't realize just taking bites of food could be so exhausting."

"Me, neither." Tess pulled out a folding chair and sat. "I need a break." She was a heavy woman with round, rosy cheeks that normally looked jolly. She was one of those who often felt a need to pinch a few leftovers after others had left the table, and felt it necessary to taste the cookies before offering them to her family. Today, however, despite the potato bites, she looked pale, her hands nervous, picking at her cuticles.

Neddie sat, too. Also tired, she went back to the topic that had been uppermost in her mind for two years, now. "You know, that fire?" Neddie's obsession wore on Tess, but she didn't let it show. They were good friends, and the fire had been an exciting event, taking its place in community lore. A mistakenly identified log, which turned out to have been pure pitch, had at last doomed the dignified old ranch house. At the time, Neddie stood stunned and barefoot in her flowered cotton nightgown, watching the first slow flames bloom into a conflagration that seemed to destroy all hope. Then neighbors flowed to her, kind and risk-taking and breathless, and brave people from the local fire house, looking like kids to the aging Corbits, and Neddie's memories shifted from desolation to having been loved past anything she could ever return. This was what she tried repeatedly to express to Tess, this inexpressible thing, and Tess in her turn tried to understand it once more, no matter how many times she had heard it.

Today, however, there was something else on Neddie's mind. It was very private, just between her and Freddy and the girls, and she wouldn't have thought of telling even Tess if it hadn't been that she had been acting so darned down in the mouth all day. Neddie had been thinking about it while she was tasting, and she thought maybe sharing this private news might perk Tess up, distract her a bit. The woman needed it, lord knows. So Neddie continued. "You know, that fire? Well, Tess, that fire woke me and Freddy up. We could have died that night. Then what? We been talkin' it over and decided that we have to have a will. We're not like you and Gus. We got no kids to obviously inherit, no big family. So where's our ranch gonna go when we kick it?"

Tess looked up with mild interest. "Sure. A will's a good idea." Her gaze drifted tiredly across the laden tables. "Everybody dies, don't they? Some time."

Neddie scowled, studying her friend. This was bringing her back to her health issue theory. Did Gus or Tess have cancer? That would account for the distracted behavior. Now Tess added, "And I suppose there are some who should be helped along. Some that need to be dead before what we might call, you know, natural."

This threw Neddie. She was silent. Abruptly, Tess focused again. "Evil," she said, "Should go." Then, "So what were you telling me about your will?"

"Oh, I..." Neddie cleared her throat, rattled. Irrelevantly, her mind told her that there was still steam coming off the pots of potato soup. Gathering herself, she drew up a smile. "The girls. We have Ed's girls, our nieces, and they aren't a bad lot. Our little Katelyn, she took up with that Toño Romero, Cammy's boy, and they make a cute couple. With Fred's brother, Ed, passed on, we are about the only family those girls have, so we fixed the will all up right, got us a lawyer and so-on, then got them together and told them yesterday. You should have seen them, Tess! They were so tickled. Frankie Belle rushed over to hug us both, saying 'thank you, thank you,' and Katelyn burst into tears. Told us we were good people."

Trying to repeat what her niece had said, Neddie choked up again, a tear making its way through the hills and valleys of her face. She ducked her head and poked at the code spoons, pushing the two with their bowls aimed at the orange-potato pudding even closer. Tess hauled herself out of the flimsy chair and reached out, saying, "There, there," but just then there was a vigorous knocking on the door.

Kelly Gallowup burst in with a cheery, "Now how you ladies doin'? You 'bout done? These two have a question for you."

Larry Gallenas and his girl, Pewter, were directly behind her, their bright faces peering over her shoulder. "Hey, smells great in here! We want this job!"

"You can have it. What do you kids need?"

"Just wondered." The teens wriggled their way past Kelly's husky back, and Larry's hand slipped to the bowl of potato donuts as he talked. His fingers didn't come back empty, despite a mock slap from Kelly. "Anyhow, we been lookin' for the Ripper's kids, you know, Syd and Spook. You seen 'em anywhere?"

"Ripper? Syd and Spook?"

Pewter chose to clarify. "He's talkin' about Nola Rippe. You know. We babysit her kids while she irrigates, but yesterday when she picked 'em up she was really blowin' wind out her ass. We were afraid she'd rough 'em up or somethin'. We thought if we could find 'em, we'd take 'em to go explore the stalls, maybe get 'em a toy or a hot dog or burger."

"It's too early for burgers," Larry corrected. "We'd have to get 'em a pancake at the fire department booth."

"I know, Larry. Shut up. That's not the point." Pewter punched his arm, which reminded him of his big brother, Luke. Oh, well, whatever.

"Oh, you know what I mean. Anyhow, we saw that meth head, Nola the Ripper, coming out of the porta-potty, but no kids with her. I hope she didn't stuff 'em down the hole."

"Larry, for god's sake! Anyhow …."

The old women, sharp-eyed, had been taking it all in. Neddie said, "I know that damn Nola. She's a trouble maker. But Kelly knows we've been in here all day. We couldn't have seen the kids."

Tess, behind her, had been filling paper plates. "Here, people. Taste these for us. We've just about got it narrowed down, but we'll take another opinion." Fair judging conditions had clearly fallen to the needs of hungry teenagers.

The room fell silent as Kelly, Larry, and Pewter attempted to look professional rather than just hungry. Suddenly, Pewter burst out, "What is this? It tastes like orange pudding. It's delicious. Does it even have potatoes in it?"

Neddie winked at Tess, who fingered the spoons that had pointed to it. "Yes, indeed, it does. Mashed potatoes, oranges, almonds … even rum. Kinda unique, right?"

"Yeah, I think you should pick it. Come on, now, Lare, let's go find the kids."

13

Gordy Finds Toño

"Yeah, I seen ya' up here yesterday." Toño hadn't said anything yet. His approach had been hesitant and cautious, but Gordy's words surprised him so much that he came to a complete halt. When he spoke, Gordy's upper half was buried under the hood of the old Bronco. Toño wondered how he even saw him now, much less yesterday. Gordy emerged, tossed his wrench loosely toward his toolbox, and scrubbed at his hands with the greasy rag that he'd laid on the fender. "What I haven't been able to figure," he continued, "is why you keep hangin' out in that dirty old shed?"

"Well, I ... I ..." Toño stammered. "Look, I'm sorry. I didn't mean to intrude on your property."

Gordy grinned at him. "You act like you're hidin'." He had a blond cowlick that was just long enough to drop into his eyes. He shook it back and peered at Toño, who, in his turn, was finding it such a relief to talk to a human being again that he returned the grin in spades.

"Yeah, I'm hidin'. Tryin' to. I guess I didn't do such a hot job of hidin' from you, though."

"Well, I try to help Gramma and Grampa when I'm over here from Denver. They're so damned old, and they got that guy Frickles on that drives 'em nuts. He fucks with their water allotment, changes the settings on the divider boxes up above, and stuff. I keep watchin' for him, and caught a glimpse of you lookin' out the window over there. What are you hidin' from, anyhow?'

"An ICE agent. You know what an ICE agent is?"

Still holding the rag, Gordy scratched his head, leaving a streak of grease across the cowlick. "Nah, can't say as I do."

"Well, I was born in Mexico. My folks are Mexican. I been here since I was a little kid, but the government can't ..."

"Oh, yeah, I heard about you guys. You're called Dreamers. Kind of half Mexican and half American."

Toño was offended. "Well, actually, I'm pretty much all American. I think it's just the government that's mixed up, can't make up their f'ing minds. They told us we could stay, but lately they been sending those ICE agents to put us back in Mexico. I didn't lose nothin' in Mexico."

"Mmmmf." Gordy seemed unimpressed. "I'm hungry. You got any food with you in the shed?"

"Well, I ... well, I got a granola bar you could have." It was the last granola bar in his pack. He hadn't expected to have to extend hospitality from his hiding place.

Gordy laughed. "Nah, you don't need to feed me. I was thinkin' of feedin' you. I bet you ain't been eatin' so good lately. When did you start hidin' from that ICE agent?"

"Oh, I ... I got here Thursday. Thursday night."

"Couple days. Bet you could use a roast beef sandwich and some hot coffee." Gordy tossed the rag back onto the Bronco fender. "Come on down to the house."

Toño sobered immediately. "I, uh ... I'm in a pretty dangerous situation. My folks, too. I don't think I better let everyone know where I am. For sure not your grandparents."

He wondered if Gordy knew his grandfather was a *mischlinge*. "See, I was just gonna ... could you somehow get this note to Katelyn for me?" He extended his shed-dirty hand, holding a folded piece of paper. "She needs to know I'm safe, and I can't text her. They could trace my phone."

"So whaddya plan to do?"

It hit Toño now. He stared into Gordy's kind, questioning face and rubbed at his own fuzzy chin. His empty stomach growled threateningly, and his eyes got shiny with the suppressed tears. "You know, Gordy," he said, "You know, Gordy. I'm not sure. But I can't face your grandparents. That won't help. I gotta think."

The grin was back, and Gordy picked up a bolt he'd laid on top of the engine, tossing it from hand to hand. "Ah, no worries. They're not even there. They're down doin' stuff at Potato Days, and Gram left a pile of good eatin' right where we can find it. Come on, we'll go down to the house and talk about asshole ICE agents and big plans and stuff, then maybe, if we need to, we can set you up somewhere with some decent food and blankets or somethin' for a couple days. You'll think better with food in your belly." He suddenly threw the bolt at Toño, asking, "Know where the hell this should go?" Toño's hand shot out, a reflex, snagging the bolt mid-air as if it were a fast ball. He started to answer, but Gordy was already walking down the hill, still talking.

"So here's the deal. That was my great-grandpa's Bronco. He liked to go fishin' in it. Grandpa Gus says if I can get it runnin' I can have it. So far my success has been shit. Maybe you can take a look, see if you got any ideas."

Toño had caught him and was keeping pace. "Sure, I could try." He juggled the bolt, looking around them: the field, the lane, a friend — all in broad daylight. He felt exposed. He felt hopeful.

14
Sheriff Pat Garrett Enjoys Most of the Parade

What Sheriff Pat Garrett felt could only be described as smug. Not in a conceited way, mind you, as that would be contrary to his character, but rather in being, finally, totally satisfied with his personal life. Here was a man who described himself as 'butt-ugly'; a man with big jug ears; a man with a large, disfiguring scar that roamed down his left cheek, traveled along his neck, headed for his chest, and disappeared furtively under his shirt; a man with a pointless, pale, drooping mustache draped on each side of his chin; a man who had lost more than one desirable woman to his handsome brother, Lyle (a couple of Garrett's earlier girlfriends had even married Lyle, but quickly divorced him); at any rate, Garrett was a man on whom the passing years had begun to have a noticeable effect. He'd given up on finding that special woman who could love him for what he was. The courage to woo and win had long since been deleted from his résumé. He'd come to accept his lonely state, but now, lo and behold! An unpredictable shifting of fate, a change in kismet, and here he was, standing along the Potato Days parade route holding the hand of the woman he considered to be the most beautiful in the world, Jenny Threewinds, and on that hand he was holding—he could feel it!—there was a pretty engagement ring, the best he could afford. Normally an observant man, today Pat Garrett saw nothing. Nothing, of course, except Jenny. Jenny, that miracle! Jenny, that amazement! Jenny, the one who had accepted when he asked, accepted as if she thought it was about time. The look she had given him last night, once he summoned his courage, made him forget there was ever a brother Lyle who stole women. This woman was his, and she had no intention of ever leaving him.

Garrett had put one of his best deputies, Louie, in charge in the big town, Riversmet. He could trust her to keep a lid on things there. Across the street he spotted McCracken, his regular sidekick, and her boyfriend, Red, both good deputies. They were here mostly for the fun of it. Garrett and his team had worked up here a couple of times on cases involving murder, but basically Croysant was a small town and these festivities shouldn't require much law enforcement except for maybe a drunk or two at the dance tonight. Business as usual was the furthest thing from his mind today. He relaxed next to Jenny and smiled dopily at the people who greeted him as they passed to find their own place along the sidewalk. Jenny kept showing her ring, flashing it, if you will, and he didn't care. He just let it happen. Life was good.

They had a good spot. The flat-bed truck on which the announcer and judges did their thing was about two car lengths away, to their right. It was a ringside seat, because as the parade entries passed, they would stop in front of the judges to strut their stuff. Garrett hadn't been to Potato Days before, but Jenny was a fan, and she expected the Brownie Troop to stop there and do cartwheels, the church ladies' auxiliary to burst into song as they accompanied themselves by strumming laundry scrub boards and beating on tin rinse tubs with wooden spoons. There should be at least one pack string that would stop, throw the pack saddles off their side-stepping mules, set up a "wilderness camp," then demonstrate how quickly they could pack up again and be on their way. Teens on floats would pick victims in the crowd and squirt them with water guns; old codgers sitting on hay bales on their reunion floats would do the same; little kids on fire trucks and forestry vehicles would feverishly fling candy into the crowd, always undershooting or overshooting their target. Dog trainers would pass, stopping at the judging truck to have the canines show their stuff. At the end of the parade there would be gunslingers and a shoot-out, the bad guys falling with great care a few feet away from the steaming piles of horse manure, the floozies shrieking in mock dismay at the loss of their men. Jenny couldn't wait to share. Garrett wouldn't say much, but she knew he'd love it.

John and Agnes Michaelson and Gus Westberg were sitting on folding canvas picnic chairs in front of Garrett and Jenny. They were reserving three empties for Tess and the Corbits. The Michaelson granddaughter, whom they referred to as 'Pickles,' a college student at San Jose State, was expounding to Gus about the philosophical merits of what she termed 'Ethicarianism.' Jenny could overhear just enough of the conversation to catch on that the young woman was getting teased by the two old geezers sitting on either side of her. Her grandfather, whose cadaverous cheekbones, lined cheeks, and short graying beard recalled Abe Lincoln, leaned a large ear in her direction, listening attentively over the rattle and bang of parade preparations, while on her other side was Gus, a solid man with a round, unshaven face under a Stetson that looked as if it had gone ten rounds with an enraged bull and lost. Gus's face was saddle leather, with smile lines etched in contrastive white where they had attempted to take refuge from the high country sun. Now Gus leaned toward Pickles and said, "So let me get this straight. Ethicarians ain't vegetarians, right?"

Painfully serious, Pickles replied, "No, we eat beef and so-on. Vegetables don't like to die, either. We are just careful that the food we eat has been treated with the utmost humanity and with the least possible damage to the environment."

Gus chimed in. "That's a damn good idea. You're just about as smart as your old granddad there. He teach you all that?'

"No, I ..."

"Here's how I see it, though. Gotta be fair. Cows gotta treat us right, too, wouldn't you say, John?"

Michaelson nodded solemnly. "Don't matter, though. They're concoctin' fake beef now. Pretty soon we can all just eat chemical burgers, and since our cows'll be useless, we can drop 'em all off in Central Park. Those people know how to treat a cow."

Pickles was annoyed. "Seriously, in India the Hindus ..."

Gus interjected. "I still say it ain't fair. Like I said, last year after my surgery I was innocently forking hay to those greedy bovines, and a old steer butted me right in the belly, right on my stitches. Set me back two weeks. Under your system, an animal like that oughtta get jail time."

"You bet. And what about the carrots?"

"Grandpa, for pete's sake, what about the carrots?"

"Well, you can't eat 'em raw. All that screamin' with pain and all. How you gonna mercifully kill 'em ..."

Pickles had had enough. She narrowed her eyes at her granddad and said, "Grandpa, you wouldn't know what it meant to be an ethicarian if the directions were written in dumb-dumb talk and hangin' out the end of your nose."

Briefly thwarted but very pleased, Michaelson spluttered as he rummaged in his repertoire for an appropriate response to his granddaughter. There must be several, but unfortunately the potentially witty exchange was interrupted by the arrival of Tess and Neddie and Fred Corbit, who took the vacant chairs. Jenny shifted on her feet, looking around at the gathering crowd. Following her gaze, Garrett commented, "Lots of people for a little town."

"Yeah, I see a lot I know. There's Tiffany Gallenas. Remember her? She must be on call; she's staying pretty close to the ambulance. And there's the Weinant women, Carmen, Alma, and Gritty. That Gritty, she's always game for anything, in her wheel chair."

Garrett said, "Oh, yeah." He knew Alma well; her knowledge of community had helped him with a couple of murders here in the valley. Boy, she was getting old. Now he added, "Oh, there's the Clarys and the new vet and her kid."

"I'm glad to see Annabelle with Doc." Jenny continued to examine the crowd. "But there's people I'm not seeing that we usually see. Where's Lew Harris? Have you seen him? And there's a little group of Mexicans, I think, but I don't see any of the Romeros. They almost always come. And speaking of Lew, what about Patch? There's talk about Patch and Nancy Jane Barnswallowper, that they have a thing. Isn't that cute? But I don't see her here, either."

Garrett said under his breath, his tone pleased, "And we have a thing, too," but no one heard him.

Neddie Corbit had overheard Jenny. She turned around to comment. "You're right. Nancy's usually right here in the middle of things. Maybe she's in the parade today."

Tess turned, too. "She could be, I guess. But you're right. Where are Ed and Cammy Romero? Cammy usually has an entry in the Potato Recipe contest, but not today."

John Michaelson laughed. "She probably got worried about torturing the potatoes."

Tess and Neddie looked puzzled, but Pickles said, "Grandpa," and punched him in the arm. "You should read ..."

Before she could finish, the speakers on the flatbed truck crackled to life, the noise making people nearby jump. "Ladies and Gentlemen! Ladies and Gentlemen! Welcome to the eighty-eighth annual Potato Days festivities!" The announcer, called Spud ever since he'd taken this job 25 years ago, was a chubby, exuberant guy; he danced back and forth across the truck bed as he shouted joyfully to the crowd, the loudspeakers roaring with the exertion. Garrett looked down at Jenny, who raised her eyebrows, spread her hands, and shrugged. Unleashed, Shriner clowns riding tiny motorbikes and throwing candy buzzed up and down the street, and Spud yelled, "First of all, Women and Men, look up! Look up! Yes, over there to the west, here they come, the famous Potato Days flyover team."

Spud looked at his notes. "That first plane you see approaching is a Cirrus SR20. It belongs to Henry Sachen, Mathew Koober, Phillip Gardner, and Jan Mons. It takes a village to raise the money to buy a plane, and that is one classy plane." The crowd obediently tipped their heads to watch the little plane grind toward them. Spud continued, reading, "It is the first such plane to have a parachute that would lower the whole plane safely to the ground in case of loss of control, mid-air collision, or other accident." The plane had reached Croysant and was circling, then saluting by tipping its wings. Everyone clapped. Spud, full of chortling good humor, said, "Of course, no chance of a mid-air collision with the next plane. It seems to be having trouble keeping up. Ah, here it comes!"

"Well, as they say, Grandma was slow, but she was old. Ha ha. That plane has an excuse just like Granny. It was built from scratch by Arthur and Becky Zimmer. The plane is an Easy Eagle, built for under $10,000 with parts from Great Plains Airline Supplies." The first plane was receding into the distance and now this plane approached the town to buzz the crowd and wave. "The Zimmers tell me they use that little sweetheart to commute around the valley and sometimes to just go up and look at the sky. Becky is piloting today, and doing a fantastic job."

Garrett was continuing to look into the west, waiting for the next plane. Jenny nudged him. "That's all, honey," she whispered in his ear. "Croysant is a two-plane town."

Fred Corbit, sitting by Gus, compensated for his poor hearing by shouting loudly, "Not much rain the other night. Wish it'd come on in — ain't seen it this dry since '87."

Shouting loudly to return the favor, Gus responded, "My dad always said, 'two things you never turn down, a new calf and a little rain.'"

Spud, done shuffling his papers, stepped back to the mike and once more drowned out individual conversation in the crowd. "So now, Ladies and Germs, what we've all been waiting for! Here comes the parade!" Reading from his notes, he went on, "As you know, the elevation around here is too high for growing most fruits and vegetables. Our old-timers couldn't organize an apple days or a strawberry days, like the folks down in the valley do, but they sure could do potatoes." Mumbling. "Let's see. I've got some statistics here — where did I put those statistics?" Louder. "Well, at any rate, we grow a heck of a lot of potatoes here in our little town."

At the far end of the street, the American Legion appeared, their banner carried smartly by two of the younger veterans. Spud continued, "There used to be enough rain in this area to grow potatoes up on the mesas without irrigatin'. Couldn't do it nowadays in this dry weather, but wait'll you see the spuds over in the community building. Big as cantaloupes." The veterans had reached the announcer's truck, where they now stopped.

"Well, here they are, our brave American veterans carryin'

our flag. You all stand and pay proper respects while our talented Alyssa Potsdorf sings the national anthem."

And so it went, a short parade, but satisfying. Floats, horses, donkeys, service vehicles blasting sirens, political groups passing out campaign literature, and a mock baseball team vigorously tossing potatoes to each other with occasional shouts of, "Hey, watch it! That one was rotten!" to the laughter and catcalls from the crowd.

Suddenly there was a volley of shots from the east end of the street. Garrett dropped Jenny's hand and stiffened, but she laughed. Leaning into him again so she could be heard, she said, "It's okay, honey. It's just the gunslingers. They're at the end of the parade and my favorite part. They're all big hams." Garrett aimed his bushy eyebrows down at her, still scowling, but she continued. "They're shooting blanks, of course. Mick Woodard organizes them every year. He knows his guns—he's careful of the load. They stop a couple of times along the parade route and have a shootout. You'll see. They'll stop here by the parade judges and make a really big show."

Garrett was nervous now. He didn't like the idea of the guns. This seemed to be a tradition, but not a good one, he feared. He squinted down the street, watching the progress of the gunslingers and ignoring the intervening floats. Others were leaning toward them in anticipation, and there were ripples of laughter from the spectators as the gunfighters exchanged insults. The group of over a dozen heavily costumed locals stopped in front of the announcer's truck, and Spud said with mock sorrow, "Here they are, just the people to spoil a good day for all of us. Dastardly Black Bart and his band of hooligans. Why, I fear they may have robbed the bank. I hope you people have some gold buried in your back yard to cover your losses, as it looks like old Bart plans to ride out of town with your hard-earned money."

Mike Woodard, the 'Black Bart' of the group, yelled up at Spud, "Shut up, you chicken pickin' dog kisser," then he pretended to aim toward the truck, shot twice, and said, "Oh, great calumny! I have missed!" Spotting Kelly Gallowup near the announcer's truck, he shouted, "Kelly, my girl, shoot that cross-eyed excuse for monkey breath," to which Kelly roared with joy, "It'd have to be for real, Bart! Can't do it—Sheriff's watchin'." She gestured at Garrett and winked, then added, "But at least I wouldn't miss like you did!" The crowd was swollen with pleasure, and Garrett had to admit that the rambunctious, spontaneous display taking place in front of him was working on his funny bone.

Part of the fun hinged on the fact that the scene was being played out by locals; the sheriff recognized several of them. Duz Weinant, of all people, was there, and he was shouting at another surprising participant, Lew Harris's reticent son, Clint. "Put up your hands, Black Bart, or your days on this earth are numbered." Duz had a large, fakey star on his vest, and Spud solemnly announced, "Oh, thank goodness. It looks like another sheriff is in town." Jenny, holding Garrett's hand, giggled. Clint Harris, always quiet, thrilled the crowd by bellowing, "You got the wrong man, Slippery Dick!"

Sienna Fowler, having turned 13, had been allowed to participate in the shootout, but she had not been allowed to carry a gun. She was a spicy child, and this infuriated her; she was vigorously brandishing a butter knife. She started the parade shouting, "I'll get you, you piece of shit," but her father had nixed that language, too. Parents are no fun. Resentfully, she resorted to bouncing along shouting, "You are a dirty, unclean wad of bear's underwear." This epithet, for some reason, resonated with the small fry along the route who ran along the parade route beside her chanting, "Bear's dirty underwear! Bear's dirty underwear!"

Meanwhile, behind Clint, Cesar Rodriguez and Larry Gallenas were shouting, "We got your back, Bart old Buddy," while Katelyn Corbit flounced up to Duz and clung to him, squealing, "You can take him, Dead Eye Dick." Weinant shot his guns vigorously, and the sound was, to Garrett, unnervingly real. Larry crumbled dramatically to the street while Pewter, her western blouse dipping dangerously low across the chest, knelt beside him, giving hysterical, whining wails and crying out, "Now see what ya' gone and done! Ya' asshole! Ya shot an innocent man!" This was a little too much, and Spud said, "Hey, watch your language, young lady. We got some standards here."

The organizer, Mick Woodard, rushed to the middle of the

shootout, both guns blazing, yelling, "We gotta get some real law and order in this town," while his wife, Nita, pulled at his coat and shrieked, "Don't go in, Deadly Dog! Don't go in there. Oh, my love, stay safe with me!"

At this point, Duz shot Woodard, aka Black Bart, saying, "Your kind are nothing but frass."

'Bart' fell dramatically, floundered about, then raised himself on his elbow and said, "Wait! Before I die, I need to know what 'frass' is!"

Pushing him scornfully with his toe, Weinant said, "Meal worm poop, Bart. Your kind are all meal worm poop." Then he blew on the barrel of his gun, holstered it, and bowed toward the crowd, shouting, "We learn something new every day, don't we?" This performance met with enthusiastic applause, then shouts of, "Watch out, Sheriff!"

Behind Duz, Garfield Fourier, Tess Westberg's second cousin, was doing an elaborate, sneaking walk and enjoying himself immensely. Now he shouted, "Draw, you clump of mustard weed! Reach for your iron, you noxious patch of leafy spurge!" These were bad insults for a rancher to receive, and the crowd was beside itself. This all went on for some time, to the great satisfaction of everyone, with much ado being made over robbed banks and trains and fights that must be finished, while dead bodies piled up, all to the cheers of the onlookers.

Meanwhile, Frankie Belle Corbit was as happy as she had ever been. She was dancing in the group of players, flinging her floozie skirts about, singing 'Frankie and Johnny,' and very much in her personal zone. Yesterday she'd learned of her Uncle Freddy and Aunt Neddie's will, and the future had opened up to her. Better yet, on Thursday she'd gotten rid of her biggest problem. It felt like an omen. Prancing in the street and watching the gunslingers play, she made no real effort to give a show. She just sang to herself, shook her skirts, and thought, "I'm gonna be rich! I'm gonna be rich! I'm gonna have a ranch. And best yet, I'm free! I'm rid of that dirty old S.O.B. forever. I'm gonna head for the big time! Yessirree, next stop, Vegas!" This was the last thought she ever had.

All the gunslingers had expired in clumps in front of the

judge's truck, and all the floozies bent over them in theatrical anguish. The spectators burst into applause, and one by one the troupe got up, dusted off their breeches and dresses, blew on their gun barrels, bowed, curtsied, and laughed with their audience. Everyone had had a good time. It was several minutes before the festive group grew quiet, realizing that something was wrong. One of the floozies wasn't getting up. Before anyone else could react, Leigh McCracken, Sheriff Garrett's main deputy, had elbowed her way through the crowd and was kneeling beside Frankie Belle Corbit, who was lying quite still, in a pool of blood.

15

Lew Also Loses Something Important

For the first time, Lew Harris was worried about being senile. It had been a while back now that Patty had sent Clint to have a word with his father. It was the wrong person to send. Quiet Clint wouldn't say 'shit' if he had a mouthful, anyhow, and on top of that he'd never found it possible to just talk with his cocky little banty-rooster dad. There was a session of coffee and fig newtons and a goodly number of comments on the weather and the amount of hay still available to feed, then finally Clint had broached the topic with, "Patty and I been talkin', and we know you're gettin' kinda old. Happens to us all." 'Happens to us all' seemed strange to Lew, coming from Clint, whom he always thought of as a kid. Had now for over 50 years. But Clint forged on now that he'd started. "So maybe a few more achin' bones, and then there's that trouble you have once in a while, rememberin' and all. Like leavin' your oatmeal pan on the burner and all. And Lucky." The 'and Lucky' was barely audible, as Clint knew the invisible dog could be a bone of contention. "So, we wondered if you wanted us to find someone to come in. You know. Kind of a helper." Clint was also avoiding the word nurse, as that could cause problems. Now he added, an afterthought, "Like Alma has."

For a minute, the oatmeal comment was convincing to Lew. He had left that burner on, and he felt pretty guilty about it. But didn't young people make mistakes, too? And why was Lucky always a problem for people? You'd think nobody else could even see her. She'd kept him company for years, best bird dog he ever had. Some people were just blind; lord, even the sheriff and his cute red-headed deputy, that McCracken, could see that dog. And in addition to that, why would he want to be like Alma? She used to be his baby sitter when he was a kid, and she was pushing a hundred now, sometimes she claimed even more. Surely Clint could see that his own dad hadn't even hit 90 yet. Or had he? Lew tried to think. Anyhow, he had to say to Clint, "Nah, son, tell your wife I don't think I need help. Real sweet of her to think of me, but not necessary for a while. I'll let you know if I get dementia or anything." Relieved to have done their duty by the topic, the two men changed the subject. They talked about cows.

That old age conversation had made Lew uneasy, though, and by today he wasn't so sure about his mental faculties. It had taken him all day Friday to get squared away, and he still couldn't figure out what had happened. He would have sworn that on Thursday Eddy had called to ask him to get his little boy, Jesus, over at Alma's. And that is what he thought he did. Then he drove to the Cowpath — didn't he? — and got food from Jenny to feed the kid. He left Lucky in the car to guard Jesus, and when he got back there was Lucky, all normal, waggin' her tail, happy to see him, like always, but no Jesus. He looked everywhere, in the car, under the car, around the parking lot and nearby brush, but no kid. He hollered, no reply. Finally, doubting his sanity, he got back in the car and drove home. He remembered that clearly. Didn't he? But on the lane that led down to their ranch, there were two little kids.

Two kids. Like little ghosts, looking up at him in his headlights. Didn't Eddy just have the one little boy? Maybe Eddie had asked him to pick up some other kids and he got mixed up. He really felt confused. How could there be two little kids out here in the middle of the night unless it had something to do with his responsibility to Eddy? There shouldn't be any kids at all in this lane, and the little boogers were crying. Maybe he was late. Maybe he was supposed to pick up these kids, then go to the Cowpath. But then Jenny would have closed it for the night, and he wouldn't have been able to feed any kids. He wrestled with the mishmash of thoughts pushing around in his head.

Pulling over, he said out the window, "You kids need a ride?" and they piled in without hesitation, the big one pushing the little one up, as if they belonged. Who the hell were these kids? He tried to remember the conversation with Eduardo and all he could be sure of was that Eduardo had said, "This is top secret, Lew. Like when you were back in the war. Don't tell anyone for a few days, because it is really serious. Promise me you'll be careful, and we'll pick him up soon. He can eat chips and carrots and stuff, pretty much anything." Ed had said 'him,' he didn't say 'they' or 'them.' Did he? Had Eduardo told him to pick up some kids here in the lane or something, and he misunderstood?

He drove to the house, unloaded the kids, and they trudged right on in. He put them in Clint's old bedroom, found blankets and pillows, and they curled up like puppies and went directly to sleep. Lew did not. He wondered if the kids were really in the bedroom. Would other people even be able to see them? Shit, he knew for sure they were there. He stared at the ceiling and tried to puzzle it all out. He'd never been quite clear about why he was supposed to take care of Jesus, anyhow, but at least he knew Jesus. Were these kids Eddy's relatives or something? And why the big secret? He couldn't remember Ed's words. Something about ICE. But this was summer. Still, outside at night, the kids would probably get cold. Maybe that worried his Mexican friend.

In the morning, he decided they were cute kids, but they didn't resemble Eduardo. Eddy must not be the father. Unable to confer with Clint and Patty because of the secret he had, he thought, pledged to keep, he bathed and fed them and parked them in front of the TV, where he set Lucky to guard them. Cautioning them to stay put, that he'd be right back, to which they nodded solemnly, their eyes wide, he took off in his car and headed back to the Cowpath.

He looked for any sign of the mysterious Jesus. There was nothing. He greeted the breakfast patrons going in and listened for possible comments about lone little boys. Nothing. Where was Jesus? Now Lew was worried as much about his own head as he was worried about the little boy. Had there ever been a

Jesus, or was he just a figment of an old man's aged and faulty imagination?

16
Garrett Takes Charge

Jenny was wearing a visored sun hat, straw, with an adjustable strap rounding the back of her head, the strap set just above her graceful neck. An opening above the strap released her long, dark, luxurious hair, its unruly beauty controlled in a thick braid. As with so many things about Jenny, something about that lovely hair slipping out of the small, practical hat possessed Garrett. He wanted to touch it. He was not a publicly demonstrative man, but as the crowd along the parade route relaxed, laughing, talking, and gathering themselves to leave after the gunslinger display, he stole the opportunity to slide his hand into the dangerously tempting tresses. His fingers had just located the lovely hollow in the nape beneath when Neddie Corbit, who was sitting directly in front of him, stood suddenly and threw out her hands. One hand smacked his shoulder, and she said, "No!" but the exclamation had nothing to do with the shoulder. Her hands dropped in a reaching-out gesture as she said again, "No!" then "Not Frankie Belle!" and started across the street. Shaken from his private obsession, Garrett followed the direction of her gaze, then stiffened. Somebody was lying beside the pavement on the other side of the street, and his deputies were pushing through a rapidly assembling crowd. His tumble back into reality was painful but automatic and swift.

His hand dropped to Jenny's arm. "Jenny, quickly. Ask that loud guy on the truck to settle people down and get them to stay put a minute. Tell them there's been an accident, and for everyone's safety they need to stay ... that the sheriff is telling them to stay where they are." A quick nod from Jenny. Garrett didn't pause, but as he made his way toward the fallen woman his eyes were alert, studying the scene.

Tiffany, the paramedic, was already there, kneeling with Deputy McCracken over Frankie Belle. She looked up to say, "She's gone, Sheriff," but he had to read her lips because the loud speaker on the truck had crackled into action with a roar as Spud delivered the Sheriff's message to the crowd. Garrett waited until he finished, then turned to ask a question of his other deputy, Red. Spud, on the truck bed and eager to help, began to repeat and elaborate on the sheriff's message. At this, Garrett wheeled around and headed for the truck, the crowd parting like the Red Sea in front of him.

Garrett could see that people were torn between fear and curiosity. Fear. Here in this tiny town. Hell of a world these days. At the truck he held out his hand for the mike, interrupting Spud mid-sentence. When he was doing his job, Pat Garrett was a person with presence, and he was doing his job now. Surveying the crowd, his voice steady, he said, "This is not a terror attack." Quite frankly, at this moment in time, Garrett wasn't one hundred percent sure that it was not, but he knew what he had to say, and he said it. People carrying coolers and chairs, hurrying toward their trucks, hesitated. People pushing forward to see the fallen woman stopped, their heads going up, alerted to the possibility of a danger they hadn't considered. Garrett repeated the assurance, driving it home, the fact of it, but also the hidden possibility of it. "This is not a terrorist attack. A woman has been shot. It is probably an accident. As most of you know, I'm your sheriff, Pat Garrett. Across the street there you see our medical people and also my deputies. Things are under control. Now we want your help to sort out what happened here."

Having heard it was "just an accident," people began to shuffle and mutter, anxious to get on with their day. Jenny, on tiptoe, murmured a suggestion into Garrett's ear, and he handed her the mike. Jenny was a singer at the Cowpath, and she, too, had presence, a voice that could muster good volume. "Hey, people. Those who maybe saw something, go talk to one of the deputies, okay? Tell 'em what you saw. If you don't think you know anything, we'd appreciate if you'd leave your name and contact info with us up here on the announcer's truck, okay? Just in case, you know? Then you can head off for a burger at the Cowbelle booth or something, right? Time for lunch. Drop off your info right here with Spud and the ladies here."

Red stopped Garrett, who was already halfway across the crowded street. All he said was, "Hey, Chief."

"Yeah, Red. Get hold of Edith. Of course, we need Thompson, but we need Hobbs asap, and we could use a couple more deputies. Anybody Louie can spare." Mick Woodard and his wife, Nita, had pushed up behind Red. Mick's face was belligerent with innocence.

"Look, Sheriff. I checked each and every one of those guns. Those were blanks. I will guarantee it."

Bristling with spousal support, Nita said, "I saw a gang of Mexicans right over there. Not our locals. Slunk away right after Frankie Belle dropped. She was into drugs, you know."

The two gunslinger organizers were obstructing Garrett's progress toward McCracken and the other people bent over Frankie Belle. Woodard wanted to continue speaking. "Mark my words. this was no accident."

Looking past Woodard, Garrett said, noncommittal, "Uh huh." Then, "Look. Woodard, isn't it? Look, Mr. Woodard, you gather up every single one of those gunslinger people and have them wait up there in the room next to the town office. Do it now. Oh, but leave me Weinant and Harris. And who's that girl?"

Garrett was indicating Katelyn, dressed as a floozie and enfolded in her Aunt Neddie's arms, both shivering with shock. Looking over, Nita said, "Oh, that's Neddie's niece. She's a good girl, wouldn't hurt a flea."

"All right, leave her for now. Get the rest before they take off." Garrett made a beeline for McCracken, who was engaged in crowd control near Frankie Belle's fallen form. "Deputy, we need some help."

Glad to have him take charge, McCracken snapped to attention. "Yes, sir, Chief. What's up?"

"We need those guns, and with a minimum of smearing of

prints. See if you can't get some of these people we know, like Duz Weinant, Clint Harris, maybe Fourier over there, get them to locate the guns and gather them up. Get a sack or something — warn them about touching."

A small, pushy person had been vigorously shaking the sheriff's elbow. "Me, too, Sheriff. I can gather guns, too." Garrett looked down to recognize Sienna Fowler, one of the cheekiest little teenagers he'd ever met. He knew her from the chicken case he'd dealt with up here in Croysant. Before she could say more, McCracken saved the day.

"Hey, Sienna. No. I need you with me. I think we're gonna need some supplies from my vehicle, like the fingerprint kit. Right, Chief?" And, without pausing to hear an answer, McCracken knelt in front of the child and formally patted her down. From under her shirt, pushed into the belt, McCracken extracted a sophisticated appearing toy gun. "First, just what is this, kid?"

"Don't tell my folks. It's not real." Sienna's face had gone stubborn. "Sometimes I wish it was but ..."

"No, you don't. And I'll keep this toy one, too, for now."

Garrett turned toward the group of emergency medical people standing protectively by the body. "Sorry, Sheriff, we didn't wait for you to actually secure the scene. Your deputies were here, and it just looks like an accident, anyhow." Tiffany shook her head regretfully, looking at the limp form at the edge of the street, now covered with a blanket. "She's gone. Nothing we can do for her. Shall we go ahead and load her up?"

Stepping past the paramedic, Garrett lifted the blanket, looked at the body, then eyed the lay of the street near where the woman had fallen. "Nah," he said, "Nah, not yet for a little bit. Gotta wait for Detective Hobbs." He dropped the blanket and stood back. Dragging his hand across his mustache, he began with his wrist and ended with a smoothing motion from the tips of his index and third fingers. Red, nearby, knew his boss, and he knew that gesture. It meant Garrett had issues. This death was, after all, no accident.

17

Nancy Jane Barnswallowper Visits the Vet

Solitude was Nancy Jane's natural state. She'd been a socially detached woman most of her life, and she needed that privacy now. She was stressed. She didn't even consider going to the parade. What could she say when people asked her about the Romeros? She could just imagine it. "Nancy Jane, where's your old buddy, Ed? You workin' 'im too hard—makin' 'im irrigate while you party? heh heh." What could she say to that stupid kidding around? She was a shy person in the best of times, and now she had big problems that she felt she must work out for herself. The last thing she wanted was to deal with the jostle of humanity, no matter how well intentioned people might be.

Even though she came up with no plan of action while she was avoiding the Potato Days crowd, at least on Saturday morning her lonely deliberations were uninterrupted. She tackled her broken four-wheeler with zest, then when it was fixed she made a point to go check out the upper divider box. She told herself that maybe Frickleson had been up there, changing the water allotment settings again. The trip to the box took her away from the house, with its associated problems, and up into the serviceberry bushes and quakies. Her dog, Dope, rode joyfully behind her on the four-wheeler, tongue lolling. At first, Dope was perfectly happy to be alone with his mistress, but then he messed up. Dope's misadventure returned them both into the company of humanity.

At the box, Dope jumped off the ATV to nose about; he soon disappeared into the brush while Nancy Jane worked, cleaning out sticks, mud, and rocks that the water had brought down from the mountain. She was just finished and was hooking her shovel back on her vehicle when she heard his screams of pain. Frantically she called him, and as she pushed through the bushes he finally slunk to her, tail between his legs, embarrassed and whining. His face, jaws, and chest looked like a pincushion.

Nancy Jane stared. "You god damned, stupid son of a bitch. Porcupines are damn near extinct around here, and you had to go and find the only one still livin' in a thousand miles." Then she knelt and took the contrite, wounded animal into her arms, saying over and over, "Stupid Dope, stupid Dope," ignoring the redundancy.

As awkward as it was, she held him in her arms while she drove back down the mountain. Once she reached the house, she made a brave attempt with pliers, but poor Dope cried and snapped at her with each tug. She could even see quills up inside his mouth, thick as a bed of spruce needles, hooked into the soft, tender tissue there. Discouraged, she gave up and, cursing steadily, loaded the sad dog on the seat beside her in the pickup and headed for the vet's.

When she arrived she found Jack and Betty Sacks and Sophia Bailey all clustered around the exam table, watching with great interest as Doc Clary inspected little Sneaker, Sophia's dog. Jack and Betty had a ranch up on Peaseford Mesa, and they had a huge cat named Toughy, who wasn't quite as tough as he thought. The trouble for him today seemed to have involved his right front leg, as it was encased in a tidy cast, and Toughy was lying limp as a dead daisy in Betty's motherly arms. Sophia, eight years old at best, was the precocious daughter of Dr. Bailey, the new vet who was trying to help Doc retire. It wasn't easy. Doc liked the animals and he liked the clients, and Dr. Junee Bailey didn't always get a chance to relieve him of the vet work that needed done. Well, she tried.

This cluster of people all looked up as Nancy Jane entered and, seeing Dope, whistled and commented appreciatively. Doc said, "Got into it, didn't he?"

Nancy Jane stomped to the exam table, nudged past Jack, gave Sneaker a gentle but not appreciated push to the side, and set Dope in the place of honor. Sophia snapped, "Hey! Wait a minute! Don't push my dog!"

Doc rubbed the back of his neck and said, "Ah, it's okay, Soapy. Looks like poor old Dope made a big mistake, and now he's payin' for it." Dope whined, providing appropriate sound effects. "Tell you what," Doc continued, rummaging in a drawer at the side of the table. "We'll give him a little something here to help him relax and quit hurtin', and Nancy Jane, you take him over there and keep him on your lap, nice and safe so he don't hurt himself, while we finish takin' care of little Sneaker here. Okay, you two?"

Sophia said grumpily, "'K," but Nancy Jane looked suspiciously around the room. "Where's the lady vet? Couldn't she do somethin' for 'im?" Doc Clary had already given the shot with no objection from Dope, who felt at this point that one needle more or less was not a problem. His head was lowering to the table.

Jack said, "Ah, Nancy Jane, lady doc's gone to help them poor critters in that cattle truck that rolled over on the Stoney City road," while at the same time Doc said, "I think you better move Dope, Nancy Jane. We are just in the middle of getting a cuterebra bot out of Sneaker's neck, and I don't figure you'll want it to get on Dope."

Now, Doc Clary wasn't really worried that the worm would get on Dope. That's not how cuterebra works, and he hadn't even started to extract it yet, but his warning had the desired effect on Nancy Jane, who hurried Dope off the table and sat in a nearby chair, tense and watchful. Dope's head flopped across her thighs and he emitted something that sounded like either a groan or a snore. Jack and Betty turned back toward the surgery table and to what had turned out to be a great afternoon's entertainment.

Doc was talking as he worked, educating Sophia. He'd assessed the lump on Sneaker's neck with his fingers, and now he made a couple of small cuts at the top, fully exposing the head of the larva. "You see, what happens, Soapy, is that the cuterebra, or what is commonly known as a botfly, lays her eggs — a lot of eggs — around a rabbit or squirrel or prairie dog burrow. When the animals come out, the eggs get on them. Your little Sneaker is really interested in those animals, so whenever she gets a chance she sniffs around their burrows. That's how she got some eggs stuck on her hair, and she's warm, so the eggs hatched. Now you know Sneaker ..." Doc grunted, probing and pushing on the worm inside the hole. "... She likes to lick her hair to clean up, and while she was licking she swallowed the larva." Doc was now carefully manipulating the repugnant creature out of the hole. "So this little worm made its way through Sneaker's body and got itself a nice, cozy home right here, under the skin on her neck. It was planning to get out before it turned into a fly again." Sophia was making a disgusted face.

"Eeeiuoo, Doc! Just pull harder! Get it out of her now! It's really gross."

"Can't, Soapy. Can't break it. Could cause trouble if we leave a piece in there." Doc chuckled and added, "It doesn't think it's gross. It thinks it's pretty."

Sophia snorted, and Betty was leaning in, enthralled, Toughy dangling loose and oblivious over the surgery table. "So that's what's in those things we call warbles."

Nancy Jane saw movement in the hallway behind the surgery. She gasped, "Eddie," and tried to jump up, but was constrained by the drooping Dope. No one had heard her. Eduardo made a shushing motion and continued to move out of sight past the door. Doc was putting the intact worm on a paper towel, and Sophia was asking, "Are there more?"

"Probably just this one." Doc Clary killed the worm and treated the hole in Sneaker with an antibiotic. At the death of the worm, everyone except Nancy Jane released held breath. Nancy Jane was staring at the door where Eduardo had disappeared. At this point, Jack, continuing to enjoy himself, decided it was time to discuss cattle with the vet.

"So, Doc, I heard you say Doc Bailey went out to that big cattle truck that rolled. That was what was left of Spike Oglehozer's herd, wasn't it? Heard he had a heart attack and decided to sell out."

"I heard that," Doc said, slipping past what he recognized

as the common, but mostly innocuous, rural practice of gossip phishing. A little information here, a little there, and one might learn, for example, of cattle that were going to be sold below market value. Instead of answering further, Doc just patted the surgical table and nodded at Nancy Jane. She got the message and carried Dope, now a sleep-induced dead weight, over to plop on the table, then she looked hopefully back at the door where Eduardo had slipped past. No one there. Jack wasn't ready to give up.

"Well, I suppose if old Spike is feeling poorly enough after the heart attack, he was right to sell out. Like I've heard said before, cows can't stand too much heat, so it's too hot in hell to take 'em with us. Heh heh. Yup." The last, the 'yup,' was in full appreciation of his own joke. "I heard that driver was texting when he rolled that truck."

Doc repeated, "I heard that," then said, "Nancy Jane, push down on his jaw right here, and we'll try to clean up this side first." Jack wasn't ready to give up on the conversation.

"I guess this will be the insurance company's loss, if a bunch got killed. You heard yet how they come out on the number of dead ones?"

Working out another quill and dropping it into the growing pile by Dope's ear, Doc emitted a noncommittal grunt. Jack continued, "Well, probably at least 60 head in that truck, knowin' Spike's herd. I reckon the rest'll be in pretty bad shape. What do you think, Doc? Reckon the stress'll bring on a bout of shippin' fever? I think at the least they'll sustain a lot of weight loss. Not sure I'd wanna buy 'em." This was a hint.

Dropping another quill, Doc looked up and met Betty's eyes. She rolled hers. Doc said, "You know, Jack, Toughy's gonna wake up very shortly, and when he sees what happened to his leg he won't like it much. You might better get him on home before he makes more trouble." Jack looked at the cat and then at Betty, who gave a firm, wifely nod.

"All righty, then. You ready, Bet? Well, it's been good chatting …"

To the departing backs and closing door, Doc commented, "Try not to let that old tomcat attack that mower again." With that, he and Nancy Jane buckled down to work in earnest, Dope occasionally whimpering in his sleep as the quills came out, and Nancy Jane giving anxious glances toward the hallway door. Finally, she could take it no longer.

"Doc, I saw ... Well, I saw Ed Romero over there." She didn't know how to put this, so she blurted, "I didn't know he was staying here with you."

Doc Clary paused mid-pull and looked up sharply. "You didn't?! Well, I'll be damned. I didn't think about it. I just figured ... Well, Nancy Jane, Eddie showed up here yesterday morning, asked if he could hang out for a couple days. He said the immigration department was after him, and what with all the politics going on, he wasn't sure he had his papers straight. He said just a couple days, and you know Ed. He's been all over the chores around here, cleaning cages, helping Annabelle with the horses and so-on. I figured you knew."

Nancy Jane had become very still. Finally, she said, "I kind of knew. Knew the ICE guys were after him. Have you got ... has he got Camilia and the kids with him?"

Doc scowled. "No, he never mentioned them. I just assumed they were with you."

"Nope. Not with me." Both Doc and Nancy Jane grew silent, processing the Romero information, pushing the limp dog around to get at the more elusive quills. Finally, Nancy Jane said, "You know, I'm kind of worried. Long time ago, Ed worked with some gang in Mexico. He told me he hasn't been in trouble for years, but he's afraid of them. He says they've got a long memory."

"You mean they might still come after him for leaving them?"

"What if they decided to get to him, somehow, through Camilia or the kids?"

Both Nancy Jane and Doc grew silent again, each considering what little they knew about Mexican drug cartels. Decapitated bodies and bullet-ridden cars crossed their minds, but they were spared dwelling on those gruesome thoughts by the entrance of a bustling Sophia. "Hey!" she said, pleased with herself. "I biked over to Patch's to show him and Buddy where that cuterebra thing was."

Hidden Treasure (or) Where is Jesus?

Distracted, Nancy Jane said, "You biked?"

Doc grunted. "Yeah, her and me and her mother have a system worked out. Which side of the road, no strangers, and so-on. It's a different world these days, more dangerous. Never had to make a fuss, could bike anywhere, when I was a kid." He filled a syringe with milky fluid and shot it into Dope, who was raising a wobbly head. "Antibiotic. You keep an eye on him, Nancy Jane. Don't let him start shaking, temperature, won't eat, and so-on. And let me know if you hear anything about this other, too. The Romeros." Nancy Jane, a little pale, nodded.

Sophia was extracting Sneaker from her backpack. "So anyhow, I told Patch you were here, Nancy Jane, and he said he wants you to stop by before you go home."

Scooping up her dog, Nancy Jane snorted, but Sophia continued. "He's got a ..." Her voice wavered, and Doc looked over at her through narrowed eyes. He'd seen her do this kind of hesitation before, when what she had to say wasn't quite the whole truth. She continued, "He's got a ... he's got a great, big rooster he wants you to see. Really big!" Now her story was coming with more confidence. "I've seen it, Ms. Barnswallowper. It's a dandy. Real *big,* and pretty feathers. And Patch wants you to see it. You *need* to stop on your way home."

She paused. She was unaware that Nancy Jane had started to redden from her neck up, but Doc, glancing over, picked up on the blush. Sophia gave it her best shot. "And I figure Patch'd be real glad to see Dope, too. You gotta go. Patch says it's important, Ms. Barnswallowper."

18

Toño and Gordy Talk Things Over

Gordy Smith was not an excessively chubby teen, but he was a large and growing one, and he appreciated good food. Dangling off a stool by the kitchen counter, Toño watched him lug a regal feast from the pantry. He'd offered to assist, but Gordy said, "Nah, this'll just take a minute," so Toño checked out the big living area in the Westberg ranch house while he watched the food accumulate. The room was cluttered and peaceful, the kind of place where you would feel at home if you felt as if you belonged there. Which Toño didn't. There was a wood-burning stove in the corner, cool now in the heavy August heat. There was a stack of little kids' flip-flops by the sliding glass door, a colorful, crocheted afghan flopped on a wooden rocker seat, a box of motor oil, a rope, and somebody's duckbill hat on the table. The counter where he sat had renegade bowls and spoons, scattered magazines, a comb and coin purse, a wrench, a screwdriver, and other droppings from a family that passed by in a hurry, people with no time on their hands to waste in restoring order.

Wrestling with a pickle jar lid his grandma had tightened, as usual, with excessive force, Gordy glanced over at Toño, who was drumming his fingers on top of a Macbook that looked as if it had been tossed recklessly among the counter junk while its owner was on their way to somewhere else. "So, you play games?"

Toño moved his hand off the computer. "Sure, when I'm home."

"You ever play 'Fortnite'? Come on, let's eat."

"Yeah, I like it. I got a squad I play with. Did have. My PC's at Nancy Jane's. That's one reason I need to reach Katelyn. She's on my squad, and she'll wonder why I don't check in."

"Cool. About the squad, I mean. I got a 'Fortnite' squad, too." Gordy had set out large paper plates. "Couple friends from Denver, guy from Peru, girl from Canada. Know a guy from France that goes into beast mode. We can't keep up with him." The boys now settled into roast beef, macaroni salad, homemade bread, and a full sack of potato chips. Gordy was apologetic. "No soda here. Gramma doesn't approve of it — she calls it 'that sugar shit' and says it may as well be poison." He laughed. "She doesn't object to all the coffee you can drink, though. This stuff is pretty strong; add a bunch of half'n'half and sugar, then nuke it. It's pretty good if you do that."

Toño was ravenous. He kept pace with Gordy's seconds and thirds. With a full mouth, he groused, "I always play 'Clash of the Clans' and 'Rules of Survival' when I get bored. Now I can't use my phone either; they could trace it."

Gordy nodded in sympathy. "That's Gramma's Mac there. My PC's in my room. I don't know if she'd let me borrow hers if I made an excuse; then you could take mine up to the shop. Then you could do some 'G Mod' and 'Ark of Survival Evolved.' That'd help with the boredom. After I irrigate is when I get on, and then you could join my 'Fortnite' squad. It's p dub. Like I said, we got players from all over. When the time is right, there's a guy from Chicago, but he works part-time, can't always get on. What's your game tag?"

"I'm usually Jaguar Jake, but we better not mess with that. It's too risky."

Gordy shrugged. "No reason to trace my computer. No more than the government has its nose in everything else these days."

Toño laughed. "Nah, I just meant I'd be afraid of breaking your PC. I can be a klutz sometimes. Anyhow, look at this. Your grandma's gonna wonder where all her food went." He rubbed his belly. "I ate too damn much."

Looking crafty, Gordy held out a cherry pie. "You real sure now?" he said in an exaggerated coaxy voice. "My Aunty Jeanne brought this, and there's two more. They'll never miss a couple pieces."

"Shit. Your gramma won't believe it was just you ate all this food."

Gordy shrugged. "My gramma's got other stuff on her mind. The way our family comes and goes around here, she couldn't keep track of who ate what if she tried."

They ate the whole pie.

"So, tell me what the hell's going on, anyhow, with that guy. I think you called him an ice man or something. Does that mean he kills people, or ices them, as they say in gang lingo?"

Belly full and encouraged by a friendly listener, Toño opted to start at the first. "See, my dad's family, they have a ranch in Mexico, but way back when my dad was my age, he got mixed up with the Barrio Azteca cartel. He was the second son, and always felt like his big brother was favored, like his dad thought his big brother knew more and so-on. He won't talk about those years, but he says he got to be a troublemaker and finally ran away from home. That's how he always nags me; he tells me not to be a troublemaker. I guess he was a smuggler, smuggled drugs across the border for the cartel.

"Anyhow, you have to know my dad. He's tough and brave, pretty smart, but he's a good guy at heart and he didn't want to be involved with, well, for him back then, it was marijuana and cocaine. Back about 2000 he stayed in the U.S. and hid from the cartel. He pretended he was a farm worker and did field work, which he says is pretty much like slave labor. He didn't think he was getting very far; he moved around a lot."

"Sucks. So what happened? Did the cartel catch up with him?"

"Kind of. But first ... see, what happened is my mom's dad and my dad's dad were big amigos all their life. You know, amigos. Friends."

"Oh yeah. That's pretty much an American word."

"Sure. Well, anyhow, my mom's dad was an Indian from up in the mountains in Mexico. He was a Raramuri. The Raramuri just have one name, and my grandpa's name was Suré in Raramuri. Suré means 'had heart.' He did have; he had a lot of heart, and Grandpa Romero admired him, how strong he was and the stuff he knew about nature."

"Cool!"

"Yeah, that's my name, too. Suré. Antonio Jorge Romero Suré. That's how they do it in Mexico. Your first name, your dad's name, then your mom's name."

"That's cool, but you said the cartel caught up with your dad?"

"Thing was, after 9/11 my dad got worried about his family back in Mexico and he quit the farm where he was picking and went back to the ranch in Mexico to see them. He knew my mom when they were kids because my grandfathers were buddies, but now they were grown up and so they fell in love, I guess."

"All right! Sounds pretty romantic to me."

"I guess it was, but then the cartel found my dad there in Mexico and he had to run again. It was romantic, though, because he left my mom pregnant. With me. When he left he didn't know, though. He didn't know he had a kid coming."

"Wow, he left your mom high and dry. That's why you were born in Mexico."

"Well, long story short, my dad hid out back in the U.S., then gradually made his way to Colorado and the Corbit ranch. And you know, after that fire, the Corbits wanted to retire, so he started working for Nancy Jane. He's been working here in the valley now for what, about 15 years? Anyhow, I was born in Mexico all right, but the border was tightening up, so when the Romero family and Grandpa Suré saw that my mother had a kid and wanted to be with my dad, they all got together to help her pay for a decent coyote, and he brought her into America okay. My folks say they couldn't do it now, but it was possible back then."

Toño chuckled and added, "I guess when she finally found her way to my dad and he discovered he had a kid, that was a big surprise. Ha! Maybe then it was romantic, right?"

"Cool. That's a hell of a story. Is the mob still after your dad?'

"Not the mob. It's a cartel. Kind of the same, I guess. But I don't really think they care about him anymore. He's just a rancher now, and he fishes and stuff, and my mom volunteers up at the school. We got lots of friends at the Catholic church down in Peaseford. Near as I can tell, we got kind of a normal American life."

"Sounds like."

"I don't think the problem for us is the cartel. I think it's that we're not legal and we can't get legal. Back when he first got here, my dad tried to get a visa, you know, a green card, but you can't get 'em. They will give out short-term visas for seasonal work, and special visas for people with university degrees, you know, stuff like that, but it's really impossible for people like us to get to be legal citizens. My mom even has a university degree from Mexico, but she doesn't want to apply for anything and maybe drag my dad into the spotlight. I'm not even sure my folks are legally married, anyhow. I know my dad knows people that can get him fake documents so he can do some stuff, but that's about all I know."

Gordy was pensive. "That sucks. So what you gonna do, now that that immigration guy is chasing you?"

"I don't know. I been tryin' to think." Toño looked worried.

"Are you legal yourself?"

"I guess not. You know that DACA thing, the dreamer thing that is supposed to allow kids like me that were born in Mexico a way to become citizens? Well, you can't apply for that when you're too young, then when you get old enough to get a job or go to college, you're supposed to apply. When you are 18, you start to 'accrue illegal presence,' but I don't know what I am now as far as legal, and I don't know how to protect my folks if that guy takes after them. I think they are just lookin' for a way to call us illegal and make us look like criminals."

"So you don't know if you're for sure legal now?"

"Shit, no. That's what drives us crazy. Politicians fighting. I don't know if I'm safe or not. I guess the only for sure legal member of our family is Jesus."

"Who's 'hay-soos'?"

"My little brother. He's three, and he was born here, so that makes him an American citizen."

"So where is he now?"

"I don't know. My dad just told me to hide, then later come

find them to figure out what to do next."

Gordy stood up. "We really gotta talk to my grandparents. They'd know what to do. They are V smart about that kind of stuff."

Agitated, Toño also jumped up. "Oh, no. No no no no no. I can't ..." He didn't want to say he was afraid of Gordy's *mischlinge*, probably Nazi, grandfather. Grasping for reasons, he said, "Look, I don't think my folks would want it spread around that we are trying to hide. Maybe they'll want to just ... to just get back to Mexico on their own, before they're arrested."

"That'd be okay, I guess." Gordy looked thoughtful. "I guess Mexico's a cool country, the part like in that movie, *Coco*. If you can stay away from the gangs. So, brings us back to square one. What're you gonna do?"

"Well, I ... I'm not sure. You care if I hide here a little bit more? Up in the shop? I could pay you for the food."

Gordy was appalled. "You ain't payin' for no damn food. We'll get you some meat and stuff to take up to the shop for now, and I'll drop some stuff off when I get a chance, but you need a better plan than that, Bud."

Toño reached in his pocket. "Here, take this phone and give me that note I was gonna send Katelyn. Instead, if you could, go see her and have her hide the phone so they don't trace it to me. You know, tell her about the ICE guy, and tell her I'm safe, but tell her that for her own safety you can't say where I am, okay? Then ask her to kind of look around and see if she can get any idea where my folks might be. She'd have to be sneaky about it. Maybe she could just drop in at Nancy Jane's place and look around or something."

Juggling the phone from hand to hand, Gordy looked at Toño's anxious face. "Shit."

"No, seriously, Katelyn's smart. She'll get me info if she can."

Saying "shit" again and still juggling the phone, Gordy sighed. "It'd be easier to just talk to my grandparents. They'd wanna help you."

Toño thought, 'yeah, sure in a *mischlinge* kind of way,' but he also knew he was asking a lot of Gordy. "No, I guess that ain't right. I can't ask you to do all that. Just let me have that phone back and I'll pack up and get outta your hair."

"Aw, shit. You ain't askin' that much. But I got an idea to make things easier. Let me just tell my grandparents that I met you at that community picnic by the reservoir last June, and that you are going to come over now and then to help me with the Bronco."

"You gonna tell 'em who I am?"

"Sure. They don't need to know you're stayin' in the shed, just that you're my friend." Having apparently forgotten that he had just told Toño that his grandparents were very smart and could help him, Gordy now added, "They won't figure anything out 'cause they're gettin' old, so they're not the sharpest pencils in the pile."

"Will I have to meet them?"

"Not necessarily. But it'd help if they happened to run into you. It'd keep our story straight. It'd just ... it'd just help me, you know? Make it less like I'm lyin' to 'em."

Toño hesitated, but Gordy went on. "And I'll get your phone and your message to Katelyn, okay? And I'll keep my ears open, too, for any word of your folks. I'm a pretty good spy, I think."

Still not sure, Toño said, "Well ..." but Gordy had decided that his plan was excellent, and wouldn't be stopped. What was a worrisome problem for Toño had become a great adventure for Gordy.

"So, let's get you lined out with food and blankets, then have a look at the Bronco." Gordy's phone gave an incoming text tink, and he said, "Well, speak of the devil. That's Gramma now." He ran his eyes over the text, then looked up at Toño, excited. "Shit, Toño, WTF. Things are getting complicated. Gram and Gramp are gonna be late getting home from Potato Days because that Frankie Belle Corbit got shot. Gram says it might have been on purpose. Gram says they need to be there for Neddie and Freddy. Isn't Frankie Belle related to Katelyn?"

"Neddie Corbit?"

"Yeah, that's the one. Oh, that's right. You know Corbits anyhow — that's where your dad worked. Any connection, you think, that ICE guy and the cartels and Frankie Belle? They say she was pretty big on drugs."

Toño had gone pale. "Is Katelyn okay?"

Seeing his friend's reaction, Gordy sobered. "Oh, she must be. Gram didn't mention her, just Frankie Belle. Yeah, Katelyn must be okay, or Gram would have said. Maybe she wasn't even there."

19

Doc and Annabelle Clary Visit Sheriff Garrett

The Sunday morning after Potato Days arrived with far more questions than answers. The huge forest fire in western Utah was sending a heavy overcast of smoke and fine ash into neighboring states, and Coloradans had been warned to protect their lungs. Eyes reddened, noses ran, and drawing breath produced fits of coughing. Gordy had slipped into the old Chabochi building before dawn to tell Toño that he'd be leaving soon to go with his grandparents to Corbits'. "You know how people do when somebody dies. Gramma's got a pile of food to take over to them; that whole Oozle-Onion Valley Club has organized to feed them while they deal with Frankie Belle's funeral and stuff."

He laughed. "Gram's already got the two cherry pies packed. Never even asked about the third one. Anyhow, just wanted you to know what's goin' on. Shouldn't be too long, and it'll probably be a chance to talk to Katelyn."

This left Toño at loose ends. The ranch was quiet for once, but he didn't feel he could leave to hunt his folks, not with Gordy counting on him to carry through the plan he'd put forth yesterday. He paced the broken concrete blocks that formed the floor of the building, climbed back into the attic to revisit the old yearbooks and papers, fiddled with tools and tried to put up a hoop to catch the flattened, airless ball, into which he blew a lot of his smog-filled breath, and petted the old cat, who now seemed to have claimed the status of best friend forever. BFF.

On the other side of the valley, near Riversmet, Sheriff Garrett woke up with a headache, having allowed himself to sleep with his doors and windows open. The damn smoke wasn't that bad last night, he grumbled to himself, wishing now that he could clear the room. Wishing again that he could have stayed with Jenny, up by Croysant. The problem was, Hobbs, his toad-like detective and reliable friend, had arrived yesterday at the scene of the shooting, looked around, examined the corpse, met Garrett's eyes, and grunted. Garrett, his face grim, had returned the look, spat an accurate stream of his nicotine-free chew toward the roadside and said, "From the crowd."

Hobbs confirmed. "Yuh," and pointed up the street. From Riversmet to Croysant was a goodly drive; by the time Hobbs had arrived, most of the curious had dispersed, tiring of the lack of official activity. Now Hobbs and Garrett waited another ten minutes for Thompson, the coroner. He gave an initial confirmation of their assessment. "Yeah, shot probably came from over there." Garrett pulled at his mustache. He'd have to get back to headquarters in Riversmet, start a file, and try to get some idea as to who might have wanted to kill that woman.

On that same Sunday morning, very early, Doc Clary, the old veterinarian, pushed his thin legs out from the sheets and flapped his knees, trying to get them some cool air. Annabelle said, "Talk about restless leg syndrome. You've been awake half the night."

"Mmmf." Doc made a face. "Been worryin' about Eddie."

"Then, like you said, you need to talk to Garrett. You want me to go with you?"

"You want to?"

This time Annabelle said, "Mmmmf." Then, "Take me to breakfast after we see him. Maybe the Harvest Apple will have some of this pollution filtered out and we can breathe while we eat."

"You'd do anything to get out of cookin'," Doc groused. He just loved Annabelle.

"Actually, where do you suppose Garrett is? Maybe I should call Jenny. She got her ring, you know."

Doc was struggling with his socks. He was past 80, and the bending required to get through a day tasked his muscles and joints to the limit. "I don't want a bunch of people involved."

"I know. I'll just tell her it's a private matter, and she'll think it's about the Frankie Belle shooting. I don't want to drive all the way to Riversmet if he spent last night up here with Jenny."

He hadn't. The courthouse was Sunday quiet when they arrived. Doc and Annabelle slipped in, their footsteps clattering in the empty hallways. Garrett, alerted by Jenny, heard them coming and popped up from his desk. "Well, look what the pup drug in. There's Doc and his good woman. What brings you two down to this neck of the woods so early? You need some coffee?"

"Nah, thanks." Doc scratched at his bald head. "You, Annie?" Annabelle shook her head and smiled encouragement at her husband. Garrett indicated the battered chairs and couch crammed into his office and they all sat. Doc continued. "We heard about Frankie Belle Corbit. Hell of a deal."

He had Garrett's full attention. "Yeah, I was there. I didn't see anything. You got something for me?"

"Sorry about that. Don't think I can help you with Frankie any, who shot her or what. I'm actually just kinda bringin' you more trouble. Thing is, I've got a piece of sensitive information that's been worryin' me all night. Tough decision to come see you."

Garrett nodded. In his line of work, you never turned down information, no matter how irrelevant it might appear at first. Now Annabelle put in, "He wouldn't have come to anyone else. You're the only representative of the law we can trust to do the right thing."

"Hate to dump on you, Sheriff," Doc went on. "I just thought it through, decided I've got a responsibility. But I'm breakin' a trust to talk to you. Countin' on you for some discretion."

Garrett nodded, remained quiet. Doc Clary continued. "You know Eduardo Romero?" Garrett scowled, trying to think, shook his head. "Well, Annie and me pretty much knew him since he settled here as a young guy, ten, probably fifteen years ago. He's always been a good guy, decent and stable. He worked for Corbits until their big fire, then he went on over to Nancy Jane's.

You know Nancy Jane Barnswallowper?"

This time the question prompted an audible and amused response from the sheriff. Did he ever know Nancy Jane! She was a character, and it seemed as if every time he was called out to deal with trouble up by Croysant, she was somehow in the middle of it. He just said, "Yeah, I met her couple of times."

"Okay, then. Yeah, Eddie's a good kid. Well, looks like a kid to somebody my age. He's probably 35 or 40. He's got a wife, Camilia, and a couple of boys, one in high school and one just a little squirt. And see, that's what brought me down here.

"The problem is, Eddie isn't legal. I know he tried a couple times to get a green card, but what people don't realize is that's damn near impossible. In the end, he just settled in with Camilia and fit into the community. I think their boys were born here and are citizens, at least the little one. That's supposed to help against deportation, but politics these days, the Trump administration has been labeling these kids that are like that 'anchor babies' and deports their family anyhow."

Garrett scowled. "Yeah, I know about that. Kind of hard to have a future."

"Right. See, Eddie showed up on my doorstep Friday morning. Seems they'd had a surprise visit from an immigration officer. Nasty guy. I got the impression they all got away, but Eddie asked if he could hide out at our place for a couple days. Well, Annie and I didn't see any harm in it. For some reason, we thought Camilia and the kids were safe, back at Nancy Jane's."

"But they weren't," Annabelle put in. "That's why we came here, Sheriff. Nancy Jane was in the clinic yesterday and it turns out nobody knows where the rest of the family is."

"Not even Eduardo?"

"He won't say anything. After Nancy Jane left, we asked him, and he just shrugged, gave us a polite smile, and said, 'Oh, they'll be all right.' And you know, body language. We got the sense that we better not ask any more or we were apt to spook him."

Annabelle sighed. "The problem is, we got the idea that maybe he isn't so sure they'll be all right. To be honest, I was there when Doc talked to him, and I got the impression that he may not know where his family is at all."

Garrett pulled on his mustache. "So, what is it you want me to do? I'm pretty sure you aren't asking me to arrest Eduardo, are you?"

Doc shook his head. "No, what the guy needs is protection. But we thought with that Frankie Belle thing, you should have all the information you could get." He hesitated, cleared his throat. Annabelle shook his elbow.

"Go ahead. You have to explain your concerns."

"Yeah. Well, Pat, thing is, I'm hoping that while you're rootin' around up our way you might keep an eye out for Camilia and the boys. We're worried about them. Thing is …" Doc cleared his throat, then jumped in with both feet. "… Thing is, Eduardo came to the United States because he'd been working for a gang in Mexico. A cartel. That was a long time ago. He talks about them a little, hates them. Last time he went to see his family in Mexico, this was years ago, they threatened him. I'm sure he quit them cold, but I've read about those cartels. I'm not so sure they quit *him*."

Garrett scowled. "What do you mean?"

"Well, I hope it's far out, but what if they want to get even with him for quitting? Or what if they want to use him for something, like some big illegal smuggling job? They could push him into doing something he didn't want to do if they got hold of Camilia and the boys. So, long story short, Annie and I would just rest better if we knew where his family is and that they're okay."

Unexpectedly, Garrett grinned. "I'm not sure you've come to the right guy for the job. You're talking to a sheriff, and asking him to protect some illegals from the law as well as from a bunch of other nasty criminals."

Annabelle shifted in her chair, looking anxious, but Doc met the sheriff's eyes and returned his grin. "Yeah," he said, "I think we do. I think we do have the right guy for the job."

20

Katelyn Corbit Searches for Information

Katelyn knew it was a time-honored tradition to take food to the family of a deceased person, but really! she asked herself. Did having somebody die really make people that hungry? She had never been so uncomfortable. People kept coming and going, letting in the unbreathable smoky air from Utah, putting strange wienie and bean casseroles on the table, and, worst of all, hugging her while saying, "I'm so sorry. I'm so sorry." Well, she was pretty sorry, too. Having somebody shot to death right under your nose, so to speak, was a pretty shocking experience, but she was probably not as sorry as people thought she should be. Frankie Belle had never been much of a sister. She was a lot older than Katelyn, had been the child of their father's first wife, who was rather a rough old gal, in the words of Aunt Neddie, and never came around her little half-sister for any reason. Katelyn had thought Frankie was pretty, but she certainly wouldn't have shared sisterly secrets with her.

At any rate, this had been a good year for Katelyn. She'd left her awkward, worrisome junior-high body behind forever, rapidly willowing up to nearly six feet tall. That meant the basketball team and Toño's respect. In fact, her slight age advantage over Toño sent her to the courthouse for her driver's license two months ahead of him. Her eyes were an unsettling shade of bright blue, thoughtful now in a way that signaled the early arrival of exceptional maturity. Even so, adulthood hadn't fully enveloped her yet. Peer pressure still caused her to struggle, and when she was socially nervous she tended to regress into teen-speak. Today, for example, after a forever of trying to make nice at this cray vigil, she spotted a kid her age that she thought she knew but couldn't place. He wasn't from her squad, or even from their school. Only when she saw that he was hanging with Gus and Tess Westberg did recognition click into place. Oh, right. He was that grandkid of theirs that came out from Denver to spend the summers. Not a bad looking guy with that dumb cowlick, but not as fire as Toño. So now what? He was weaseling his way across the room toward her. WTF? This could be V embarrassing — she couldn't begin to think of his name. She'd just have to keep it 100.

When he reached her, he held out his hand and said, "Hi, you're Katelyn, aren't you? Toño's girlfriend? I'm Gordy, the Westbergs' grandkid. We need to talk." Ah, Gordy. A name. That helped. She wasn't sure why they needed to talk, but he looked so serious that she could tell he was FR. Looking around, she said, "Okay, maybe out there? On the porch? Or over by that tree?"

Outside, he told her the full story of Toño as he had learned it, and gave her the phone. "I guess you have to bury it. Just kidding. But don't put it where it would help them to trace it, okay? I really don't know if that's possible, but Toño seems to think it's a problem."

Unlike the death of her barely known sister, this news had brought a teary look of concern to Katelyn's blue eyes. "So where is he now? I need to go see him."

"No, he said for your own safety, he didn't want you to know where he is. He just wants you to know he's safe and see if you can hear anything about his family. Like maybe you could mingle here, for example, and see if anyone says anything."

Katelyn snorted. "That's crazy. What if I do find out something? How do I get word to him?"

Momentarily taken aback by this possible flaw in their plan, Gordy stammered, then said, "Yeah, you're right. I guess ...well, just call me. I'll give you my number, and I'll ... well, I should be able to reach him."

Hidden Treasure (or) Where is Jesus?

"Okay." Katelyn pulled out her phone and entered Gordy's number, but she was clearly exasperated. Toño was obviously hiding at Gordy's. Where else would he be? At least, this was the opportunity she had been looking for. Something this important, she wouldn't feel guilty about getting away from the wake, or whatever this was.

As soon as Gordy left, she slipped to the table and snagged a large paper plate full of cookies. Leaving by the back door, she made a beeline to her car and headed to the Barnswallowper place. She found Nancy Jane in back, feeding her chickens. Putting on her friendly-neighbor face and clutching the cookies, she said, "Hey, Ms. Barnswallowper. Remember me? I'm Katelyn Corbit, Toño's girlfriend. You've seen me up here a couple times, hanging with Toño. You have any idea where I could find him? I've got cookies."

Nancy Jane's response was brusque. "No. Haven't seen 'im lately." Katelyn thought she looked worried.

"Well, anyhow, maybe you know about my stepsister, Frankie Belle? About her gettin' shot and all?" Nancy Jane stepped out of the chicken pen and closed the door, giving a curt nod and a barely audible, "Sorry to hear it." She turned her back and headed toward the house. Katelyn, not easily put off, followed and continued, "So people are bringing a lot of food, and my Aunt Neddie wanted to share. She sent these cookies over."

Nancy Jane kept walking stolidly, and Katelyn added loudly, "And also, I know all about that ICE agent."

Stopping abruptly, Nancy Jane turned, saying, "What do you mean, 'all about'?"

Katelyn pushed the cookie plate at her, and, distracted, Nancy Jane took it. "By 'all about,' I just know some crooked Fed showed up here and caused trouble the other night. I need to talk to Toño and Eduardo or Camilia to see what I can do to help."

Her eyes narrowed, Nancy Jane looked grim. "You oughtta just stay out of this, girl. It could get dangerous."

Katelyn shot back, "I think it already is, and those people are my friends. I am going to help."

"Well, Spunky Puppy, I don't know. I got no idea where they

all went, and I got stuff to do here." She examined Katelyn's face, which had gotten stubborn. "I might've heard Eddie mention the vet's. You know, Doc Clary's."

Studying her face, Katelyn said abruptly, "Thanks," and turned for the car. Nancy Jane called after her, "Well, thanks for the cookies. And you be careful. You want a gun? I got an extra twenty-two."

Katelyn stopped and turned. "Nah, not this time, Ms. B. I've already been grilled by the sheriff about the gun I had when Frankie Belle went down. Don't want more trouble about guns." With that, she gave a little wave and made for her car.

The Clarys weren't there, nor was the young vet, Dr. Bailey, or her kid, Sophia. The clinic was locked up tighter than a drum. On a hunch, Katelyn went up the hill from the clinic to the Clarys' home and headed back to the horse barn. Sure enough, she saw Eduardo's back, retreating past a stack of small alfalfa bales. She didn't think he'd seen her. Breaking into a lope, she shouted, "Hey, Mr. Romero! Hey! It's Toño's girl, Katelyn. I need to talk to you." For a minute, she saw him brace and thought he was going to run away from her. He turned, though, and said, "*Hola, muchacha. Qué pasa?*" Katelyn was relieved. She was gasping when she reached him, her lungs unhappy with the smoke filled air, her blue eyes watering.

"I'm sorry. I didn't mean to bother you, but I heard about the ICE guy and I was worried about everybody."

Eduardo leaned on his pitchfork and frowned at her. "How did you hear about that? How did you find me?"

Dodging the question, Katelyn asked, "So where's Toño? And his mom and Jesus?"

"I don't know." Eduardo seemed to deflate. He sat on a bale and Katelyn sat beside him.

"Did you know somebody shot Frankie Belle yesterday? They don't know who did it, but I think they think it was on purpose."

"Doc told me. But I want an answer to my question. Who told you about the ICE agent?"

"I went up to Nancy Jane's. I wanted to tell Toño about my sister, but when I saw none of you were there, well, I kind of just

Hidden Treasure (or) Where is Jesus?

kept asking and Nancy Jane finally told me a little. She didn't want to, kept saying she didn't know where any of you were, then finally hinted you might be here."

Eduardo ran his hands up and down the pitchfork handle, staring at the ground, and said, "*Mierda.*"

Katelyn smiled. "Yeah, for sure. Shit. Toño taught me *mierda*. So you really don't know where they are, either?"

"It's safer that way. And you aren't safe, Katelyn. I think this could be dangerous business. You need to go home and just play dumb for a while." He laughed. "Probably not easy for somebody as nosey as you, *niña*. But just don't make a big deal out of the fact that you know about us. Don't tell people you talked to me or saw me."

Katelyn was suspicious. "But you really don't know where they are? Aren't you worried about them?"

Normally an even-tempered man, Eduardo stood up and snapped, "Of course I'm worried. But my family is doing what we have to do, what we think is best."

Mollified, Katelyn stood, too. "Right, I understand." She hesitated. "I can help a little, I think. I heard ... I heard from a friend of a friend, and Toño is okay. I don't know where he is, but it sounds like he's safe."

The look she received from Eduardo was long and searching. Finally he said, "Thank you, then, *muchacha*. It helps to know he is safe."

Driving from the Clary home, Katelyn should have turned left on 46 to return to her Aunt Neddie's place, but she dreaded the hugging and fussing. She was eaten alive by her conviction that Toño was at Gordy's. The more she thought it, the more she wanted to see him and get it all cleared up. She turned right. While she drove, she rationalized her decision—Toño needed her; she would understand more of what she should do if she could see his body language; she herself was a *woke* person and deserved respect; she could count on Toño because her *ship* with him was *trill*; and so-on—but after she had passed Alma's, she turned into the Oozle-Onion Valley Club House parking lot. She still wasn't sure. She wasn't worried about her own safety. She had, after all, the psychological invincibility of the young.

She just was afraid that Toño was trying to get across a secret message, something encoded in his sending of Gordy or ... or in his phone. Plus, what would she say to Tess or Gus if the boys weren't there? Gordy had said Toño didn't want to involve them.

She pulled out the phone and ran through the messages and numbers, feeling rude and invasive. Shit, well, *mierda*, this was *cray*, all this that was happening. There wasn't anything on the phone since last Thursday night, when Gordy had told her the Fed guy had been to Barnswallowpers. Well, all right then. She jumped out of the car and walked briskly to the back of the clubhouse. Looking around, she spotted the box that had been used for firewood since the old days, when the building was a school house. It was up against the back door, under the eaves. The phone could stay safe, dry, and secret, there. She stuffed it down in, next to a couple of sticks of kindling, and, dusting off her hands, headed for her car.

Across the way was that Frickleson's place, the gross *sus* Toño had told her was a creeper and water thief. The place looked deserted, but in back was one of those toddler tricycles and a beat-up, yellow plastic toy ride-in car. That felt wrong to her. She was getting *TFW* something is out of place. The way Toño described him, the guy was just a warped, single-guy creeper asshole without kids, somebody she should avoid. The kind of guy who would be hung up on pictures of naked women.

Then it hit her. OMG! Toño was trying to send her a coded message. It wasn't just the ICE agent. Frickleson had kidnapped Camilia and Jesus, and Toño was trying to find a way to ... to ... well, she wasn't sure. Slowing down her racing thoughts, she got a grip on her imagination. Maybe speculating about a kidnapping was going too far. Still, she knew that, as she had heard her Aunt Neddie say, something was rotten in Denmark. Children's toys in a nasty old bachelor's yard didn't make sense, but neither did anything else: Frankie Belle shot; Eduardo claiming he didn't know where his family was; Toño hiding, probably at Gordy's, of all places, and telling her to stay away for her own safety. Seriously? *Her* safety? Well, maybe she had better respect his warning until she knew more, but, well, Gordy's place? And *her* safety?

Even so, she really needed to talk to somebody. The only people she knew that she felt she could trust in this situation was her *fam* from school, her squad, Pewter, Larry, Cesar, and the rest. She felt P good about them. She'd cowboy up and go home now, but she'd find a way to get in touch with them soon, on the down low.

21

Snoop Makes an Exciting Discovery

Tess Westberg's hand tried, without success, to finger her absent knife. The thing was, she was glad that Frankie Belle Corbit had been shot. This had nothing to do with Frankie Belle personally. In fact, she barely knew the young woman. About all she knew of her was that Frankie Belle had a reputation for spending too much time at Old Johnney's Bar B Bar in Peaseford, in the bar part of the Bar B Bar, in the back. If she remembered right, Frankie Belle had hooked up with that reprobate, Mickey Rippe. Mickey was a lot older than Frankie, harmless enough, but well known around Peaseford and Croysant for being a sloppy drunk. Frankie was pretty enough; she surely could have done better, so why hadn't she? Tess had heard from her own family that it had to do with drugs. That's what people always said, 'drugs', so whatever. Still, Frankie Belle was Neddie Corbit's much loved niece, and Tess was ashamed for being happy about her sudden demise.

No, she wasn't literally happy that Neddie's niece had died. She was just relieved that there was a significant distraction from what she'd found in the culvert. It gave her something else to think about. She truly didn't know what to do about that body. It shouldn't be there, she knew that, but the horror of finding it there had crippled her ability to think straight. Once more her left hand struggled in her pocket, desperate for the little knife, but again it emerged without success. She felt she should take action soon, but what should she do? Should she try to talk to

Hidden Treasure (or) Where is Jesus?

Gus? Should she call Sheriff Garrett and play dumb? Probably not. Her poor brain spun like a rat on a wheel, trying to sort out possible consequences.

She studied Gus, looking for some clue as to whether she should approach him. How would he react if she told him about it? He'd always been a good guy, friendly, talkative, and full of fun, unless someone, herself or one of the kids, got too close to his core. Then he clammed up. For example, she knew very little about his first years in America. She tried to learn, hoping to be a full part of his life, leading with questions like, "How did people treat you when you first came here?" and he would change the subject. Then there were their other problems from way back, that Joyce. It had been well over sixty years now, and it should be easier to view it all from such a distance. Even so, it still rankled to think that Joyce had gotten herself pregnant and tried to pin the baby on Gus. Tess was so damned angry and jealous back then, sure she'd never even have a chance with him, when the next thing she knew Gus met her after class and asked her to a movie. Not long after, Joyce and her family left the country, at least for a while. Sometimes she tried to find out how Gus felt about Joyce, but he just shrugged. Once he said, "No worries, Tessie. Never was Joyce. Always had my eye on you." She let it go. And that corpse now. Maybe she should just let that go, too. Maybe no one would find it. But things didn't always have a way of working out if you didn't do what you should.

When they returned from the stint at Corbits', Gordy tussled briefly in greeting with Snoop, then said, "So, Gram, I got a buddy wants to help me with the Bronco. I think he's up at the shop right now. Have Gramp holler if he needs me." Before she could reply, Gordy had snagged a sack of potato donuts and two bottles of iced tea off the cabinet and was out the door.

Tess went to the kitchen window and stared out. She could see the culvert from there. Gus had gone down the hall to his office to do bookwork. She chewed her lip. Maybe she should go hunt her knife again. She looked around the kitchen and living area; this room was a mess. There were containers of food that needed put away, toys to pick up, towels to gather and launder. Sighing, she began to putter.

Gordy popped in the door, Snoop on his heels. "Hey, where's Gramp? I need to see if we can borrow that second-hand battery he was telling me about."

Tess indicated Gus's office and ventured, "So, who's your friend?"

Gordy was already halfway down the hall, his back to her. She heard something about 'just neighbor kid' and 'met at picnic.' She silently cursed her failing old ears and went back to stare out the kitchen window over the sink. Before allowing itself to be plunged into the dishwater, her left hand made another hopeful, unsuccessful, foray into her pocket.

She'd finished the dishes when Gordy popped back in, exuberant. "Gotta tell Gramp. She turned over! Battery got 'er goin'." Gus appeared from the hallway, and Gordy repeated his news, then said, "Thing is, she won't stay goin'. Gotta be the carburetor, right, Gramp? That grease and dirt on it looks older than you."

Gus rubbed his chin. "Yeah, I suppose it could be."

"Well, like Toño says, can't hurt to clean it up. I'm gonna get my PC and we'll google for directions how to do that."

Tess could see that Gus was hurt. He wanted to be asked about how to clean the carburetor, maybe called to the shop for a look, but he just said, "All right. Give it a go."

She said, "Why don't you bring your friend ... what did you say his name was? Tony? Why don't you bring him down for iced tea and cookies, and you boys can talk to Gramp about the carburetor."

"Nah, he's kind of shy. Gets embarrassed easy. We'll just google it, then ask Gramp if we run into trouble. Can I take up some cheese and crackers, though?"

Contemplating his grandson and remembering the youth he wished he still had, Gus ignored the carburetor question. He said, "Gordy, when you irrigate, don't forget to move the water into the waste field tonight."

Tess drew in a breath. The waste field was where they collected the water left from the upper pastures, just north of the culvert; that water drained directly into the culvert. Maybe she should say something. Maybe she should go ... Gus was continuing. "Meanwhile, you boys be kind of quiet. Gramma and I are going to get a nap. It's been a tough 24 hours, what with Frankie Belle and all, and your grandma looks worn out. You get your own crackers."

Indecision was sucking the spunk from Tess. She didn't argue. Instead, she lay down by Gus, who plumped his pillow and said, "I hope that other damn kid doesn't take over and screw things up. Gordy's a little too easy going, apt to just let somebody who doesn't know squat tell him what to do. He likes mechanics, and I was hopin' he'd learn from tryin' to fix that Bronco, think things out on his own." Tess tried to find something supportive to say, but before she could respond, her husband's lips began to vibrate, a rubbery snore.

As for Tess, she couldn't sleep. She picked up a novel, her eyes marching past the meaningless words, then finally slipped quietly off the bed. From the bedroom window she could see the boys up by the shop; apparently they'd found some kind of table and were busy with the computer and Bronco parts they had laid on it. Snoop and that pest of a shop cat, old Mush, puttered around the boys' feet, occasionally receiving a scrap of cheese or cracker. She didn't recognize the neighbor kid, but she could see them talking and laughing, so she decided it was good that Gordy had friends here as well as in Denver. She folded towels, cleaned up the bathroom, and contemplated how much longer Gus tended to sleep now than when he was younger. Her hand explored her knifeless pocket, and she was once more drawn to the kitchen sink and the window above it. There, she froze.

It was surely over. The boys, irrigating shovels over their shoulders, were walking toward the waste water field. Snoop had rushed ahead and arrived at the end of the culvert, and his tail, a frantic semaphore, was saying that he had found the most exciting thing in the world, and it was right there! Right there! She couldn't hear him, but from the dog's stance she was sure he was barking. The boys dropped down the ditch bank toward him, which inspired him to start digging, his hind legs on the bank, his front legs in the water, splashing. Tess backed away from the window, feeling faint, her heart acting up in her chest. "I should have done something. What could I have done?"

She backed into Gus, who had come up behind her. He asked, "What's going on?" Tess couldn't answer. Gus stood at the window, scowling, but Tess grabbed a cloth and began to scrub vigorously at the stove. In seconds, Gordy had burst into the house, Toño reluctantly behind him.

"Grampa! Gramma! There's a dead guy down there! He's in the culvert! He's blocking it off, and he stinks like hell. He's all covered with flies. His face is a mess; there was rocks all over him."

Toño had shrunk against the door jamb. He said softly, "I need to go home."

Gordy, turning to him, said, "No, wait. It'll be okay." With that, he pulled out his cell phone. "I'm calling the sheriff. He'll know what to do. That guy down there is gross. Gram, you don't want to see it."

Everyone else in the room was saying, "Maybe not, maybe just a minute, Gordy. No, maybe don't call yet until we see …," but Gordy's 911 call had gone through. He said, "We need you to send up Sheriff Garrett. There's a dead guy down here in our ditch."

22

Garrett, McCracken, and Red Arrive at the Crime Scene

McCracken, carrying an LCD spotlight, slid down the bank, looked closely at the mangled face of the corpse, retched, then shone her light up at Garrett and Red, who were standing with Gus and Gordy on the road above the culvert, everyone shining their lights around the area and Garrett asking questions about the culvert, its function, and about the water flow. Now he addressed McCracken. "What do you say, Mac?"

"It's a man, but his face is a mess. My guess is, he's been here a couple days in this heat. This thing is putrid. I think the bloating is going to make it impossible to just pull him out of the opening. This water isn't helping. Identification will be a problem; it looks like his hair has actually come off his head and is floating here beside his shoulder."

Garrett grunted and looked over at the Westbergs, considering them in the dim light. The kid, Gordy, was hyped up by the excitement and drama, but Gus just looked old, his face grayish and drained. Directly addressing him, Garrett said, "Mr. Westberg, I'm afraid this is going to be more of a production than any of us want. I'm sure sorry for the trouble to your family. We're gonna have to get some tape up, and bring some personnel here to watch this tonight, and I'll be contacting a good forensic team before we even try to remove him, then I suppose we'll need an excavator."

Grim-jawed, Gus stared down at the culvert. "You people want to come up to the house to talk? Tess'd make you some coffee."

"Oh, nah, thanks, that's good of you, but no. Red and Mac need to get a crew organized for now, and I only have a couple questions for you. Mostly for Gordy, isn't it?"

Gordy was on, with an eager nod. Garrett continued, "I understand you found him. You and a friend, right? You mess with anything here when you did?"

"We moved the rocks off his head. We wanted to see who it was."

"And do you know who he is?"

"No, sir, Mr. Garrett. That face is too much of a mess."

"Understood. So that's all you did?"

"Yes, sir. Then we went up and told Gramp and Gram, and called you."

"That's good. So, where's your friend now?"

"Uh ..." Gordy looked at his shoes. "I think he ... I think he went home." He hesitated, cleared his throat. "I think he needed to get back to his family." He paused. "It was gettin' late."

McCracken, having climbed back up the bank, pulled out a notebook. "So. What's your friend's name?"

Taking a deep breath, Gordy pushed at a rock by his toe. "Suré. His name is Suré."

As far as McCracken was concerned, this was not an appropriate name. She wanted 'Tom' or 'John.' She tried to repeat it, but Garrett said, "Where does your friend live?"

This might be safer ground. "At Barnswallowper's. He ... he's been staying at Nancy Jane Barnswallowper's. For right now."

Garrett eyed Gordy, half visible among the flashlight beams and headlights on the police car. "So he went back to Barnswallowper's?"

More firmly, Gordy said, "Yeah, that's where he probably went."

"And does he have a car, this Suré?"

"Nah, he's a good runner. On the track team, I guess. He probably ... he probably just ran home." For good measure,

Gordy added, "His mom gets worried about him if he's late."

Garrett pulled on his mustache. There had been a tiny light in the old, ramshackle shop. It was there briefly, then blinked off when the sheriff's car turned in. He considered Doc Clary's visit earlier today. Hmmm. Perhaps, he thought, perhaps we have discovered where at least one of the Romeros is hiding.

Gus and Gordy were sent back to the house while the deputies went about securing the site and Garrett made calls to Jenny, Hobbs, and Thompson, the coroner. Red walked over and waited until he got off the phone, then held out something in a cloth he was using to protect for fingerprints. "Found this over there on the ditch bank down in the grass. The flashlight beam kind of glinted off it. Thought you might like to see it before I bag it."

Garrett held his own light on it, squinting. It was a little brown pocket knife, about four inches long. He could just make out the initials TFW engraved along the side.

23

Law Officers at the Cowpath

The Cowpath was empty. It would open at 6:00, but Jenny let the sheriff and his team in early so they could have an uninterrupted cup of morning coffee while they talked things over. All of them looked haggard. Their sleep had been short and disturbed. Jenny brought sweet rolls, set them in the middle of the table, then pulled up a chair to sit next to Garrett.

For some reason, Deputy Red Hargrove was wearing dark glasses, incongruous in the dim light of the early morning restaurant. He pulled them off now and set them by his cup, then rubbed his red, sleep-deprived eyes. "Hell of a mess, the dead guy. Looked to me like somebody wanted him that way — he ain't gonna be easy to identify."

McCracken chuckled dryly. "Asa, you're the face wizard. You see anything in that gob of washed-out gore that you could recognize?"

Detective Asa Hobbs snorted. He liked to chew gum, a lot of it, thinking that the wad in his mouth might help rein in his persistently run-away food cravings. Now he pulled out the wad and wrapped it in his napkin, then stowed it next to his fork. He snorted again and took a large pull on his heavily creamed coffee. "Wasn't a face there to recognize. I called NecroSearch."

Snagging the gum-filled napkin, Jenny made a quick trip to the wastebasket at the serving station, then returned with the coffee pot as McCracken commented, "I heard that those people are great, but don't they just hunt for corpses that have been missing for years, not corpses that are new and we know where they are?"

"I talked to the guy there. They can help us get that thing out of the pipe with as little loss of evidence and clues to his identity as possible." He added cream to his coffee refill and took a second sweet roll.

Red thanked Jenny for the coffee, then asked, "So when they gonna get here? Don't they work out of Denver?"

"Yeah, their company owns a little plane now, though. He thinks he can round up a crew and get here about mid-morning today. Wants to borrow a car or a car and driver, have somebody meet 'em up at the Croysant airport."

"Can do." Garrett blew on his coffee, recalling with amusement the air show at the parade. "What time?"

"They'll call. Anyhow, boss, let me just make sure you're up to spin on the family involved in your other murder." He grinned. "You do recall that you got another murder on your hands, right?"

Garrett grunted. "Unfortunately."

"Right. Anyhow, maybe there's a connection. So, just in summary. Your victim, Frankie Belle, was a step-sister to Katelyn, the teenage girl you talked to after the shooting. Katelyn was one of the gunslingers. She's a niece to Neddie and Freddy Corbit. Seems like old Mrs. Corbit, Freddy's mother, got on a roll when she was naming her kids. She called them Eddy, Heddy, Teddy, and Freddy. They're all dead now except Freddy, but back in the day they all worked together to run that big Corbit spread.

"Freddy married Nadine, who got into the spirit of it all and had them call her Neddie. Heddy and Teddy never married, but Eddy married some gal that apparently had quite a reputation back then. She birthed Frankie Belle, then died young. Could have been something venereal, but you won't hear gossip from me. After she died, and as he got older, Eddy met a sweet young thing just out of high school and that seemed to be a case of tender, ill-fated love all around. They had Katelyn, and shortly thereafter the young wife was out helping work cattle. Her horse shied. No one ever knew what spooked him. They were on the slope of a steep gulch, a narrow trail, and the horse lost his footing when he jumped. Both he and Eddy's little wife rolled down the gulch. It broke her neck and it broke the horse's leg. Eddy shot him, of course."

The group at the table were shaking their heads and murmuring comments of "I'll be damned," and "Damn dirty deal." Hobbs continued. "Anyhow, Eddy went ahead and raised the two daughters, but they said he was never quite right after he lost Katelyn's mother. A little goofy. Chronic depression. He died a couple of years ago, and Freddy and Neddie took Katelyn in."

"That's a pretty heavy history there," Garrett said. "You think any of it's related to either murder?"

"Here's the deal. First of all, out of all those Corbits, Freddy, Neddie, and the girls are the only ones left. After the fire, Neddie and Freddy got worried about the ranch, so they just now made a will. They wanted to be sure the ranch and all they had went to the girls."

Thoughtfully, McCracken said, "That means that, with Frankie Belle gone, Katelyn would inherit everything." Everyone turned to stare at her, and she shrugged. "Yeah, I know. Sweet, dear little Katelyn. The only one with a motive."

Hobbs grinned. "Maybe. Or there's a guy called Mickey Rippe, older guy, hangs out at these local bars, drinks a lot, could be on meth. Scuttlebutt says he and Frankie Belle were very close."

Jenny scowled. "But why would he kill her?"

"I dunno." Hobbs shifted his large, toad-shaped body. "Might be worth checking into, though." He chortled. "And your 'little' Katelyn is now approaching six feet tall, and pretty athletic."

"You suppose it's Rippe over there at Westbergs', stuffed into that pipe? Well, no," Red corrected himself. "Timing would be off — Frankie Belle was shot Saturday. That guy's been in there too long."

"We could use some gossip." Garrett addressed Jenny. "Look, honey, why don't you go have an informal chat with Alma?"

Hidden Treasure (or) Where is Jesus?

Jenny was taken aback. "Alma?! Why Alma?"

"Whenever I'm around that old woman, I realize she knows more about this community than people give her credit for, even in her addled state. She's old as dirt, but she's got great interest in the world."

"But what do you want me to do?" Jenny was baffled, thinking 'I'm not the law officer here.'

"Well, first make an excuse. tell her you wanted to show her your engagement ring or something like that." No one at the table had realized that Jenny was sporting a ring. Everyone's eyes traveled to her left hand, and a glance at Garrett's expression told them there was no mystery as to the source of the ring. Jenny, the sudden object of an excess of attention, blushed. Pleased, Garrett continued. "Then just chat. See if she's heard of anyone in the community who's gone missing. Some local rancher or something."

Responding to comments such as, "So, the old boy finally opened his pocketbook," (this from Hobbs) and "Congratulations, you two," Jenny beamed. "Thanks. Thanks, everyone." Then she added, "Sure, I can do that, Patrick." Garrett was checking the time. Nearly six, and he had one more piece of business to get to before the restaurant filled with the breakfast crowd.

"Good, Jen. Look, now we gotta move along. I got information I want to get to you people only. I don't want this to get out, and I mean that, but I need heads up from those here. We do have some missing people. An ICE agent hit Nancy Jane Barnswallowper's last Thursday night and tried to take the Romero family, or at least some of them. They managed to get away, and we know where Eduardo is, but ..." Garrett hesitated, thinking of the flicker of light in the Westbergs' old building. He continued carefully. "We don't know where Camilia and Jesus, the wife and toddler, have gone, and we also don't know if Antonio, the teenager, is with them."

Hobbs regarded the sheriff, his look shrewd. "So what do you want us to do, boss? Arrest 'em, rescue 'em, protect 'em ...?"

Garrett returned his steady gaze. "I can't see as they did anything wrong, can you? Maybe if you hear something, just tell me." He paused, thoughtful. "Mac, why don't you see if you can

125

locate somebody close to Mrs. Romero, Camilia, maybe a friend or co-worker. See if you can learn anything without giving out a bunch of information. Be covert as hell." He grinned; he knew McCracken liked assignments like this.

The discussion was interrupted. It wasn't quite six, but there was a loud, heavy banging on the front door of the restaurant. Jenny jumped up. "Oh, gee, that's right. There's old Lew again." She hurried to unlock the door, then took two bulging paper bags off the counter and handed them to Lew, who thanked her, turned, and left.

When she returned, Red said, "Wow, what was that all about? Harris need morning take-out real fast?"

"Well, kind of." Jenny smiled. "You know Lew. You know how he's got that dog, Lucky, that nobody but him can see? Well, the other night he stopped by — Thursday, I think it was — and said he was involved in some big top-secret thing that he couldn't talk about. He said he'd picked up a kid at Alma's, and he needed food for him."

In one voice, the law officers said, "Jesus? Jesus Romero?"

"No, honestly, I think this is something else. I don't think there was ever even a kid there. I never saw one. I think it's kind of an invisible kid, like Lucky is an invisible dog. See, he came in later and said he'd made a mistake, that there wasn't just one kid, but two. Of course, that wouldn't be Jesus. So now I fix him take-out every couple days for him and invisible Lucky and the two invisible kids. I guess it's his business, whoever actually eats it."

24

Toño and Gus

Toño was scared shitless, to put it bluntly. He was convinced that it had to be the ICE agent down there in the culvert. The guy must have died, after all, when Toño hit him with the safe, and his dad and Nancy Jane had tried to hide the body. This meant he and his family were in a lot of trouble, and the problem wasn't going to be just deportation. He had to get out of here and find another place to hide until he could find his family. He deeply regretted telling Gordy anything, and now Katelyn was involved, too. His head throbbed. He couldn't think.

After a nightmarish night spent with *chabochi*, skinheads, neo-Nazis, gangs, and you name it, morning finally arrived. Toño watched out the old, broken windows of the dead house. The ranch was busy last week when the Westbergs worked their cattle, but today's bustle made that previous family activity look like a peaceful convention of meditating Buddhists. Yes, today it was a kicked-over beehive out there. Official cars came and went; the Westberg family swarmed around; neighbors, unable to contain their curiosity, pulled down the lane, tried to find parking spaces, failed, and drove into the fields. As for Toño, he packed, simultaneously sluggish with worry and frantic, trying not to forget anything he might have scattered in the old shop, pushing what was left of the food Gordy had brought into his backpack.

Here's what he would do, he decided. Everyone was focused

on the taped-off area down by the waste field. He'd slip outside, make sure he'd left nothing important near the Bronco, then slip into the trees and brush to the west. At least Gordy had given him an excuse for being here if someone tried to talk to him. He could just say that he was supposed to meet Gordy today to work on the Bronco and play dumb about all the activity. That should work. He eased out the door and set his backpack next to the crumbling cement step.

He found his Leatherman while he tidied up the tools he and Gordy had left on the table. He thought maybe he'd better check inside the Bronco for anything else he might have misplaced. The doors were worn and needed lubricated; none of them opened smoothly. Walking to the passenger door, he gave it a good yank. Stumbling back, he suppressed a horrified scream. There in front of him was another corpse. It was sitting slumped, head dropped forward. Then it jerked up, as startled as Toño was, and emitted an exasperated, "Hey!"

Now Toño truly was appalled. This was no corpse. This was Gus Westberg, Gordy's fearsome, probably Nazi, grandfather. Toño took two more steps backward, but the old man growled, "Hold on, you. Who the hell are you?"

All Toño could manage was, "I ... I came to help Gordy with this Bronco, remember?"

The old man was coming fully awake. He started trying to pry his legs out of the narrow seating space and said, "You nosy little bastard. Ow! Damn it, cramp!"

"I'm sorry. I'm sorry." Then, incongruously, Toño stepped forward, saying "Can I help?" thinking to lift the old legs out from where they were wedged underneath the glove compartment.

"No, Jesus Christ, kid, back off. Last thing I need is help. I came up here just to get a little peace, get away from that overly helpful mob down there." He made his voice falsetto, mimicking his offspring. "'Dad, are you hungry?' 'Dad, eat more oatmeal,' 'Grandpa, is it time to irrigate?' Natter, natter natter. And Tess is the worst of all. 'Don't worry, honey,' and on and on, all the time fidgeting and stewing. 'It's going to be okay.' Well, of course it is. Why the hell wouldn't it be, I ask you?"

Toño opened his mouth and closed it, having no idea what

Hidden Treasure (or) Where is Jesus?

to say. The cranky old guy seemed plenty put out. He'd finally dislodged his feet and was dropping them toward the ground. He growled, "You may as well come on down and get something to eat, too. Everyone else is. Eat me out of house and home."

"Uh, no, I can't, I ... thanks for the offer, but I can't. I ... I gotta get on home." The old guy's hair was standing up, pulled by the static electricity of the Bronco seat. It was white now, but Toño could see it had once been blond. German. Nazi.

Gus straightened his back and gave Toño a piercing look. "You know, buddy, I think that's kind of a fucked-up statement. My guess is you haven't been home for a while. My guess is you got problems at home, and Gordy, with his big old heart, has been hidin' you in that shed." Toño lowered his eyes, and the old man looked across at the backpack by the shed. "Yup, I think I'm right. What's your name?"

Toño couldn't find his voice. The old man prodded. "Look, you're already in it up to your neck, aren't you? You may as well tell me your name."

His dad would have stood up to this guy, Nazi or not. From what he'd learned on social media, that's what you had to do with these people. Bullies. Squaring his shoulders, Toño said, "Look here, mister, I'm Toño Romero, and I'm gonna get my backpack and go."

Toño turned and started away, but Gus said, "You hold on a minute. I don't think we're done here. Aren't you one of those Mexicans from over at Barnswallowpers'?"

Stopping, Toño said, "That's not your business." This came out somewhere between a snarl and a whimper.

Sounding sour, the old man said, "Maybe it's not, and maybe it is. You involve my grandson in anything? What's your big hurry? What you hidin' from? You act scared to me. Does this have something to do with bein' an illegal Mexican?"

Slowly, Toño turned. "It's how you see it. I'm not scared of Gordy. And I didn't bother Gordy. Or like you say, involve him in something. We're just friends."

"But you're scared of me? What is it you think I'm going to do? Beat you?"

Toño looked back over his shoulder at the old *Chabochi*

129

house that had almost come to seem like a home, then at the solid, white-haired German. It all came to a head. "Or maybe worse. You're a Nazi, right? A *mischlinge*. You people have never let up. Your whole deal is to get rid of all the brown people, like me. It just builds up and up and up. You got no way to know what it's like, what it's like to be American all the years of your life, but never to really have the right to be an American. Always just part American, part nothing. What the hell do you think I am, anyhow, if not American? You tell me."

Gus released something that sounded almost like a wheezing laugh. "Oh, boy. Oh boy, oh boy, oh boy. Settle down, Señor Toño. You and I really do have some things to get straight. You kids. You kids and all your high tech devices. Did it ever occur to you to google *mischlinge?* To get a definition? Where did you come up with that term, anyhow?"

Toño stammered. "I … I was in the shed and … and I was bored, so I saw some of your papers. I didn't mean to snoop — it looked like you threw that stuff away. There were mice all over it … it was some kind of certificate. Plus, I can't google." Flummoxed, Toño took a cautious step closer, and repeated, "I can't google. I don't have my phone."

"And Gordy wouldn't know, would he? He never asks me anything. You little farts. You kids always know so damn much and so damn little at the same time. Pull up that chair over there, and you sit. We're going to have a little talk."

The chair was a rickety lawn chair, and old Gus was still half in and half out of the Bronco. Just north of them, people continued to throng around the house and yard and lean into the yellow police taped area containing the corpse. Someone had brought a big excavator and unloaded it from a trailer, but it wasn't doing anything, just sitting idle as people carrying duffel bags poked their heads in waiting police cars, then returned to the culvert carrying various kinds of equipment as they flowed around the crime scene.

From where he was, Toño thought he could see someone taking pictures. Everyone was busy, and this would be a good time to run. Gordy's ancient grandfather would never catch him. He looked at his backpack, then at Gus's face. The old man seemed to read his thoughts; he tipped his head at Toño and raised his eyebrows. His expression was a kind of challenge. It asked, "So, what are you going to do?"

Picking up his backpack and going would get him away from all this. Listening to the old man, staying here in the midst of the trouble, that was what was scary. That would take courage. Roughly, Toño reached for the chair and dragged it to a few feet from Gus. The old man smiled. Toño couldn't interpret that smile. He snapped, "So go on. Talk."

Gus started with, "I was born in 1937, in Germany. Do they teach you in school what was going on in Germany at that time?"

Struggling with his memories from history class, Toño said, "Well, America wasn't in the war until ... until 1941 or something like that, right? So I ..."

"In 1935," Gus interrupted, "In 1935, Germany passed the Nuremberg Laws. Those laws were intended to obtain the blood purity of the Germans—they wanted only people of pure Aryan blood in their country."

"Oh." Toño shifted forward, listening.

"Anyone with Jewish ancestors was denied citizenship and all other rights, no matter how many generations they'd been in Germany, no matter that Germany was as much their home as it was anyone else's. And Aryans could go to jail for mingling with them or helping them. Helping Jews." Gus looked toward the house, watched the activity there, then continued. "My father was Aryan. He was a full, white German. He looked a lot like Gordy. Even had the same blond cowlick."

"So, uh, was your father a Nazi?"

Gus looked at Toño and shook his head sadly. "My father loved my mother. My mother. Her name was Rebecca Boesch, and my mother was Juden. She was a full-blooded Jew. Not all Jews are dark, but she was dark, her hair and skin maybe more like yours than mine. She was beautiful, my father told me."

'His father told him.' Toño felt his stomach tighten; this story was not going to end well. Knowing he must ask, he said, "But you didn't ever see your mother?"

Looking across the fields, his eyes searching for a different world, Gus replied, "Not to remember her. The Nazis called my parents' relationship 'blood treason.' They married in 1936, after the Nuremberg laws, and because of the marriage, they were evicted from their home, sent to live in a crowded apartment with many other people, told to divorce. My father was threatened with imprisonment for associating with the *volljude.*

"I was born in 1937. At first I was given a place in the Reich because I was half Aryan. They called those of us who had this mixed blood *mischlinge*. That's where that word comes from, Mr. Romero. It doesn't mean Nazi."

Toño's eyes were wide. "I'm sorry. I'm really sorry."

"What you found up in that dirty old shed was probably my *Abstammungsnachweis;* that's a 'certificate of pedigree'. It classified me, Gustof Westberg, as a *mischlinge,* half Aryan, half Jew. It worked for a while, kept me safe while my family tried to find a way out of Germany.

"Hitler, though, he was tightening things up. You're a rancher, I think, Toño. You know how we bring the cattle from the field to the corral, then into the smaller pen, and finally into the lane and the squeeze chute, where we can get them to be still while we vaccinate them or treat a sore eye or whatever. That's how Hitler worked, a little at a time, and that's how dictators or men and women who want to be dictators work now. First they call names, then they separate people out. They make walls and slums and ghettos. They call people rapists and thieves and gangsters, and they use the labels to say that the people they want to control are making it so the other people in the country can't get ahead, that they are taking other people's jobs. Gradually they gain full control; they have the whole country in a squeeze chute." Toño was nodding. This was the truth. He could feel it. Gus continued. "Hitler started calling the *mischlinge* monstrosities. He said we were halfway between man and ape. It wasn't long before we were subject to all the persecution of full blooded Jews."

"Oh, god! What a *mierda!"* Toño had forgotten the activity around the house and culvert. "But you escaped?"

"There were plenty of Germans who didn't like what was happening to their country, but Hitler had them in the squeeze chute, too. They were scared. It was hard; they didn't know how to help and not be in trouble, themselves. My father had an old friend, Eva Baader. He made me memorize her name—he told me to remember her because she was a true hero. Anyhow, at great risk to herself, Mrs. Baader got him some forged papers, and my family were able to make it as far as the Swiss border. This was in 1941, just before America entered the war. The way my father told me, the border my family arrived at was on a road patrolled by the *Wehrmacht*, and they were stopping people there, turning some back, taking some. I wasn't yet four, and my mother was carrying me. Just as they reached the Swiss border crossing, she sized up the situation, saw soldiers there taking people. She threw me at my father and screamed, 'Run, Kurt, run,' then turned to the troopers and said, '*Ich bin Jüdisch*. Take me.'

"So my father ran; he crossed into Switzerland. He tried to pull Mother with him, but she struggled, creating enough confusion that he could get across. He saved me. He was able to save me because they were shooting at my mother. He saw her fall. He hated himself. After that, he made it to America, just with good luck, and he tried to be a good father, but I think he always hated me a little, too. We try to be reasonable, but we can't always control our hearts."

Toño sat slumped in his chair. Finally, he looked up, meeting Gus's eyes. "I don't know what to say. I'm way sorry, man. So damned sorry."

Gus smiled, and now Toño knew it was friendly. "Ach, it's okay. We're alike, you know. They didn't want to let me be an American for a while, either. It was that wartime atmosphere. Kids at school used to beat me up and call me a Nazi."

"Like I did," Toño mumbled.

"I used to think if everybody had a kind, forgiving heart we could get past some of the horrors in this world, and that I should start with me, at least try to be compassionate, but there are just things that scare us, and stop us, things we can't learn to forgive. If that guy down there in the culvert turned out to be, just happened to turn out to be, one of those White Supremacists, I'd be glad. Real glad that that's where he ended up. So that's how it is with me, Toño."

Toño swallowed. "I guess ... I guess in a way that's how I'd feel if ... if it turned out to be an ICE agent."

Gus studied the boy. Quietly, he said, "Well, I guess we'll find out who he is before too long, the way they're going at it down there. Let's go get a bite to eat. I'll help Gordy watch out for you. Us *mischlinge* and you wetbacks should stick together, right?"

25

Katelyn and the Squad Make Plans

Larry spotted him first. "Holy crap, speak of the devil! He's right over there." Of course, Larry hadn't seen the devil. He'd seen Toño. Like everyone else in the community, the teens had gotten wind of a corpse having been found at Westbergs', and like everyone else, curiosity had drawn them over to check out the situation. Two dead people in two days! This was a lot for Croysant, and people wanted to be on the front lines for information. Like everyone else, Larry, Cesar, and Pewter came up to "offer their help." Katelyn, on the other hand, brought a load of the food that had been delivered to Corbits' the previous day in the interest of helping that family grieve for Frankie Belle. Neddie had bustled around, filling two large boxes with casseroles, salads, and desserts, saying, "I think Tess will need these now more than we do," and saying, "That poor woman! Who do you suppose it is? Some stranger, died on her place and crawled in that pipe? But why? Was he thirsty?"

Meanwhile, Tess was commandeering her children and grandchildren in her own kitchen, calling on them to produce more food, all to be set out on folding tables in the yard, complete with paper plates, iced tea, cookies, and coffee. Food production, Tess found, was a great distraction.

Having clustered near a table, the squad members looked in the direction of Larry's gesture to see, sure enough, the topic of their current discussion: Toño, across the yard and in deep conversation with Gus Westberg and Gordy. "WTF!" Cesar exploded. "What's he doing, anyhow? He hasn't been on Fortnite since Thursday, hasn't returned my texts …!"

"Shhh," Katelyn cautioned. She'd turned pale, her knees jelly. She grabbed for Pewter's elbow and spoke intensely. "Look, people. This is serious. This is trill. It goes deep. Something is way off here, and we need to get somewhere private, somewhere we can talk. I mean, V private." She indicated the people milling around them, some looking curiously at the agitated teenagers.

Catching her tone, Larry said, "Okay, okay. Maybe my place? Nobody's there right now. Mom's here, doing some kind of paramedic standby."

"That'd work, I guess," Pewter said, always supportive of Larry, "But what about Toño and that Westberg kid?"

"What about them?"

"Should they come with us? Should Toño know we've spotted him?"

"Huh," Cesar grumped. "I say ignore 'im. He's been ignoring us." One of the Westbergs walked by with a plate of cheese and crackers, and he snagged a fistful.

Katelyn's mouth had formed a tight line. "No, we take them." There was an implication that the two would be shanghaied, if necessary. Glancing at her face, the others didn't argue.

Delegated to do the retrieval, Larry threaded his way through neighbors and tapped Toño on the shoulder, spoke a few words, and gestured toward the rest of the squad, now clustered with heads up like a nest of alerted prairie dogs. Toño nodded, faced the group of friends, threw his hands out in a 'not my fault' gesture, then spoke briefly with Gordy and Gus. The squad saw, of all things, a warm handshake with Gus, then both boys joined the others, Toño and Gordy looking worried.

The kids managed to squash into Larry's noisy, rattle-trap F150, the ones in the back seat sitting with knees to chins. On the way to Gallenas's place, Toño filled them in, telling them the whole story of the ICE man, while Gordy supplied back-up whenever a detail went missing. Their obvious tension spread throughout the truck.

Pewter, not one to mince words, summed it up. "So you

Hidden Treasure (or) Where is Jesus?

think you killed him, and that's him in the culvert, and now you're scared to death."

"That pretty much says it all, yeah. And I'm worried about my family. I need to find them, so I can warn them and we can get the hell out of this country fast."

They pulled into Larry's yard. Ever the thoughtful host, Larry took them to the kitchen and got out soda, ice cream sandwiches, and potato chips. They ate, but no one sat. Cesar, leaning against the sink, started with, "Well, Toño, if it helps, I think we can tell you where your dad is."

"You can? God, yes, it would help! Where is he?"

"Yeah. You know, that lottery ticket, how your dad won a bunch of money, and was scared to cash it in because of immigration, and had us hide it?"

"Yeah, we put it in the baby Jesus at Alma's."

"We did. But anyhow, we got worried about you when we didn't hear from you, amigo, and then worried that maybe there was a time limit on that ticket, that maybe your dad needed to cash it. You know, we didn't know all the rules."

Toño was impatient. "Yeah, yeah. So anyhow, where's my dad?"

Determined to keep his story in order, Cesar said, "Well, anyhow, this morning we went up to Nancy Jane's and of course nobody was there. Well, Nancy Jane was, but not anybody from your family. So we wheedled and wheedled, and she said she had to go, that she had stuff to tend to over at Patch's. She's getting pretty hung up on him. But we kept after her, and I think she's worried about that corpse, too. Anyhow, she finally just said, 'I gotta go. If you kids want to keep causin' trouble, go over to Doc Clary's.'"

Anxious to move things along, Pewter cut in. "So, of course, we took the hint. That's what we did, was go to Doc's. It was early, so we headed over there and we caught your dad in the surgery helping the young doc, Doc Bailey. We don't think they expected anyone that early, and he was right in the middle of it, so he couldn't drop everything and take off. That little blabbermouth, Bailey's kid, Sophia, was there, too, so your dad wouldn't say much of anything. We tried to ask about the ticket, and he just headed us off, said, 'Yeah, sure, bring it to me. I may need the money.' Of course, Sophia was all ears, asking 'What money? Did you win some money?' and we just decided to cut our losses and leave. Told him we'd be back. I don't know how he dealt with Doc Bailey and her kid."

Toño was gnawing on a finger. "Was my mom there?"

Larry, Pewter, and Cesar all shook their heads. "We didn't see her." Cesar continued, "I don't think she was there, bud. I didn't see any sign of her." Toño sat, looking drained, and Larry, wanting to comfort, started with, "But maybe she was ..."

Katelyn interrupted. "Or maybe not. I want to talk about some other stuff. I don't want to worry you too much, Toño, but I think we need to get on this. Like now. Like yesterday. And we need a plan."

Concerned about Toño's state of mind, Larry snapped, "So what is it, Kate? What's your big deal now?"

"Well, I'll tell you. It's that Frickleson. I had to park at the clubhouse for a few minutes yesterday — that's where your phone is, by the way, Toño. That's why I stopped, was to hide that phone, like you asked. Anyhow, I hid it, and then looked across the road ..."

Cesar interrupted. "His phone?"

"Yeah, my phone." Toño nodded. "That's why I haven't been texting and stuff. I think they can trace it. The feds. Gordy and me asked Katelyn to hide it."

Irritated at the interruption, Katelyn continued, her voice louder. "So, *any*how. Over at Fricklesons', there's some kid toys. Toño, didn't you tell me he's an asshole bachelor? A sus? Not the daddy kind of person."

Pewter and Gordy spoke at once. "A real creeper." "Steals water, probably other stuff."

"Well, what would he be doing with kids' toys? Has he got Jesus and Camilia? Is he holding them hostage?"

"That's too far out."

Larry, sharing eye contact with Pewter, said, "But there might be other kids missing, too. We're supposed to babysit Nola Rippe's kids while she goes on her irrigation rounds, and she didn't show up today, or even Friday."

Hidden Treasure (or) Where is Jesus?

"We haven't seen the kids for three days," Pewter added. "They're just little ones. Syd and Spook. She's mean to them."

"Maybe he's got them all," Katelyn volunteered.

"Is he the kind of guy that would be in a gang? Toño, you said that there was something fishy about that ICE agent. Maybe there's a cartel thing." Cesar was worried.

Katelyn was getting worked up. "There's more. I was watching when I drove up to Gordy's place today, and I saw another car there when I passed Fricklesons', and some skinny, hairy guy walking around the yard. I was driving, so I couldn't see much, but I don't think he was from around here."

This comment brought on generalized conversation, everyone talking at once. Cesar said, "Don't gang members usually have shaved heads?" Someone responded, "Oh, you don't know. That's probably just a stereotype."

Gordy said, "This is a mess. Don't we need some theory of the crime? I'm not even sure which crime."

Katelyn said, "Yeah, Gordy, you're right. There's the guy in the culvert and then there's my half-sister, and I guess what worries me most is where is Toño's mom, and where is Jesus? Is he with her? And I guess we need to worry about those Rippe kids, too. That does drag in my sister, because Nola Rippe was Frankie Belle's boyfriend's daughter. Frankie Belle and Nola were close to the same age, but the boyfriend was older. In a weird way, Frankie was like Nola's stepmother."

Everyone was trying to follow. Pewter said, "Oh, I knew that. Frankie Belle lived with that Mickey Rippe, didn't she? Young enough to be his daughter. And then I didn't think about it, but I guess his real daughter's name was Nola." She threw out her hands. "So what do we do?"

Katelyn was ready to lay it all out. "We need to stake out that place, the Frickleson place. That Frickleson is the suspicious one. Everyone knows he's a crook, so what else is he up to? Could you help me? Let's make a plan right now, stake out Frickleson's day and night until we're sure he hasn't kidnapped somebody or killed somebody. There's six of us here; we can work in pairs for safety. Maybe that's why Toño's dad needs that lottery money right now, to pay ransom to Frickleson."

Hesitantly, they all acquiesced, but Cesar said, "There's something else you all need to know. Pewter and Larry and me already stopped at Alma's this morning to get that ticket. It's not there."

Toño, already at the end of his rope, jumped up. "What do you mean, it's not there?"

"Just what I said. We hid it in that baby Jesus, the hollow part like those kind of figurines have inside, and now it's gone. Not just the ticket. The whole baby Jesus is gone."

26

Evidence and Clues

NecroSearch had gone back to Denver armed with photos, soil samples, pebbles, tubes of water, pieces of vegetation, a shred of baling twine, and various measurements that might prove helpful; the corpse was loaded in the coroner's van and taken down county to be studied by Thompson; the Westbergs had been courteously requested to respect the crime scene until the sheriff's office notified them that they could return to normal. At the sheriff's office, Detective Hobbs, Deputy McCracken, and Sheriff Garrett eyed five items that the sheriff had carefully removed from evidence bags and laid out on his desk to study, wondering if seeing them together would give them any new insights.

McCracken was fascinated with the wadded blob of dark hair that the NecroSearch guy had handed her, saying, "All right, deputy, you may want to bag this."

She'd flinched, thinking the guy's hair had already somehow rotted right off his head, but catching her look, the researcher grinned. "It's a wig. I think the guy was bald." Staring at the wig now, McCracken tried to think what it meant. Hobbs, however, was the one doing the talking, and he was absolutely enthralled with the gun. Hobbs had an eidetic memory, and he was a gun aficionado. He could talk chapter and verse about most guns now on the market, as well as those no longer being sold. This particular gun had been found taped under the seat of one of the metal folding chairs used to seat the crowd for the Potato Days melodrama. The excited clean-up volunteer called Garrett immediately, but alas, there were no fingerprints on the beautiful, laminated rosewood grip nor on the fine, stainless steel barrels. No fingerprints, meaning Hobbs felt free to do what he craved, which was to handle the gun and point at details while describing its merits to Garrett and McCracken.

"My friends, this mighty derringer is a Bond Arms Cowboy Defender. It couldn't have been a better choice for our shooter's purpose. It's very small. It'd fit in your pocket, easy." Holding out thumb and index finger, he showed them the measurement. "You see, the barrels on this little beauty are just three inches long; the whole gun is about five inches. This is one of the handiest concealed-carry weapons you could have for self defense."

"Or to kill someone," McCracken interjected sourly.

"Well, in this case, that's what happened," Hobbs conceded. "But just look how well made this is. Smooth, no sharp edges, strong. You could hit somebody with it if you needed to."

"Huh." McCracken took the gun and looked it over. "I don't get the two barrels, Asa. Why two barrels? Do they both shoot at once?"

Pleased to inform her, Hobbs said, "Nope. This one is a .45 LC. The 'LC' stands for Long Colt. The other one is a 410 shotgun barrel, should be used with two and a half inch shells if you don't want too much kick. That's what makes this gun fun. The barrels alternate. When you pull the trigger, it shoots one barrel; then you cock it again, and it's ready to shoot the other. Our suspect was a crack shot; he or she had one chance. Frankie Belle was shot with the .45 LC barrel, from maybe twenty feet away. The other barrel, though, had been shot and not reloaded."

"I'll be damned." Garrett took the gun, examined it. "So. The spent shotgun casing isn't in here."

"No, it has an automatic extractor. We'll be keepin' our eye out for that casing while we continue with our detectin'." Hobbs took the gun from Garrett and dropped it back in the evidence bag. "That, but our priority now is to run the trace. See who could afford to carry such a snazzy little killer."

"Yeah." McCracken poked at the other items on the desk:

the pocket knife, a business card with the writing mostly washed out, and a small figurine, a baby which looked like a baby Jesus from a Christmas creche. "Wonder if your trace will turn up anybody connected to the dead guy so we'd know why he was carryin' this other weird stuff. He must've been religious. That looks like baby Jesus."

"Mmmf," Hobbs reacted, not a great contributor to speculation that didn't involve the gun. Then he said, "Well, what's with the knife?"

Garrett suppressed a smile. "Looks like it belonged to somebody dyslexic."

Both McCracken and Hobbs stared at him. "What? Why?"

"Well, it says 'TFW' there on the side, but that could be a dyslexic person's version of 'WTF'." He was now thoroughly amused by his own joke, but the other two groaned. Garrett spread his hands. "Hey, isn't that what kids these days say about a screwed-up situation like this? WTF?" He waited while they groaned again, then said, "Okay, wet blankets. Seriously, I don't think the knife relates to the case. It was on the ditch bank, not in the guy's pockets. Tess Westberg probably dropped it there on the bank when they were working cattle or something. TFW probably stands for Tess Fourier Westberg, one of the dozens of related Fouriers that live up that way. Anyhow, we'll see."

"Well, whatever." McCracken ran a cranky hand through her runaway red hair. "I've got something else for us, some info that we need to add to our bundle-o-facts. I talked to one of Camilia's co-workers, like you suggested I do, Chief. Her name is Flor Torres. I've known that lady for a real long time; we hike and climb together. She's not really Mexican. She came here years ago with her parents. They were asylum seekers from El Salvador.

"So, at any rate, she works in the Montessori hot lunch, but when school is out for summer, she works part-time at the Peaseford Market delicatessen. Now, I found out that Camilia is a steady volunteer at the Montessori, so I figured her and Flor might know each other, and sure enough. Good buddies. I went to the market and started chatting with Flor about flan recipes, kind of drug Camilia into the conversation as another good cook, and 'just happened to wonder' about Camilia's status as an immigrant.

"Flor backed me off of that. Just made a comment about Camilia being worried, mostly for Toño, because of the current political climate. Flor said, 'You know, I gave her a card for a good family immigration lawyer that Hugo and I know in Denver.' Flor said Camilia took the card, but probably didn't do anything about it. Anyhow, she had a couple more of those cards, so she gave me one. Said if I saw Camilia to maybe tell her again, because it's getting more dangerous here for Mexican migrants."

Garrett took the card, looked it over, then handed it to Hobbs. "Listen, Asa, besides the gun trace and so-on, why don't you do some digging, see if Camilia tried to contact this attorney. I'd sure like to know where that woman and her kid are."

"Sure thing. And what about that other business card you got there?" Hobbs pointed with his chin at the illegible card on the desk. "Not for the same outfit, by any chance? I guess it's too damned washed out to tell."

"You'd be surprised." Garrett pulled some tweezers out of his desk drawer, gingerly picked up the ragged card and held it to the light. "See, there are still some letter shadows left. This was in an inside pocket; remember, the guy had on a uniform. The uniform jacket had lettering sewn on it that said 'ICE' and 'POLICE'. Now do you see what those card letters spell out?"

Leaning up toward the card and squinting, McCracken said, "Oh, yeah, 'Immigration and Customs Enforcement,'" while Hobbs expelled a breath, saying, "Interesting."

Carefully, Garrett turned the card over. "Now, can you get any of this other side?"

Hobbs squinted. "There's an 'R', then something, then maybe a 'Y'? Maybe 'Ray' or 'Roy'?"

"After that probably another 'R' or a 'P', then something, something, a 'V' or 'Y', and then more clear, 'E' and 'R'." McCracken leaned back. "That's what I get."

"Yeah, that's what I get, too." Garrett laid the card back on his desk. He didn't look happy.

"So, you gotta call ICE, see if they're missing an agent, Ray or Roy somebody."

Garrett pulled on his mustache, sat back in his chair. "Maybe not. Maybe give it a couple days." He knew he had to answer the questioning looks he was getting. "Okay, I know you people give me a bad time about my hunches, but I've got some problems with this deal. Things that don't fit anywhere neat right now.

"First of all, I think I know where the Romero boy is. I'm pretty sure, anyhow. Yesterday while we were looking at stuff at Westbergs', working with the NecroSearch people, I see this Mexican kid talking with Gus Westberg and the Westberg grandkid. The two Westbergs just acted interested, involved, maybe a little concerned, but the Mexican kid was fidgety as hell, shifting foot to foot, looking around, nervous. Then he saw me, met my eye, and looked away, quick. Not long after that he was gone, and so was the Westberg grandkid. The Westbergs must be hiding that kid. That corpse must surely be the guy that came after the Romeros, and that just leaves you to imagine what that kid is feeling."

"You may be right," Hobbs growled, "He must be one poor, damn, scared kid. But you can't just ignore ..."

Garrett cut him off. "The thing is, something about the ICE guy is fishy as hell. I'm not sure ... I need to check. The wig. And do ICE agents carry business cards? Shouldn't we be finding a more official, maybe laminated, federal ID? Something clipped to his uniform, or in a wallet? It's ... I can't put my finger on it. Something here is just too damn slick. ICE agent stuffed in pipe. Baby Jesus in his pocket. Mexicans on the run. And another weird death done with a derringer. I need time to sort this out."

Hobbs said doubtfully, "It would have been pretty easy to get a fake ID, though. But I guess illegal as hell; it'd be a felony."

McCracken got up and gathered up her papers. "You know, Chief, I haven't seen you wrong yet, even when you go psychic on us."

As he exited, Hobbs chuckled under his breath, "Or psycho, maybe."

27

Jenny Learns Something at Alma's, But What?

It was August, after all, hot and smoky, and the creche shouldn't have been there, but then, Alma was past the point in her life where she had the energy or interest to move Christmas decorations in and out of storage. The CNAs who tended her, or her 'girls', as she called them, had picked up some of the Christmas things, but a couple of nativity stars still hung in her windows, and angels peeked out among green geranium leaves. Knowing Alma, which Jenny did, having been friends with her for many years, she no doubt appreciated the shy angels and the sparkle and glow of big stars catching the morning light. Alma was a woman well touched by her world.

Jenny had been too busy during the last twenty-four hours to do anything about Garrett's suggestion that she visit Alma to find out if the old woman knew of anyone in particular missing in the community. The Cowpath relied on Jenny: she played guitar there often, frequently worked as a hostess, and when needed, filled in for the regular waitresses. This week, following the law that everything happens at once, she had provided music on the weekend, helped with the sheriff's meeting on Monday morning, then, as she prepared to go home that day, Shalene, the waitress who was expected to work on Mondays, called in. Cookie picked up the phone. She told him that both her twins were emptying stomach contents all over the rug, and she didn't feel so well herself. Should she come in? Cookie replied, panic in his voice, "No no no no no, we'll get Cherish!" After which he handed the phone to Jenny, passing the problem along with it, and returned to mixing batter. The Cherish solution did not pan out. Most apologetic indeed, she told Jenny, "Oh, dear, I'm so sorry. I can't come now. Miss Bluebell is having her baby, bless her heart, and I must stay with her. Don't you just love babies? Bless your heart. I'm so sorry. I will try to come when she's done, though. Okay? Thanks, Jen. Bless your heart."

Right. Fair enough. Well blessed, Jenny accepted reality: Cherish would never be pried away from her beloved, birthing donkey. Even so, her face was a bit grim as she gathered up the order pad and went to work. She was drained by evening, and grateful to find Garrett at her trailer, ready to spend the night. She was used to him now, and slept better with him near. It was a good night; alas, he left for Riversmet very early the next morning, needing to do paperwork and go over evidence with Hobbs and McCracken. He'd discussed what was in the evidence bags with Jenny: the knife and gun, the washed-out business card and tangled, pony-tailed wig. And that Jesus figurine. Working her way through her morning chores, Jenny pondered those items, trying to make sense of them, but she came up with nothing. Finally, rooms tidied, dogs fed, and garden tended, she finished marshaling her forces, located her only cookies to bring along, and headed for Alma's.

Alma was always pleased to have company. The CNAs came by three times each day, and her grown children, Duz, Duz's wife, Carmen, and Gritty, kept a tight rein on her needs, but her short-term memory was gone. Often she told guests that no one had been there for days, and that such neglect was making a good deal of extra work for an old woman like herself. The guests humored her, knowing that she was mostly immobile and thus unable to do any work except in her own virtual realities. She craved fish, fresh brook trout, well-floured and fried in bacon grease, such as those which she'd eaten in abundance as a child, and she craved strong coffee. She daydreamed about cooking these things, then eating them with Doug, her husband, long since passed. Sometimes the neighbors helped out by bringing fish, although they were never able to cook them up to Alma's standards. Still, they tried. As for the coffee, the CNAs certainly didn't get it strong enough. She yearned for it to be so thick it would need chewing, as she tried to explain. Her children knew how to get it just right, and often did, and Jenny, also, having been a routine visitor for several years, also knew what was required. Today, Jenny puttered in the kitchen and brought Alma a cup that was so fierce it almost threw the spoon out on the floor. Then she brought herself a wildly effective wake-up cup also, and the two women sat together, eating the butterscotch cookies and chatting up a storm.

The conversation often went in circles, as Alma tended to get hung up on one topic. Today she discussed her sister, the one who had died several years ago. Struggling with the chewed-up brown-sugar cookie mass in her teeth, Alma told Jenny several times that, "When Elaine died, she still had all her teeth, like me, but she had gotten so that she repeated herself and repeated herself. It was time for her to die, I think."

Jenny thought this might be a good point to interject, saying, "Yes, a lot of people we used to know are missing from the community these days." She stressed the word 'missing.' "I wonder who else we know who maybe we haven't heard from in a while."

To this, Alma replied, "You know, Elaine was the one who always stirred up the fights between us, so I don't miss her much. I miss my friend Hallie Flute more than I miss my sister. There was that time ..."

At that point, Jenny spotted the creche, and thought, "Someone is missing." Mary was there; Joseph was there; there was a band of Angels, plus Wise Men, sheep, a donkey, and so-on. But the point of the whole display, the central figure, was missing. The dresser hadn't been dusted for some time, meaning there was a small clear spot, not dusty, in front of Mary and Joseph. That space should have contained Baby Jesus, tiny hands and feet up, eyes on his holy mother. Jenny felt a thrill of discovery! That ICE guy had been here before he died. She couldn't wait to tell Garrett.

Half listening to the description of the aggressive elderly

Hidden Treasure (or) Where is Jesus?

and dead Elaine, she got up and picked up a small stuffed bear that was wearing a santa hat and cowboy boots, and that was sitting near the creche. Holding it up, she interrupted Alma with, "My! This is really cute."

Her flow stopped, Alma said, "Oh, yes, I suppose. One of the grandkids brought that. Squeeze its hand."

Jenny squeezed its hand and the bear began to wiggle vigorously and deliver a version of Rudolph, the Red-Nosed Reindeer, in a hearty cowboy twang. She had to keep holding the bear because there didn't appear to be a way to turn it off, and she was afraid its lively jigging would knock over other keepsakes on the dresser if she put it back down. Speaking over the loud bear, she pointed to the creche. "It looks as if you have more Christmas things here, too."

Rapidly losing interest in the current topic, Alma said, "Oh, somebody gave me that. Don't remember who. My girls should have gotten that put away by now — it will be spring soon, won't it? Anyhow, did I ever tell you about how my sister got so that she repeated herself and repeated herself before she died?"

"Oh, yes, Alma, I think you did once." Jenny persisted. "Now, this is odd. This Christmas scene is missing the Baby Jesus. Whatever happened to the Baby Jesus?"

Annoyed, Alma glanced over toward the display, shrugged, and said, "I think Elaine's mind was going. I should have felt sorry for her, but when we were little, she wet the bed and I had to sleep in a puddle half the time."

The bear had, mercifully, stopped. Jenny set it down, and deliberately kept her voice loud. "I really, really wonder who took your Baby Jesus."

As if it were common knowledge, Alma said, "Oh, you remember. Lew Harris took him when he was up here. He was going to take care of him for a while." Alma looked into her empty cup. "I wish I had more coffee."

Well, she may have been a tad unforgiving of poor Elaine and her bed wetting, but she was old, and of course, she could have more coffee. Taking her cup to the kitchen for a refill, Jenny's head seethed with questions. Why would Lew Harris, of all people, take Alma's little Jesus? They had always been good friends, but why the little Jesus? Was it so his imaginary boy would have something to play with? This whole scenario was stupid. How did the ICE agent, dead in a culvert, end up with it? How did he get it from Lew? If, indeed, Lew had taken it.

Returning with the coffee, Jenny said, "So, Alma, why did Lew take that little Jesus, the little figure that was supposed to be part of your Christmas scene. See? Right over there. It's missing."

Alma was confused. She strained her head up to see. "Oh, it is, isn't it? Well ... and you say Lew took it? Why, I thought I moved it. I suppose he took it to keep it safe. You know, those boys hid something very, very important in it. They told me not to tell anyone that they hid anything there, and I won't. I won't even tell you. I don't know what it was, but they said it was very important. But I see it's missing." She nodded her head thoughtfully. "So, you say Lew took it, to keep it safe? Well, that's good."

She contemplated the creche, and Jenny contemplated her. Finally, taking another butterscotch cookie, Alma sipped her coffee and said, "So, speaking of missing, did I tell you that I feel bad, because I don't miss my sister Elaine nearly as much as I should. She wet the bed, you know."

28

Garrett Receives an Interesting Visitor

Garrett continued to consider the items on his desk after Hobbs and McCracken left. A wig. Was the guy disguising himself for some reason, or was he just bald and vain? The stupid, incongruous, washed-out business card—it just didn't sit right. Would a government agent carry business cards like that? Really? Really? Maybe he should ask Hobbs to follow up; for all he knew, maybe they did. Then the baby Jesus. As inconsistent as the card. Garrett had poked his little finger into the hollowed-out space inside it, thinking something might be hidden in there, a phone number or safe combination, but nothing was there. At least, not at this point. The knife, Garrett dismissed. But the gun held interest. It had been found in Croysant, but two shots had been fired. Where? Maybe someone hadn't been such a crack shot after all. Maybe they had issues with immigration enforcement, and they had shot the ICE agent with the first barrel, the shotgun barrel, then intended to shoot someone else with the second barrel, the .45, and missed, shooting Frankie Belle by accident. It was clear the ICE man had been shot, but they were going to have to wait for the coroner's report for details. So maybe ...

A sharp knock on his door interrupted his speculation. "Yeah. What is it?"

Edith peeked in. "There's an hombre down in reception. He wants to report a missing person."

"Look, Edith," Garrett snapped, "I'm trying to think here. You know that. Missing persons are routine—just take down his information so we have it."

"Well, Chief, normally I would. *You know that*," she countered, mimicking his cranky tone. "But see, the missing person problem is up in that area where the murders just happened, up out of Croysant." Now she was ready to tease her boss. "I just thought a normal, efficient sheriff might like to meet this guy. Geez, I forgot who I was dealing with, didn't I? Not normal, not …"

Garrett cut her off with a dramatic sigh. "Ah, what was I thinking? How could *any*thing I am doing here in my office be *nearly* as important as the work you find for me?"

Edith (Garrett had finally learned to pronounce it 'A-*deet*') Ovieda giggled at his fake sarcasm. "Ah, Señor, you forget. Jenny showed me the ring, and I agree. You are one man who needs a wife."

Putting the evidence items back in their bags while he talked, Garrett said, "Anything you want to tell me about this person who is missing someone before I meet him? Or her?"

"I said 'guy.' Him. Not much. Buggy eyes, needs a bath, fade-away voice. I kept having to lean in to hear what he was trying to tell me, which wasn't a pleasant experience. Kind of *basto*, you know, a creeper. You'll sort it out when you talk to him." And she knew he would. Despite her teasing, Edith, like McCracken, had a good deal of respect for her sheriff. She was well aware of his intuitive hesitation to move too quickly to report the missing ICE agent, and she appreciated it. She knew the Romero family from church, and didn't think of them as illegal criminals, just as fellow Mexican immigrants trying to get past bureaucratic obstacles, like everyone else.

The concerned party entered the room sideways, adopted an air of jovial friendship, and held the missing person form out toward Garrett, who ignored it. For a flicker of time, Garrett questioned Edith's 'creeper' assessment. The man was skinny and bearded, with longish hair and a tee shirt that was slightly soiled at the armpits, but Garrett's beat was rough and rural; you could find a guy like that on any street in Peaseford or Croysant, and even here in Riversmet. Then the man spoke, and Garrett never knew just how he knew these things, but he did. The man said, "Nice to meet you, Sheriff. I'm Percy Bush." He tapped

Hidden Treasure (or) Where is Jesus?

the form, indicating where he'd filled in his name. "I came to Western Colorado to visit my nephew."

Yes, somehow, Garrett knew. None of it was true. This guy's name wasn't Percy Bush. He never found it nice to meet a law officer. And there was no nephew. Someone missing, maybe, but not a nephew. Garrett indicated a chair, and as the man sat, Garrett saw his eyes. They were a confirmation. Above the friendly, brown beard were green eyes as hard and murky as frozen swamp water. His manner formal, Garrett said, "So what can we do for you?"

"Perhaps not so much, this being a small town operation here." The man was looking around the battered office, its well-worn furnishings, and his tone had become condescending. He'd decided he was talking to a hick. "But I suppose you could try. My nephew, Paul Frickleson, was supposed to meet me at the … oh, what is that place called? The Cow Patty? Or … no, the Cattle Trail, I guess. Something like that. Up in Croyling. You know Croyling?" Garrett didn't know any place called 'Croyling,' but he didn't respond, waiting for the man to continue. "At any rate, Frickleson, uh, Paul, didn't show. I was … uh, well, I was naturally concerned. I went to his house, you know, and his car is there, but no sign of, uh, Paul."

"I see. Well, maybe he just went out with friends?"

The cold, green eyes assessed Garrett. "I heard there have been murders there, there in, uh, Croyling. I am naturally worried."

'I'll bet you are,' thought Garrett. 'Naturally worried, naturally concerned. Smells like unwashed socks to me.' To Bush, he said, "Neither of the victims in those murders would have been your nephew. One, in fact, was a woman."

Happy to have received this info-bit, and trying to look relieved, Bush said, "Oh, yes, yes, I see. Who were they? Maybe I knew them."

Garrett scrutinized him. Why would he think he knew them? He couldn't even seem to think of the right name for the town. "Well, Mr. Bush, I'm not free to divulge the identity of the male victim at this time. You can, however, learn the lady's name from any local newspaper. She was a young woman, and her name was Frankie Belle Corbit." Then, just to bait him, the sheriff added, "Had your nephew had a quarrel of some sort with Frankie Belle Corbit?"

A strange little flitter of the green eyes, and "I'm not sure. I'm not sure. I may have heard the name from my nephew, but ... but I don't recall a face. Catching on, he added, "No. Oh, no. I don't think Frick ... Paul would have shot this Frankie, uh, Ms. Corbit."

"I see." 'I see' was a comment Garrett was fond of using when he preferred not to contradict someone who he knew was wrong.

Bush shifted in his chair. "My nephew, you know, Paul, he said he had something for me. In the way of a gift. A late birthday gift. But I don't see anything like that at his house, and his emails have stopped; this is why I'm worried; he hasn't been in touch for almost a week."

Again, Garrett said, "I see," thinking, 'This cocky S.O.B. just piles it higher and deeper.' Now he continued, "Look, go back to the reception area and finish filling out the missing person report, leave it at the desk with Edith. We're a small department here, not too busy...." He said this on purpose, his Gomer voice, watched as the affirmation of his being a hopeless hick cop appeared in the squirrelly fellow's eyes. Good. It was always better if people like this underestimated you, and he reminded himself not to make the same mistake. Now he finished, "So, we're a fairly rural place. We should be able to watch for your nephew, and we'll let you know if he shows up." He made the last sentence sound country friendly.

Following Bush out the office door, he turned right as Bush turned left toward the reception area. Garrett made his way at a fast clip to Hobbs's office. "Asa, on your feet and into the street. That guy that just left my office, we may need to locate him later, but I don't think any information he gave or is going to give us is correct. Maybe tail him, see if you can get anything we can use to trace him later. License plate. Anything."

For a heavy man, Asa Hobbs could move from one spot to the next with amazing speed when necessary. He was out the door before Garrett had finished his last sentence.

29

Red and Louie Look for the Missing Person

A car and a pick-up truck were parked at Frickleson's place when Deputies Red and Louie arrived to check out the missing person report. Peering at the vehicles as they pulled into the yard, Red said, "Looks like our missing boy may be back." They'd brought a search warrant after what Garrett told them about his visit from the phony Percy Bush, whom the two deputies now referred to as 'Perp,' but now they figured they wouldn't need it. Nephew Frickleson was no doubt home, safe and sound, and without a missing person, this wasn't a crime scene. A brief check of the vehicles revealed a shotgun in the rack above the back window of the truck, but nothing else of note. Louie directed a shrug at her partner, said, "Let's go."

They knocked politely on the front door, then rang the bell. Finally, Louie said, "Look, I'll check around here to the left if you've got the east side. Meet you at the garage." Just as they turned to search along the sides of the house, the front door behind them was smashed open with a loud thwack. Both deputies had their guns drawn by the time they turned back, but they found themselves facing a .22 rifle pointed directly at them and held by an extremely indignant Nancy Jane Barnswallowper.

"The son-of-a-bitch ain't here," she snapped.

The deputies had encountered Nancy Jane before. Louie held out a conciliatory hand. "Put the gun down, Nancy Jane, darlin'." Red added, "Nancy Jane, it's okay. We just need to talk." Nancy Jane ignored them, apparently figuring it was she who needed to talk.

"I've shook down every corner of this dump, and he just plain ain't here. Damn lucky for him, too, because I'd kill his sorry ass if I caught him. That's his car out there, so I figure he got his handy ride outta town with one of his doxies."

Red said soothingly, "Yes, this could be true. Could you please lower the barrel of that thing, then we can figure this all out."

"Oh," she said, looking with surprise at the gun aimed at the nervous law officers. "Sorry, Deputy." She lowered the gun, but continued, "That fuck-head has offended every single person in this community. He's just plain crooked. He steals water, tampers with the divider boxes, messes with everybody's rights. The Fouriers, the Fowlers, the Johnsons, the Westbergs — we have to fight him every time we turn around for every cubic foot of water we're entitled to. He's probably working with that hellion Nola Rippe. Calls herself an irrigator. Ask me, that ain't all she's up to. He must have figured something was gonna happen soon to get it all stopped, maybe at the water board meeting. And it ain't just irrigatin'. This morning I went out to water my livestock and not a drop. This is the third time that's happened. Something's really wrong with that guy. He's a psychopath. What kind of person would deprive people's animals of their drinkin' water? He even took the water from Cherish's donkeys. God, when that happened that poor woman was fit to be tied!"

Still eyeing the .22, Louie said, "So you thought you'd come settle things with him?"

Nancy Jane snorted. "Well, Deputy, if you mean shoot him, then no. I ain't never really shot anybody in my life. I sort of shot Fowler once, just in the foot, but he was tryin' incorrectly to claim a piece of my land. I just thought I'd insist that this asshole lives here would have a little chat with me, try to see what kind of shit he's really up to. I think all the water shenanigans are just to distract us neighbors so we don't actually notice what sort of felonies he's truly engaged in."

Left speechless, Louie and Red tried to think what to do with her. The sheriff was secretly tolerant of Nancy Jane. He saw her as a person with a good heart but bad social skills. If they charged her with breaking and entering, or threatening law officers with firearms, he might see that as an annoying interruption of his main murder investigations. On the other hand, if they sent her on her way, that would clearly be a dereliction of their duties. As they tried to sort it out, Nancy Jane continued, "Let me see, I guess the only other thing might interest you here is what the hell those kids up there in the sagebrush on that hill think they're doin'. They been watchin' me ever since I pulled in here."

Both deputies' heads jerked around. Sure enough, two boys were crouched low in the rabbit brush, but not low enough. Red barked, "I got 'em, Louie. You stay here with Ms. Barnswallowper." Scrambling up the hill, he struggled to catch his breath. The boys stood and made to run, but he yelled, "Hey! I'm the law. You two don't take off, or you'll be in a shit-pile of trouble. Get on down here. Deputy Nickle and I need a word with you."

The boys started down the hill. Red, sucking air, watched them weaving through the sage with their hands up, stumbling as the hill dropped. They looked comical. He knew these kids, Cesar Rodriguez and that Westberg grandkid, Gordy something or other. Last name wasn't Westberg. Seemed like it might be Smith. Cesar shouted, "Look, Red, we didn't do anything wrong."

His lungs finally re-inflated, Red hollered, "I don't suppose you did. Put your hands down, for pete's sake. You look stupid. What is it you are doing, anyhow?" Then, he couldn't resist adding, just to give them a goose, "You know you're trespassing. Doing that just for fun?"

They looked at each other, then Gordy said, "Well, uh, our friend, Katelyn ... you know Katelyn Corbit? ... Katelyn and everybody, they don't like the guy that lives here. We all don't. She thinks he kidnapped Camilia and Jesus Romero. And that he's holding them hostage."

This explanation left a lot of gaps. They'd reached the house, and Red addressed Louie. "These people think Mr. Frickleson might have, uh, kidnapped somebody. Maybe ... Camilia and Jesus Romero." He looked at the boys. "Why in the world would you think that?"

There was a big pause. Then Cesar said, "The toys in the yard. And the way he is, always trying to cheat people and stuff."

Louie knew kids. She had six of her own. These kids weren't saying everything. She started to push, asking, "What else?' but before the words left her mouth, she knew. She remembered Garrett's briefing about the ICE agent, and his concerns about the entanglement of the Romero family. These kids were covering because, well, of course. They were hiding Toño. Before she could think how to handle this insight, Nancy Jane snapped, "I told you. I told you Frickleson was no good, up to worse than we thought. And you should see the drugs he's got stockpiled in his garage."

This got everyone's attention. Two deputies and two boys swiveled to stare at her. "Drugs?"

"Well, yeah. Figured you knew. Figured that's why you came. The guy has boxes of Codeine, Dilaudid, Demerol, Percocet, the works. Pretty sure they're all opioids. Sure as hell a lot more opioids than you'd need for your average pain prescription."

Red and Louie looked at each other. Well. This was turning out to be a lot more interesting than they'd expected. Louie said, "Well, all right then, Ms. Barnswallowper. I suppose we better go see this cache of drugs."

The officers headed into the house, the others trailing behind. Red growled, "Look, you people. I won't argue with you, but you keep your hands off anything, understood?"

They trooped through the house to the kitchen. Stepping into the garage, everyone stopped to stare. Sure enough, at least a dozen large boxes sat on a shelf, all marked, all apparently opioids, all evidence. Red whirled. "This just became a crime scene. You people get on back outside the house."

Louie said, "Boy, we need to call the Chief," and pulled out her phone. The boys had started to back out, but Nancy Jane was walking across the room. She took down a small plastic sack of powdery-looking material that had been barely visible behind one of the boxes.

"I wonder what this stuff is. Heroin, you think?"

Cesar said, "You need to be careful, Ms. B.," but Louie was

Hidden Treasure (or) Where is Jesus?

alarmed. "No! You don't touch that, Nancy Jane, it's evidence!" Nancy Jane, very curious, had already opened the sack and was squinting into it at the contents, shifting it to better see in the weak garage light. Puffs of dust rose from inside the sack.

Red started toward her, no longer calm. His voice had become heavily official. "Put it back now, Nancy Jane."

Taking a deep, exploratory sniff, Nancy Jane said, "Well, it don't smell like much," and set the sack back next to the boxes of prescription opioids. To Red and Louie she said, "This stuff can't be legal, can it?"

Louie responded, "Come on, we all need to get out of here. The sheriff is sending people." They made their way to the outside step, the deputies still unsure what to do with two trespassing teens and an intrusive ranch woman. They just knew that the cache of drugs warranted a lot of attention from the office in Riversmet. It was at that point that Nancy Jane Barnswallowper collapsed.

"Long day," she murmured, sitting on the step. "So tired now." Then she lay down in the open door, smiling in a friendly fashion at the world as she sighed, "So sleepy." This ended in a gasp and she added, half guilty, "Can't seem to get my breath."

"Ooooh, Jesus!" Louie exploded. "Fentanyl. That was fentanyl in that sack—she sucked up a gob of it. Call 911—hurry up! Tell them to bring naloxone, if they can." Nancy Jane had started to thresh around, struggling for breath. "Hurry, damn it." Louie started CPR. "Water. Maybe get cool water!"

Both kids were calling frantically, and Red dashed for the kitchen. It was only later, when the ambulance had pulled away, that his subconscious finally burped back up the anomalous thing he'd seen on the table as he rushed in for cold water. A computer mouse sat there, but there was no sign of a computer. What did that mean? He digested it. Didn't it mean that the apparent criminal Mr. Frickleson had left in a hurry? A big hurry? He'd grabbed his computer and high-footed it, no time for details like the mouse. Why? Had he seen 'Perp,' and needed to run? Or had 'Perp' picked him up? Red glanced over at Louie, but she was leaning against the hood of the police car, filling Garrett in on the details.

30

Same Day, More Police Work in Croysant

On Wednesday morning, after dispatching Louie and Red to follow up on Perp's missing person report, Garrett had ambled over to McCracken's desk and pulled up a chair. Her bright red hair was a mess as she pawed it in frustration, staring at her computer screen. "Hey, Chief. Hate this thing—it's so damn slow."

"Could be time to get away from it for a while. Say, here's what I think, Mac. Yesterday Jenny visited Alma, and she noticed that the baby Jesus is missing from a Nativity scene Alma hasn't put away since Christmas. It looks like the figurine was moved fairly recently; dust all around it, but clean where it was sitting. She asked about it, and Alma insists that Lew Harris took it."

Prying her eyes from the trudging Web site, McCracken said, "What? You think it might be the same one? The one in that evidence bag?"

"Well, it's quite a mystery, isn't it? If it's the same Jesus figure that we have here, how did it get from Lew's possession to our corpse's pocket? Maybe we need a trip to Croysant today, go talk to Lew."

Intrigued, McCracken nodded. "Maybe. Or maybe just another Alma thing: she picked it up to dust and forgot where to put it back. Maybe we should target Alma." She twiddled a pencil across her fingers like a baton. "Personally, I wonder about the Corbits. Romeros worked for them for years, and now Camilia and her little guy are apparently missing. At least probably more missing than that Frickleson guy. Maybe Camilia's hiding at Corbits'. Plus, I was just trying to look back in the files here to see if there was anything suspicious about that fire."

"So, was there?"

"Not at the time. Not what I can get to pop up on this donkey."

Sympathetic, Garrett said, "Well, then, let's head on up to Croysant. Get away from the deadly computer screen. We'll do some fancy police work. We'll hit Corbits' first, since it's on the way, then go on up to Lew's, and maybe Alma's. I'll be 'chatty cop' and you be 'snoopy cop'."

The Corbits lived in a well-designed modular home that was complete with all the bells and whistles: chandeliers above the dining area for lighting that could be dimmed when desired, a kitchen island containing a modern propane-fed stove top, two sets of bay windows, one accommodating pillowed seating in the guest area and, next to the kitchen, the other encompassing a breakfast nook. Social conventions gave 'chatty' Garrett and 'snoopy' Mac all the openings they needed. First, they expressed, once more, their condolences for the loss of Frankie Belle, and assured Fred and Neddie that they were working day and night to catch the shooter. The Corbits tended to talk at once, affirming, correcting, and supplementing each other's statements.

They responded to the sympathy with, "Oh, dear, yes, that was terrible!" (Neddie) and "But it may have been for the best," (Freddie) and "Yes, you say that, but we didn't want her to go that way," (Neddie) and "But there were the drugs and she may have had a worse end in store because of them," (Freddy). All this came in rapid fire succession, the law officers balanced on the flowery, seldom-used couch, sipping coffee, nibbling on the inevitable cookies, and their heads twisting back and forth as if at a tennis match while they tried to follow the conversation.

Now there was a pause as everyone caught their breath, and Neddie said, "You're right, dear. I think the drugs were becoming a problem." She turned to Garrett. "I worried about her. She kept bad company."

Freddy said, "Especially Frickleson and Rippe." This launched them again. "It wasn't natural, how much she loved that song, 'Frankie and Johnny,' like as if she'd like to shoot her Johnny, too," (Neddie) "And we never knew which Johnny. She had more than one," (Freddy) "But basically two, Fred. You are making it sound like she was a slut," (Neddie) "I suppose. Well, she got around, but I think she was a good girl at heart," (Freddy). And then, Neddie, directly to McCracken: "Like I said, she actually lived with Mickey Rippe, whose real name was Michael John. Sometimes people called him Mickey-John. But she also spent a lot of time with John Paul Frickleson. See, that's another John. I hated him."

Now, Fred kicked in again. "You see, why Neddie is so radical about that Frickleson is we think he is a real thug. Old Mickey-John is just a drunk, I think. Mostly harmless. But Frickleson strikes us as crooked as a two-peckered owl."

McCracken and Garrett exchanged looks, and Mac decided this might be a good time to do her snoopy cop thing. "Neddie, you have such a beautiful house here."

Neddie Corbit beamed. "Would you like to have the tour?"

Would she! McCracken contained herself, just saying, "Oh, my, yes, I'd love to see what you've done with it."

And then the formalities: "Would you like to come along, Sheriff?" followed by, "Mighty nice, but I'll just visit a while with Fred, here," and as the women moved away, "How you copin' with this drought, Fred? Any hay crop to speak of?"

Driving away, the sheriff and deputy compared notes. Garrett said, "I didn't get much more. I asked about the fire, and Fred confirmed that he and Neddie made a mistake, threw a big chunk of pitch into their wood stove instead of a regular log. That stove got melting hot. They couldn't get it under control before it set everything around it on fire. They had things piled too close, anyhow: kindling, newspaper to start the fire, a rocker with some crocheted items on it—it all just caught into a big blaze and went up in flames. Fred was sort of shame-faced about it, said they both should have known better, and bemoaned the fact they were old and careless."

Hidden Treasure (or) Where is Jesus?

Mac, who had taken a shine to Neddie, grunted. "Hmmf. I guess somebody could have planted the pitch log."

"Maybe. If so, probably another crime, another time. What'd you learn?"

"Unless it was actually planted by careless Frankie or one of the Johnnies," she fired back. "Anyhow. What'd I learn? Well, I got a good look around. Absolutely no trace of Camilia or any little kid. I got a good look into Katelyn's room, too, and it's real typical of a modern young woman — messy bed, gym shorts and shoes scattered around on the floor, couple of groupie posters, pop cans in the wastebasket and a potato chip sack on the desk. Only thing I noticed was a laptop on that desk and when I made a casual comment that it looked like a good one, Neddie told me that it wasn't Katelyn's. She said that Katelyn's is small; I assumed she meant a notebook. She said that Katelyn, as she put it, drags it around with her all the time. She told me that Katelyn told her that she is just keeping the one I saw for a friend, that she needed it for a few days for gaming. So I guess that's not too strange. Not suspicious. Neddie assured me that Katelyn likes to play games on her computer and so-on, so ... well, typical teenage stuff." McCracken scowled. "Maybe."

Garrett also grunted. "Yeah, I suppose. They didn't think much of our missing person, Mr. Frickleson, did they?"

"Maybe he shot Frankie Belle before she could shoot him first."

"That's possible, absolutely. That would leave us with the ICE agent. Any ideas about who would want to murder the ICE agent? Did he have something Frickleson wanted?"

Mac had slumped in her seat. "Drugs. I suppose, drugs. Always drugs, these days." She snickered. "Maybe Baby Jesus was full of drugs and they washed away in the ditch ..."

"The figurine would be too little ..." Garrett began, then realized she was kidding, and finished, "To hold enough drugs to have us watching for symptoms in those cows that are drinking from the ditch below the culvert."

"I'll bet," McCracken continued, enjoying the fabrication, "That Lew Harris and Alma are part of a drug ring. They're receiving drugs from a Mexican cartel, all cleverly disguised as religious figures, and hiding them until Eduardo can pick them up and distribute them."

Garrett chuckled, but didn't get a chance to expand on her foolery because they'd pulled into Lew Harris's lane. Once parked, they sat a minute, gazing at his door, bracing themselves for the encounter with the rambling old man and his beloved dog, Lucky, which no one except him could see. Dealing with Lucky meant that you must be careful not to step on his tail or sit on a chair he might be occupying or ignore him, all difficult in the face of his invisibility. Sighing, they reached for their car door handles. Just then, a little boy burst from the front door of the house, ran down the steps, giggling and shouting, "Come on, Lucky!" and scampered around the corner toward the back.

Both law officers hit the ground at once, Garrett saying, "Did you see that!" while Mac exclaimed, "Hay-soos!" They tore for the yard.

It was not to be. Just as they reached the front gate, prepared to unlatch it, Garrett's private line began to ring. The cell rang with urgency and persistence, caller ID announcing Louie. McCracken fingered the gate latch impatiently as Garrett mumbled 'oh's' and 'yeah's' into the phone, then he pocketed it and said, "Sorry, Snoop. We gotta head over to Frickleson's. Louie and Red have gotten into a little more excitement than we expected. And Nancy Jane's headed for the hospital."

31

Crime Scenes

It isn't always easy to isolate a witness, especially if that witness is a teenager. When Garrett and McCracken arrived, Cesar and Gordy were hunkered forlornly on the Frickleson front steps. Red had detained them when the ambulance pulled out, telling them that the sheriff would no doubt want to speak with them, and Louie, mother of six, immediately saw what happened next. The phones were pulled from pockets and the texting started. Louie confiscated the phones. "Look, kids, this is serious stuff here. Ms. Barnswallowper may die. You shouldn't be blabbin' about this to the whole world."

Both boys protested their innocence: "Just letting Mom know I'll be home soon for chores," and "Katelyn needed to know; she's our organizer," to all of which Louie snarled, while juggling the phones, "Right. I get it. We can check," which terrified the boys, setting them to worrying about what other items might pop up on their phones for the police to examine. Gordy considered bringing up the possibility of a necessary search warrant, but decided to wait awhile. This turned out to be wise. Louie now commanded them to "*sit*" and "*stay*" until the sheriff arrived to talk to them. Then she gave them her monkey face.

Only Louie could do this face. She used it on her own saucy kids, and when necessary, she aimed it at Red, her partner. It involved pushing her head forward and showing all her teeth in a wide, fake grin. This either meant, "Don't even think of crossing me," or "We both know that everyone else in the world is crazy as hell, so we may as well play along and do what we must." It always worked. Both boys stumbled backward away from her and plonked onto the step. Which had gotten very toasty in the August heat. But had to be better than confronting Louie.

When Garrett pulled into the drive, he sized up the situation and said a few words to McCracken, who then got out of the car. Garrett drove away. After conferring with Louie and Red, who were putting up crime scene tape, Mac sat down beside the boys. She wasn't a mother, but she was a dedicated athlete and spent a lot of her spare time coaching kids' sports. She felt sympathetic toward the miserable kids. "How ya' doin', you two?"

Both mumbled, "Fine," and Cesar felt impelled to add, "Look, Deputy McCracken, we didn't do nothin' wrong."

McCracken smiled at him, and it wasn't a monkey face. She said, "Oh, no, no, of course not. We just need whatever info you might have, then you can head on home, get at your chores and stuff. You still live just out of Croysant, Cesar?"

"Yeah, same place."

"And you're livin' with your grandparents, right, Gordy? It is Gordy, isn't it?"

"Yeah, that's right. Just for a while in summer, to help out. I go back to Denver next week, but I'm here now."

"Good. No problem, then." McCracken stretched her legs, settling herself more comfortably on the step. "So, I understand you kids decided to keep this place under surveillance. What was your reason for doing that?"

The boys tensed. They looked at each other, then Gordy said, "Well, we got a friend needed some help. See, this man that lives here, he's not Gucci. He's a bad guy. We wanted to help our friend to try to see …" he hesitated. "… to see what he is up to."

"I see. And who is this friend?"

Again, not a good question. The boys checked each other out to see if they should say. Finally, taking a breath, Cesar said, "Katelyn Corbit."

McCracken said amicably, "Oh, I know Katelyn." She paused, letting it appear that she was thinking, then asked, "So when did you start this surveillance? That information could be important."

An easier question. Both boys said, "Monday. Monday afternoon."

"Just daytimes?"

"No, we've covered this place day and night since Monday." They said this with some pride. Watching Frickleson's hadn't been easy; mostly it was long, tiring hours fiddling with their cell phones while they waited, plus there were the excuses they had to make to the adults in their lives.

Encouraging their sense of accomplishment, McCracken said, "Wow! That's a bunch of hard work! I've been on stake-out before, and it can wear you down. It wasn't just you two, was it?"

Cesar said, "Oh, no, we alternated. Us and Katelyn..." Gordy poked him. "... and Larry and Pewter," he finished cautiously, omitting Toño. McCracken caught the save, and let it slide.

"So in all that time, did you see anything unusual?"

Now they were in the rhythm of this, and could respect this as an important question. Cesar said, "Yeah, Katelyn did. Last night."

Not wanting her to think they were withholding information, Gordy interrupted quickly, "Yeah, we would have told you, but we haven't had a chance yet."

"Okay, then. Let's hear it."

"Well, Katelyn said some skinny guy in a hoody pulled up and carried a bunch of boxes into the house. Now that we been in there, Gordy and I figure it was those boxes of drugs we saw."

"I bet it was," McCracken confirmed. "Did Katelyn see the guy enough to get a description?"

"No, it was too dark." Gordy had had time to think how he wanted this story to go. He didn't want to talk about the possible kidnapping of Camilia and Jesus, so now he said, "See, you know how Katelyn's sister got shot, and she would like to help catch the killer, so the other day she saw a sus guy in Frickleson's yard that wasn't Frickleson. That's why she wanted us to watch. It was a skinny guy that had a beard, and she thinks the one carrying in the boxes was the same guy."

"And the boxes were going in, not out? And the man wasn't Frickleson?"

"Right. Going in, and not Frickleson."

"All righty then, kids. You've helped a lot. You go on home now, but stay where we can reach you. You can tell Louie that it's okay to give you your phones. Got a ride?"

"Sure. Our truck is just over the hill at Gallenas's place." On their feet, the boys headed toward Louie with a certain amount of trepidation.

While the deputies worked, Garrett drove to Westbergs'. In part he just wanted to get a feel for what was going on there now that the corpse was out of the culvert, and in part he thought he might see evidence of Toño. He was convinced that the Westbergs were hiding the boy, and he would have liked to talk to him.

Gus met him at the front door, hobbling out and closing the door firmly behind him. "Pretty day, isn't it, Sheriff. I expect you came to have another look at the crime scene. Or have you got it all figured out already?"

"No such luck, Gus." Garrett worked at the non-nicotine chew he had behind his lip. He could see Tess pass like a shadow inside the kitchen window. Old Gus was shielding someone. But who from whom? Did Tess know anything about the Romeros' difficulties, or Toño, whom Garrett would bet was staying up in that old shed? Sometimes it was good to hold your cards close to your chest, but once in a while it helps to flash your aces. Pulling at his mustache, Garrett continued, "I can't get much more information out of that culvert right now. Forensics has been over it with a pretty careful hand. I just thought I'd stop by and see if I could have a word with Toño Romero."

Gus was old and experienced, not easily thrown off stride. A brief flicker of the eyes let Garrett know he'd caught him by surprise by bringing up Toño, but his response was measured. "Sheriff, I wouldn't know where Toño is right now. You got some special reason to need to talk to him?"

Now Garrett would push it. Meeting the assessing gaze of the old man, he said carefully, "Actually, I do. Someone has told us that Camilia and Jesus, his mother and little brother, are missing. I thought perhaps Toño might have some idea as to how we might find them, before they come to some kind of harm."

Hidden Treasure (or) Where is Jesus?

Gus caught the hidden meaning, the protective note the sheriff had sounded, but before he could respond, Katelyn Corbit's tall frame appeared from around the corner of the house. She was carrying a plate. Disingenuous, she said, "I brought you two some cookies."

Garrett couldn't help but smile. Somebody needed to eat those damn cookies so these people would quit passing them around the community. Gus looked annoyed to see the girl, but Garrett said, "Maybe you're one of the people I want to see, Ms. Corbit. I heard a bunch of you kids have been watching the Frickleson house. You one of that bunch?"

Katelyn was a girl with a straightforward manner. She said, "Yes, sir, I am."

Garrett nodded. "Well, then, Gus, thank you for your time. We'll try to get that area around the culvert restored as soon as possible, let you get back to normal ranchin'. And please take these cookies on in to your wife. I have a little job I need Ms. Corbit to do; she may need to take a friend or two, but this shouldn't take long, not for young people who have already honed their spying skills." Garrett was grinning, half kidding with her. "Gus, you think you could spare Gordy and Toño for a while?"

Gus snorted. He thought, 'Won't back off the Romero kid, will he?' and his expression said, 'Nice try, Sheriff,' as he turned to go in the house.

Back in his car, Garrett discovered that Edith had called. He called her back, listened for a minute, then said, "Go ahead and read it to me." Now he was concentrating on her words. When she was done, he said, "I'll be a sonuvabitch, those guys are good." Clicking off the phone, he drove back to Frickleson's.

It was past noon, and the team of law officers were finishing up. Garrett went directly to the car that was still parked near Nancy Jane's old truck. It had been there since Louie and Red first arrived. Carefully, he examined it while McCracken came across to greet him. "What's up, Chief?"

Garrett indicated a dark spot near the back door handle. "Wonder if that could be dried blood?"

Squinting at it, McCracken said, "Could be, I guess. Uh oh, what's this about?"

"We've got an early report from NecroSearch. Not a lot yet, but intriguing. It's gonna mean more work. Let's get Louie and Red and the rest, and I'll explain." Grouping near Garrett's car, the law officers were all ears. "You all know what heritage fruit and vegetables are, right? Something where the seed has been in one family forever, just passed down from season to season?" Most of Garrett's listeners were frowning, trying to find relevance in his words. Vegetables didn't seem to have much to do with crime. He continued, "You can't buy them any more in seed stores; the families kept the seeds from their ancestors, and they're unique. So, my point is, some of these old apple trees around here are like that. They were planted by Johnny Appleseed types of people that settled here in the valley years ago, at the end of the nineteenth century, and were trying to see what they could do with the land here. The trees, they're apple trees, but they're not your Galas or Fujis or Delicious or Granny Smiths. They're older, and they're unique. Following me so far?"

Everyone nodded, still looking puzzled. Garrett continued. "So when the forensics team with NecroSearch went over the corpse, they found minute pieces of apple tree leaves and tiny twigs in the seams of the pants. Those leaves and twigs had no matches with any of the trees within several hundred yards of that culvert. The NecroSearch people took what time they had here to look over the roadways nearby, and guess what. They found two matches. Look across the road there."

He pointed, and everyone followed his gesture and looked into the area by the community house. Sure enough, a scrubby little apple tree was growing near the parking lot. There were exclamations of "I'll be damned," and "Seriously, right there?" Someone said, "What the hell! Did Frickleson carry out a hit more or less in his own back yard?"

Garrett grunted. "Well, that isn't the only tree. The other tree was, as nearly as I can tell from their description of mile markers and GPS coordinates, and well, you know, but anyhow, I think if we look we'll see it along the road just south of Alma's."

Over the buzz of speculation, Garrett said, "You realize that this doesn't tell us much. It just sets us up for some more work. We need search teams to go over the areas by both apple trees.

Hidden Treasure (or) Where is Jesus?

Red, you get that set up. Look for anything, but especially keep your eyes open for a shotgun shell. Then Louie, I'd like you to get a forensics team going on that car."

"You bet, Chief." Louie shielded her eyes to consider a cloud of dust turning in from the main road. "Looks like those kids are back, or at least some of them. Want me to send 'em packin'?"

"Nah," Garrett chuckled. "They're workin' for me right now. Maybe they got a report."

Gordy bailed out of the driver's seat and Katelyn's long legs appeared on the other side, then, to Garrett's relief, a Mexican kid untangled himself from the gear shift and seat belt at the middle of the front seat, and followed Katelyn out. She was shaking her head as she approached. "It wasn't him, Sheriff. He wasn't there. We actually went in the house and talked to Lew, and he claims a couple of his cousin's kids are visiting from out of town. I don't think any of us believe him, but he went and got a kid, probably the one you saw. It definitely wasn't Jesus."

Cesar agreed, then added, "He did say something weird. He said he thought he was supposed to take care of Jesus, but then found out he was wrong."

"Yeah, but Cesar, I think that's just Lew talking." Katelyn turned to the sheriff. "You know how Lew is. We had to all stop and pet Lucky and stuff."

Toño had wandered around the yard, stopping by the plastic yard toys still sitting near the front steps. He pushed at the riding car with his toe and said to no one in particular, "Chuy likes this kind of stuff. Gets in and makes car noises like he's really going somewhere. Wonder why this old creep who everyone thinks is just a bachelor ... well, I wonder why he has these kid toys here."

No one spoke. The question hung heavy in the air like coiled thunder. Had Jesus been here?

Karen Weinant Gallob

32

Nothing Seems to Add Up

"I did everything I can possibly think of. There is absolutely no trace of her. See if she's hiding them behind her desk somewhere."

If he hadn't known his friend so well, Garrett would have found those statements to be impossible to decode. As it was, he knew exactly what Detective Asa Hobbs was getting at. It was early Thursday morning and Hobbs, Garrett, and McCracken were once more trying to do informal brainstorming in Garrett's office. Edith had chosen fiendishly to bring them a large, healthy plate of fruit instead of the box of donuts that she knew the solid detective required at this hour. The man was tortured. Garrett had mercy. He picked up the phone and said, "Edith. Mr. Hobbs would like to know if you have the donuts hidden under your desk." The phone chattered and Garrett said, "Oh, that's good. Maybe if you don't mind sharing, you could bring a few on down here." The giggles on the other end of the line were unmistakable, and Hobbs sighed. "That woman is a curse."

McCracken was at a dry erase board she had brought in. She loved binge watching murder mysteries, and it always seemed so sensible to her, to put the various victims and suspects up on the board, draw lines to connect them, and stand back to see if there might be a eureka moment from the perspective it gave. So far she had three corners of a triangle, with Frankie Belle in one corner, the ICE agent in another, and Frickleson/Perp/drugs printed in the third. Now she was standing back to mull as to where she should add other players or clues, and whether there might not be some solid, or perhaps dotted, lines that could connect something in the whole thing.

As for Garrett, he was ready to pick up on the first part of Hobbs's comment. "Mmmf. No trace. Phones? Bus tickets? Local Uber lady?"

"I've been all over it, Pat." Hobbs refilled his coffee cup from Garrett's pot and eyed the door, hoping for the arrival of donuts, but, disappointed, continued. "I put as much manpower on it as I could afford, checked bus schedules and manifests, trains, planes, all the forms of communication and transport we can think of. Her name is Camilia Romero, right? Not a problem anyhow, as we thought about aliases and just kept our heads up for someone matching her description. You know the drill. Anyhow, as nearly as we can tell now, she hasn't left the valley. She's still up there near Croysant, or at least around here somewhere. I talked to Eduardo."

Garrett looked up sharply. "You did?"

"I did. Assured him we aren't out to get him. He had her phone, and gave it to me, says he's had it since the ICE agent was there Thursday. Nothing on it." Hobbs shrugged. "He wasn't that hard to find, doesn't seem inclined to run. Just says that Camilia and Jesus will be fine. He seems resigned to the idea that he will be arrested for the murder of the ICE agent. Could be he's hiding Camilia and the kid, trying to protect her."

McCracken wanted to put Eduardo on the board, but wasn't sure where to put him. The office door bumped open and Edith came in carrying a large box of donuts, assorted styles. "About time," Hobbs grumped, holding out his hands. Edith turned to Garrett.

"Sorry to interrupt you with another missing person report, Chief, but that's what held me up with the donuts. I think this probably relates to your murders, too. In some way. It has to do with Croysant. Can I send her in?"

With a faked air of profound martyrdom, Garrett took a donut from the box being guarded by Hobbs and said, "Why not? You'll do what you want anyhow."

Edith grinned. "Damn right. And right now, I want a donut."

Hidden Treasure (or) Where is Jesus?

Leaving with donut in hand, she added, "And I'm sending the nice lady in. She's very worried. I'm sure Mr. Hobbs will want to offer her a donut."

The "nice lady" turned out to be Laura Taylor, from Social Services, and she was, indeed, worried. She was given a chair, but politely declined the donut, sitting stiffly forward and leaning toward Garrett at his desk. "Sheriff, I thought we could resolve this ourselves over in Child Protection, but I'm afraid we haven't succeeded. We seem to have a serious problem. I'll fill out a missing person report, but I wanted to give you the background of this case myself."

Dusting crumbs, Garrett nodded, giving her the go ahead.

"Last week Frankie Belle Corbit filed a complaint against a woman who lives up in Croysant. That woman is Nola Rippe, and Frankie Belle accused her of abusing her two daughters, Sydney and Sara Rippe. She's a single mother, father or fathers unnamed. Sydney is five and Sara is three; Frankie referred to them as Syd and Spook.

"We're trying to follow up on this, but we cannot find those two little girls. As you know, Frankie Belle, who made the report, is now dead. Nola Rippe lives in a place in Croysant that is ... uh, a little run down, you might say. She was there when we went there, but I think she was on drugs. She'd just laugh, then say that she 'didn't know where those kids are—probably around here somewhere.' Then she threatened us—told us to get out of her house and quit snooping in her business, or she'd get her gun.

"So, the bottom line is, we have to find those little girls ASAP, Sheriff, or I think you may need to bring her in. Either she's hiding them, or she really doesn't know where they are. In either event, they are no doubt in great danger."

Garrett's donut high had evaporated. He slumped in his chair and dismissed Laura Taylor with a promise to put everyone he could spare on the case, and to follow up to her with a report. After Ms. Taylor left, the three law officers were silent, staring blankly at the dry erase board. Finally, Garrett said, "Shit."

Eying the rapidly emptying donut box, Hobbs said, "Well, I was waitin' until I could get some real food under my belt instead of that damn fruit, but I guess now it's high time to tell you about the rest of what we learned. It'll either help you or confuse you."

"Well?"

"Well, we got lab results and the trace and so-on on that gun that was found taped to the chair at the town hall. Definitely the murder weapon, definitely no fingerprints, but we got a good solid trace. The gun belonged to your friend, Mr. John Paul Frickleson."

Garrett froze. "Jesus Christ, Asa! Half the morning gone while we dick around here eating these damn donuts. Mac, get an APB out on that creep. This whole thing stinks worse than that ICE agent's corpse. Then get somebody, I don't know who we've got left, but find out, get somebody to watch the Nola Rippe house. Shit, we don't want her to take off with those kids. And Asa, court records, aliases, you know the drill. Maybe, too, see what you can find out about cartels in this area." Hobbs lumbered out, McCracken scuttled, and Garrett got up to pace, mumbling "Shit." Idly he drew dotted lines from Frickleson to Frankie Belle to Roy or Ray, the ICE agent, and back, completing the triangle on the dry erase board. Then he threw the marker down in frustration, as baffled as McCracken had been.

Knocking softly, McCracken edged the door open, then re-entered the room. "APB out, Chief. Sent deputy to Rippe house in Croysant. What now?"

Sitting back down, Garrett frowned. "Tell me again abut the relationship between those Rippes and Frankie Belle Corbit."

"Okay. It's like this: the older Rippe, Mickey, the one Fred Corbit called 'just a drunk,' he was Frankie Belle's boyfriend. Not married, I don't think, but lived together."

"Okay. So, then, Nola Rippe, the missing kids' mother?"

"She was actually Mickey's daughter. One of those goofy, small-town relationships, because that would have made Frankie Belle kind of like a stepmother to Nola, even though they were about the same age. Mickey was a lot older than Frankie."

Garrett was tapping a pencil on his desk. "Hmm. Might have made Nola pretty angry, to have her so-called stepmother report her to Social Services for mistreating her kids. It could mean that she would lose those kids."

"Maybe. Although it sounds like she didn't amount to much as a mother, kind of didn't care whether she lost them or not."

"Hmm. Maybe. Now if I got this right, those little girls—girls, right?—they would be Mickey Rippe's grandkids?"

"That sounds right."

"All righty, then. I think what you and I need to do next is have a little visit with Grandpa."

33

Mickey Rippe is Sad

"Ah, Frankie Belle. I wouldn't have killed Frankie. I loved her." Mickey Rippe's eyes were red and watering; McCracken figured it was either grief or alcohol. "She dumped me, you know, just before she got shot. So beautiful, that day! So happy! I begged her to stay, promised I'd quit drinkin', but she was planning on that inheritance from Fred and Neddie. She said she was going to leave Croysant and everything in it and start her life all over fresh."

Mickey Rippe gave a tremendous snort, pulling a disgusting amount of mucous back into his nasal passages. He struggled to reach his back pocket, finally extracting a wadded, limp, red bandana and blowing into it valiantly, apparently aiming to clear things up once and for all. As he worked on it, Garrett and McCracken assessed him. He wasn't an old man, late fifties maybe, but life had run him through the wringer. Garrett figured he was one of those guys who could never catch a break and used alcohol to treat his pain. McCracken was sure that a decent diet and a consistent exercise regimen could work wonders for the man.

Finally satisfied with the nose situation, Mickey continued. "She thought if she got away from here, got away from me and Frickleson and Nola and all of it, that she could get away from the drugs and drinkin', too. She was probably right, but, oh, man, it hurt me so bad. It hurt so bad to think of losin' her." He snorted again, brought the damp hanky to his nose, then added, "But I did, anyhow, didn't I? I lost her anyhow. Lost her anyhow."

Now his whole face was buried in his hands and his shoulders were shaking. Mac had the unpleasant feeling that this was probably more about his own pain than about Frankie Belle's death, but even so. Letting him subside, both she and Garrett stared at the wallpaper, which had originally been loved and pretty, but was currently faded to a dull gray with flecks of pink that were probably once roses. Raising his head, Mickey Rippe said, "Sorry. Sorry."

Garrett believed him. "Tough loss."

Mickey rallied. "Nola, though. You asked about Nola, too. She's still around, I'm afraid. You won't like how I'm going to talk about Nola. You won't like it, because she's my daughter, but she is one nasty woman, that one. The most rotten apple in the barrel. I heard that nowadays women think it's good to be called a nasty woman, implies independence or something, but I don't mean it that way about Nola. She really is ugly in her soul. She takes after her slut mother, made all sorts of trouble for me and Frankie Belle and for those little girls of hers. She treated those kids like dogs or worse. Frankie and me, we stewed and stewed about it, didn't think they'd listen to people like us, but then we finally turned her in to the Child Protection Services. We think she was batting those kids around, locking them in her closet or out in the yard, stuff like that. Never heard back, though." This thought made Mickey indignant. "Typical government rip off, Social Services is."

McCracken, trying to soothe, said, "They're the ones that contacted us. They're working on it."

"Good. You should arrest her. You know, Nola stopped by the bar after we turned her in, told us those girls belonged to her and for us to keep our prying asses out of it. She was mad as a wet hen, but cold as ice, too."

Trying to sort out those mixed images, Garrett said, "You must be worried about them, your little granddaughters. Do you know where they are now?"

"No, I haven't seen them here in town. I figure she's got them up at Frickleson's. She and Frickleson are like this." Mickey held up his hand, his first and second fingers crossed. "I guess I should try to go there and check on the kids, but to be honest, I'm kind of afraid of them. They're like Bonny and Clyde, reckless. Nola says Frickleson is the girls' father. I doubt it." He snorted again at that thought, which caused another nasal explosion.

Garrett stood up, as did Mac, but both did their best to smile in a friendly fashion in order to avoid the handshake. Once in the car, Garrett said, "Well, Mac, what do you think? Those kids aren't at Frickleson's, but maybe their toys are."

"I need some time to chew this over. Wish I had my board — I'd get some stuff written in. Do you think that he was so upset when she dumped him that he decided to kill her?"

They had headed south out of Croysant, driving almost aimlessly, and Garrett was quiet. Suddenly he straightened up and with resolve turned left on Oozle Road. "Let's poke around a little. Let's go see how Nancy Jane's feeling, just make sure she's okay after the Fentanyl episode."

They pulled into Barnswallowpers' driveway and knocked at the front door, their intentions being friendly but their demeanor cautious, knowing Nancy Jane's penchant for guns. No one answered the door. The place seemed deserted. Peering around, Garrett said, "What now? Our department got a hospital report; it said she'd been released with instructions to rest. You suppose she's already out somewhere on this place, grubbing?"

Mac shrugged. "Here comes someone might know."

Garfield Fourier had a well-deserved reputation as a reliable, helpful neighbor. He pulled up next to the sheriff's car and said, "You looking for Nancy Jane? I don't think she's here. I've been doing chores for her, and I called the hospital just a while ago. They said they sent her on home yesterday evening, but she never turned up here. I'd like to know where she is, too. I don't even know how she left the hospital — I checked, and her truck is still down at Frickleson's. Of course, the Romeros aren't here right now to look out for her, either. You think she's okay, Sheriff? Is it too soon to file a missing person report?"

34

Bad News at Frickleson's

"More missing people," Garrett grumped.

"I'm hungry," Mac said.

"Me, too. Well, should be. It's damn near noon. You know, my granny wouldn't have held much truck with just donuts for breakfast."

"Come on, Chief. There was fruit, too. Hey! You just passed the Cowpath."

"Jenny's not in today. The 46 Burger okay?"

"Clear down by Peaseford? Ten more minutes yet?" Mac faked a whiny voice. "I'll surely die of hunger. You better hit the siren and get your pedal to the metal."

McCracken's phone gave a series of pops which sounded like gun shots. Incoming text. Reading quickly, she said, "Chief, Louie and Red have been trying to track us down. Edith told them we were up here, and they have information they want to tell us in person. Can they meet us at the 46?"

The deputies didn't wait for the oversized burgers to arrive from the counter. Once seated, Red said, "We got some real interesting stuff, Chief. They found the shell."

Garrett was elated. "No shit! A shotgun shell? Where was it?"

"It was in the parking lot of the community house." The burgers arrived and Red waited for the server to go out of earshot. The French fries were stacked so high in the basket that they fell off onto the table. Salads were available, but nobody had ordered one, not even McCracken. She was going to allow the thick slices of tomato on the burger to suffice. As soon as they were private again, Red continued. "So, forensics will need to get a closer look in that area for blood."

Red took a large bite of burger, which cooperated by oozing sauce and pickles from its opposite side. Louie picked up the story. "But anyhow, Chief, that's not all. Forensics has made a good start on that car, and you were right. There are blood splatters outside, along the door and fender."

Garrett said, "I'll be damned," as McCracken paused mid-chew and added, "So, there you go." Then Garrett continued, "You know that Hobbs's people traced that car's license to Frickleson, don't you?"

"Is that right?" Louie said. "Well, anyhow, there is more interesting stuff, Chief. So far, they've only got one thing showing blood inside the car; there's none on the upholstery or anything." She sipped her Dr. Pepper. "What they got is a little safe. It's the kind that needs a key, not very big. I saw it. I think it was made down here in the high school, in the shop class. My kids make that sort of thing, and I almost think I saw that safe, or one like it, when the shop class had a dinner and silent auction last year. They auction off the stuff they make, and the parents usually try to be sure it gets bought."

Red picked up the narrative. "This one is a nice little safe, solid as a rock, well made. Maybe four inches deep and four or five by eight inches on the other sides. Wouldn't be easy to break into."

Garrett repeated his "I'll be damned." Then, "And it had blood?"

"Just a little, on an edge. They've sent it on down to the lab."

"Maybe the day is going to go better yet." Garrett took a napkin from the stack in the condiment basket at the center of the table and made an effort at some catsup that had invaded his mustache. His phone rang. "Garrett here." A pause. "They what?! You're shittin' me. Okay, we'll be right there."

He shut down the phone and was quiet for several deep, calming breaths while the deputies waited expectantly, then he said, "We gotta head back up to Frickleson's ASAP. Those damn kids hacked his computer."

Hidden Treasure (or) Where is Jesus?

"They what?!"

"Apparently they took the man's computer on Monday, when they started this surveillance they appointed themselves to do. Mac, I think that was Frickleson's computer that you saw on Katelyn Corbit's desk, the one she told Neddie she was keeping for a friend."

"Frickleson's!"

"That's right. And they've been working on it like little beavers ever since. They finally broke it wide open, accessed all his files, stuff Frickleson thought he had secured."

Red was thinking about the computer mouse he'd seen on the table, the suspicious mouse with no computer nearby. He should have mentioned it to Garrett then. Now all he could think to say was, "So, did they find something important?"

"According to what Hammond said on the phone, there's enough stuff on that computer to send Frickleson up for the entire foreseeable future until hell freezes over." Garrett dropped change into the tip can and hurried his team out the door.

In the car, he put on his light bar. Behind him, Red and Louie followed suit with their own flashers. "Thing is, Mac, this is all well and good, but we are going to run smack dab into legal issues with the way those kids got the evidence, whatever it is."

"So what is it? What did they find?"

"Hammond just said to get on up there, that he could show us better than tell us. He's holding the kids there. You know Hammond, he isn't much more than a kid himself, so he speaks teen-speak. He calls them the squad, and says he's keeping the whole squad there until I talk to them. Said the kids are really stirred up, really upset, and that they should be."

McCracken shot Garrett a wicked grin. "Sounds *cray* to me, Chief."

"Yeah, it's *cray*, all right. I've heard that one before." He rounded the corner onto Oozle Road and pulled into Frickleson's, where a group of kids and cops were milling around. "It may be crazy, but now it's time to get serious. I think you young people say FR, or maybe that this situation is *trill*." Garrett's smile was smug; he was pleased with the results of having googled teen talk.

For once, the kids were not talking all at once. The deputies were keeping everyone out of the house, and the mood was hushed. Nancy Jane's pickup was still there, parked in the shade of a large elm, and they opened the tailgate to set the computer on. Everyone crowded in to see, and Cesar took control. A picture popped up on the screen, and it took a full minute for the gathered people to realize what they were seeing. When they did, a collective sound of revulsion escaped them. "I just about can't bring myself to touch this filthy thing," Cesar mumbled.

In the picture, naked and arranged in a sexually suggestive pose, was a tiny little girl, no more than five years old. She was draped against the toy car, the same one they could all see, right there in the yard. Larry touched the picture sorrowfully and said, "That's Syd. That's our little Syd. Pewter and I babysit for her when Nola Rippe irrigates."

Cesar began to move through the pictures, image after image of naked children posed suggestively for the intrusive camera. Garrett said, "That's enough, Cesar." He had a taste of bile in his mouth.

"It's not all, though, Sheriff," Katelyn said. "The other stuff on this thing, they tell who buys these pictures, where he sends them, how he gets other pictures of little kids. It's a child porn ring."

Louie, mother of six, was flushed bright red. "The dirty, stinking son-of-a-bitch," she exploded. Then she said words that her fellow officers couldn't have repeated, even in rough shod company, words like bleeding monkey pus of a human, and worse. "He's going down, Sheriff. I will personally locate this pig-feces excuse for a human being and bring him in myself, if necessary."

The other law officers were making similar sounds, and the kids were nodding with relief to have official support for their view of the horror they had unearthed. Garrett just said, "Yuh." Then, he said, "Look, you kids. You squad. Taking this computer involved breaking and entering. This means we may have legal problems getting it into court for evidence." The kids' faces fell, but Garrett continued.

"We're all on the same page here, but you kids don't keep

messing around and give this criminal a legal loophole to escape justice. We need to find this ... piece of shit, and find out everything he's been up to, and we don't want him to slip through our fingers because any of us were careless.

"Now, you snoopy little devils, give some contact information to Red there. You can leave, but you stay where we can reach you, and keep clear of this whole deal for a while. That means you, too, Toño." Toño gave Garrett a lost look, his face hopeless. This caused Garrett to add, "Look, Mr. Romero, we are all on your side on all of your other issues, too. Just try to give us some space here. We'll do everything we can about this mess."

Now the sheriff turned to McCracken. "You better package up that computer. We'll take it on down, but we may have to contact this squad to get at the rest of what's in it." Clearing his throat, he said loudly, "They seemed to know what they were doing, didn't they?" He intended that the kids should know he was praising them.

35

A Visit to Lew Harris

The sickening pictures in Frickleson's files left them all feeling gutted. How could this have happened, right here in this little community, right here under their noses? When Larry and Pewter approached him, Garrett was leaning against his police car, trying to sort out how to proceed without letting the evil son-of-a-bitch escape the grasp of the law. He would have to mend the legal slips that had already been made. The two kids were holding hands, and their "Sir?" came out tentatively. The sheriff didn't seem all that welcoming.

Garrett arced a shot of non-nicotine chew expertly toward the ground behind the rear tire, then said, "Yuh. What you need, kids?"

"You know, you sent Katelyn and Toño to see if the kid you saw at Lew Harris's was Jesus, but what if it was Syd or Spook? Katelyn and Toño don't know Nola Rippe's kids."

McCracken, nearby, put in, "What would her kids be doing at Lew's? He said it was his cousin's kids or something. Anyhow, the kid we saw was a little boy."

Larry said, "She dresses them like boys. Don't ask me why. And Lew doesn't have kids."

Starting to cry, Pewter said, "We can't let it go. Just let us go check, Sheriff. We babysit them all the time. We won't mess with ... with legal stuff. The investigation and stuff. We just need to see them to be sure they're okay."

These two were so damned earnest. Working his chew, Garrett looked around the yard and said, to no one in particular,

Hidden Treasure (or) Where is Jesus?

"All under control here, looks like." Then to McCracken, "Let Red or Louie know we're headed on into Riversmet. The two kids can follow us over for a pit stop at Lew's before we go on down." This sent the teens scurrying for Larry's truck.

When they arrived at Lew's, he opened the door with a "Howdy, Sheriff," and a swift glance over his shoulder at the living area behind him. Then he reached down and said, "Take it easy, Lucky. They ain't gonna hurt you."

McCracken, by Garrett, knelt down eye to eye with the invisible dog. Addressing Lew, she said, "I think he just wants to say 'hello'."

Reaching in his pocket for a dog biscuit, Lew handed it to Mac, saying, "All right. Try him with this."

Extending her hand and palming the biscuit, McCracken said, "Yeah, now we're friends. Look at that tail go."

Larry and Pewter exchanged significant looks, and Lew said, "What brings all you people here?"

Before Garrett could respond, Larry said authoritatively, "Mom sent me and Pewter over. You remember Mom, right? Tiffany Gallenas? She left her girls here for you to take care of, and she said they must just about have you worn out by now. She said it was time to pick them up."

This was a jaw dropper. Fortunately, Lew was focused on Larry and didn't see Garrett, Pewter, and Mac all turn to stare in amazement at their gangly companion. As it was, Lew was nodding thoughtfully. He said, "Well, she's right about that. I'm tirin' out a bit. I'm gettin' a little old to try to keep up with small fry." He narrowed his eyes at Larry. "Thing is, people ain't supposed to know they're here. Somebody … was it your mom? I thought it was Eddie. Get confused every now and then. Swear to god it was Eddie Romero told me I wasn't supposed to let anyone know the kids were here. Said it was important to keep it under my hat."

Still staring back at the astonishing teen, Garrett realized that he had such a tight grip on Pewter's hand that the knuckles had gone white. Now the boy said, "Uh, that's … you're right, Mr. Harris. You have to be real careful about this. Uh, that's why we brought the sheriff, so you'd know it's okay."

Jerking his attention back to Lew, Garrett said, "Yeah, yeah, it's okay, Lew. These kids know ... they know how to keep things quiet. They won't tip anyone off."

Lew Harris pursed his lips and nodded thoughtfully. "Well, all right then, Sheriff. If you say it's okay, I suppose it will be okay. Come on in the house, then."

The four searchers crowded through the door, ignoring the hapless Lucky, who almost couldn't retreat fast enough to keep from being trampled. In front of them they saw toys scattered around the room: an Etch-A-Sketch propped against a chair; two Weebles forced, against their will, to lie down, tucked tightly under an afghan on the couch; Stretch Armstrong draped limply over a box edge; a row of Star Wars action figures and Evil Knieval on his motorcycle, all arranged around a Nerf ball on the coffee table. There was also a real dog, a mutt that was eyeing them languidly, half-asleep on a chubby overstuffed chair. Progressing down the hall, Lew was growling loudly, "Come on out now, you little rug rats. Someone here to see you."

When the little girls emerged — and they were girls, despite the shaved heads and boys' clothes — there could be no doubt about their identity. When they saw Larry and Pewter, they squealed and catapulted themselves into the teenagers' arms. Syd, the five-year-old, hugged Larry, saying, "Come see! Come see all the stuff Lew found for us!" while Spook merely stood with her eyes wide, saying, "Hi hi hi hi hi," then she put her thumb in her mouth. Syd slapped at her sister's hand, telling her, "You ain't supposed to suck your thumb," and Pewter hugged them together. "It's okay, Syd. It's okay. It's all right if she sucks her thumb today."

McCracken was attempting to fade into the woodwork. She didn't want the sheriff to see her crying. As for Garrett, he watched the reunion, pulled at his mustache, and addressed Lew. "Good of you to take care of these kids for, uh, Tiffany. You've got a lot of toys here. Looks like they're toys a boy might like, right? You got any more kids here?"

"Them toys were my own boy's, Clint's, when he was little. These poor little devils had to have somethin' to play with. They was pretty forlorn when I picked 'em up along the road."

Hidden Treasure (or) Where is Jesus?

Garrett frowned and persisted. "But just two little girls? You got any other kids or anybody else here?"

The girls were wallowing the real dog's head, telling Larry and Pewter that "This is old Mugger. He's Clint's dog, and he comes to visit Lucky. That's another secret—Clint doesn't know his dog visits us. We got lots of secrets."

Lew answered Garrett. "No, just these two little waifs. Thought I was supposed to get Jesus, Eddy's kid, but I guess I got that mixed up. Clint says sometimes I have dementia."

Mac, somewhat recovered, asked Garrett, "What's going to happen, Chief?"

Pewter leaped up from the rug where she had been looking at a Luke Skywalker figure with Syd, and said, with shocking fierceness, "Not back to Nola Rippe. I'd kill her first. I'd kill that woman with my own hand."

Garrett said, "Nobody's killing anybody, Ms. Pewter. Now, you politely ask Mr. Harris if it's okay with him if you take these girls back to Larry's mama for a while." Fixing his gaze on the teens, he repeated firmly, "For a little while. Legal issues."

Before Pewter could respond, Lew said, "Sure, you take 'em on back to your mama now. I need some rest, and I bet she misses 'em."

'Maybe,' Larry thought, considering his busy mother. What he said was, "Thanks, Mr. Harris," and returned Garrett's stern gaze with his own steady look. "We, me and Pewter and Mom, we'll take good care of them."

Back in Riversmet, the dry erase board sucked McCracken toward it like a magnet. Garrett sorted papers Edith had put on his desk. Mac erased the board and started fresh. Murdered: Frankie Belle and Roy or Ray, an ICE agent. Missing: Paul Frickleson, Camilia and Jesus Romero, and Nancy Jane Barnswallowper (maybe). She turned to Garrett. "What about the fake Percy Bush and the loathsome Nola Rippe? Do we know where they are?"

As you get older, the adrenaline wears off faster. Tired, grumpy, and not wanting to sort this out until he could get some rest, Garrett looked up and muttered, "Yeah, I believe Hobbs has that under control."

McCracken put the two names in a separate column, then said, "Personally, I think Frickleson did the killing, but why? And where is he? Makes you worry about Camilia and Jesus, I know that."

Sighing, Garrett said, "Well, let's get some sleep on it. If you have a light bulb go off in your head, you can call me. I'll be at my house in Riversmet tonight."

He pushed at the papers on his desk. "Here's a couple of things to add to your confusion. Hobbs checked court records, and he says a couple weeks ago Frickleson filed for custody of those little girls. Claimed to be their father."

"Ugh!" McCracken dropped the marker. "Why would he do that?"

"We can speculate. Anyhow, another thing here. The coroner'sreport on the culvert corpse. The guy was probably killed about last Thursday evening, the same night the ICE agent raided Romeros. Probably the same guy, I would think. And here's the thing. He had an injury above his left eye, made by some object heavy enough to damage the bone of the skull. Thompson says the blow would have knocked him koo-koo, but not killed him. Just like we figured, he was killed by a shotgun, close range, probably there at the community house where our teams found the shell."

Garrett scanned down the report, then read some more. "Mostly bald. A bald guy. Even after several days of rotting in that ditch, they still see the marks on his soggy body where he was dragged. And despite the damage to his face, they were able to determine that he had an old scar on an upper lip. One that was there earlier, before he was killed."

"Oh, Jeez, Chief. Something to do with gangs? Did he threaten Frickleson, trying to get some of those drugs, so Frickleson killed him? I can't follow this."

"I know, Mac." Garrett shuffled the papers on his desk, looked up at the dry erase board. Camilia and Jesus must be in the valley. Where were they? Was the Frickleson perp holding them for some reason? Were they in danger? He felt tired and discouraged. "None of it fits together." Then, seeing McCracken's worried face, he added, "Not yet."

36

Jenny Visits Tess

Jenny Threewinds wouldn't have arrived at the bright idea of coming to see Tess if Garrett hadn't sounded so beat down when he called last night. Garrett had poured out his problems to her. The child porn ring had crushed his heart, and he told her that he hadn't a clue about where the missing people were, nor could he put it all together as to who murdered Frankie Belle or the ICE agent in the culvert. He didn't want to call Immigration and Customs Enforcement and tell them about their missing agent, Ray (or was it Roy?), but not calling would get him in deep shit at this point. He was full of fear for the Romeros. He would certainly be called upon to treat them as prime suspects. And maybe they were, but his gut told him that someone else had killed the man.

Jenny reassured him that he knew more than he thought he did, and that he just needed to get some sleep and approach it all fresh by the light of day. But as she talked, she kept thinking about her own anomaly, Tess Westberg. Something hadn't been right about Tess all week, and Jenny felt an urge to sort out what it was. Uncertain of what she was trying to do, but anxious to help her sheriff, she set out bravely on this task of her own. She didn't want Tess to hear her coming and disappear again, so she parked by the cottonwoods and walked down the lane.

Tess was a small, round woman with jolly, rosy cheeks. Gus, like many ranchers, could be a bit reclusive, but Tess was normally an out-and-about kind of person. She went to her grandkids' and great-grandkids' school and sporting events, dragging Gus along with her whenever she could. She was involved in the community, and she volunteered at the library. She loved to bring family members to the Cowpath; Jenny saw her there frequently. This week, however, Jenny had only seen her at the parade, then at Corbits', when everyone brought food to comfort them for Frankie Belle's death, and then the next day, when people descended on the Westbergs' out of curiosity about the corpse in the culvert. These were required appearances, and Tess had been withdrawn, her usually rosy cheeks pale. Thinking it through, Jenny reaffirmed her own sense that something was going on with Tess, something more than a dead stranger on the ranch.

Her thinking was further confirmed when she came across Tess in the kitchen garden next to the house. Standing up, surprised to see Jenny walking toward her, she made an unconscious movement toward the house, but Jenny emitted a cheery " 'Allo," and the older woman couldn't, within common courtesy, escape. Now Jenny added, "It's such a beautiful day, and I'm off work. Shalene's in charge all day at the Cowpath, so I thought I'd get in a hike. I parked up by the cottonwoods, thought I'd see how you all are doing since that dead guy showed up on your place Sunday."

It sounded flip, but it was a pretty good first move. Jenny knew it would be. Tess, standing with a cluster of carrots in her right hand and her left hand poking aimlessly in her empty jeans pocket, could hardly ignore Jenny's perky, friendly overture. She lay down the carrots and responded pleasantly, "Well, thank you, Jenny. We're doing fine. But you're right. It is a pretty day. I suppose you're curious to see what the crime scene looks like now. I could walk down with you, then I'd best get busy. Gus wanted a little help in the office."

'Ah, pretty slick,' Jenny thought. 'She's kept me from getting too settled into the house as an unwanted guest, and let me know I shouldn't stay too long.' Out loud, she responded, "Sure, I'd like to see it."

At the culvert, Jenny said, "Boy, this is a mess; the county or state or whatever had better get it fixed back for your family." It was a mess. They'd torn the road work off the culvert, then taken out the pipe and cut it apart so as to remove the corpse with a minimum of damage to the body. The water itself had been diverted. It now flowed openly in an excavation across the road a few yards past the culvert itself, an ugly, muddy ditch.

"It's really torn up, isn't it?" Tess's voice was shocked and shaky, and Jenny looked at her, surprised. Tess shook her head. "I didn't see this, you know. I haven't been down here since they called the sheriff. I just ... well, I've been in denial. It felt safer to stay in the house and cook."

This gave Jenny pause. It would be true that a body this close to one's home might feel threatening until one was sure who the killer was. Maybe that was why Tess had been acting so strangely; she might be feeling uneasy about the safety of herself and her family. The crime tape was still up, but the deputies were gone. Jenny decided she'd have to mention this problem to Garrett. Glancing at Tess, she realized that the older woman did not look at all well. Jenny said, "Oh, dear, Tess, honey! You need to sit down." Taking her arm, she led Tess, unresisting, to an array of old stumps by the gate and sat her on one. Dropping her head between her knees, Tess resisted fainting as Jenny fished in her hip pack for a bottle of water. Watching her drink, Jenny said, "I guess it's a good thing you didn't come down to see that culvert when the man was actually in it."

Tess was giving Jenny the strangest look Jenny had ever seen. Her cheeks were still ghastly pale, and she said, "But I did see him in the culvert. I saw him before anyone else realized he was there. I knew he was down here."

Jenny stared at her. She had no idea what to say. She stammered, "You what?"

Taking a deep breath and giving the water bottle back, Tess said, "Jenny Threewinds, I wasn't born yesterday. People look at me and see a fat old ranch woman with as many kids as the woman in the shoe. They never realize. I'm an educated woman. I was head of my high school class here, and when I graduated I was accepted at Swarthmore. With a scholarship. My family and teachers urged me to go, but it's back east, and Gus was going to be here. He always wanted ranching, and he wanted to study agriculture at Colorado State. So I went where I could be near him. In a way it was an unsettling time. I majored in biology. Biology is the science of life, and I was trying to find out what life is all about, but I was never a real biologist. I should have majored in philosophy or literature. Or even theology. Oh well, water under the bridge." She looked at the uprooted culvert and chuckled. "No pun intended. What I want you to understand, though, is that I know you didn't just come lipperty-lipping along out of the blue, down our lane, to take a happy hike to see me. The sheriff sent you, didn't he? He has something he thinks you might be able to find out. So what does he want?"

Completely taken aback, Jenny stammered, "No, he didn't. Patrick didn't send me! I ..."

Tess was giving her the kind of grandmotherly smile that prohibits a lie. She said, "But you came on his behalf, even so. You love him very much, and I understand that. I love my Gus very much, too. Your sheriff is also a good man, and I have something I haven't been telling, something he may need to know to move forward on this case. It's time I come clean and take the consequences. It's been torture, but I've finally come to accept that eventually I will have to, that I can't be quiet about this forever, although I can't quite comprehend the nature of the danger to myself or my family."

Not knowing what else to do, Jenny took Tess's hand. "Oh, dear, Tess! What happened?"

"You know, Jenny, I love my kids, and my grandkids, my whole family. I love them more than anything. Just think about our Gordy, for example. I hope he'll be part of this community some day, even if his folks have to work in Denver for now. I wouldn't want him or any of my family to suffer shame or sorrow because of their grandfather's actions. When you get older, you aren't looking for people's approval anymore, but you do become acutely aware of consequences."

This wasn't easy for Tess. Jenny herself felt frightened. What was this woman telling her?

"I was born to an old settler family. You know my family, the Fouriers; they've been in this area since the Utes were driven out and burned the mesas behind them. Hmmph. Sad enough. My

Hidden Treasure (or) Where is Jesus?

mother was well-intentioned, but raised way back up in the hills, you know. Her family came here in wagons, and survived off the land. She had no idea how to be close to her children, and as for telling us the so-called facts of life, that was totally beyond her." Tess gave an odd little chuckle. "So you see, before my marriage to Gus, she quite awkwardly brought me a stack of white cloths. They had been carefully ironed and folded into tidy squares. She was so shy about this, and she said, 'Tess, you need to know that men are very messy. It is nature's way. If you want a good marriage, you understand that you must never deny Gus. Even if you are tired. If you keep some of these under your pillow at all times, it will help you clean up that mess he makes when you have intercourse.'"

Tess was laughing, but Jenny was speechless. Tess continued, "So, that's the way it was, and always has been. I could never deny Gus anything, not that I ever wanted to. He's my sun and moon. And I've been cleaning up his messes ever since."

Taking Jenny's chin in her hand and turning her head to look directly into her eyes, Tess said, "You can tell your dear sheriff that it was me who put the rocks on that man's face. Looking back, I see that I wasn't being rational; I'd just encountered a corpse, after all, and I was shocked. All I could think was that somehow I needed to hide him, hide who he was and that he was there. Hindsight. Of course, I realize now that wasn't possible. But right at that time, I didn't want him to be found. At that time, I thought Gus had killed him. And I needed to clean up his mess."

Jenny gasped. "You what!? Why? Why would Gus kill an ICE agent?"

Something flickered across Tess's eyes, a glimmer of uncertainty, but it passed, and she said, "In this world, on television, on the Internet, we hear so many stories of war, of rape, starvation, violence, and death. Sometimes they diminish the simple courage it takes to live life every day. Gus was brought from Germany during World War II, as a toddler. His father brought him. He and his father watched helplessly as his mother was shot to death at the German border by the Nazi version of ICE agents." She sighed. "He's old now, and the passing years should have healed him. It's been a long life. But somewhere deep in Gus the loss of his mother in that way created a powerful ability to recognize true evil, and to resist it by whatever means is available."

Tess looked away toward the mountains and murmured, "When a child's heart is injured, the anger may appear to be gone, but it will stay, deep, deep inside."

Suddenly, Jenny was flooded with an enormous respect for her own love, Sheriff Pat Garrett. Something was askew here, and Patrick would know what to say to Tess, what to ask. He would know what to do. She did not.

37

Garrett Receives Special Visitors

On Friday, the morning Jenny visited Tess, Garrett retreated to his office. He couldn't say he'd had a great night's sleep, but at least he'd gotten away for a while. He spent the last of Thursday evening on his patio sipping merlot, listening to a favorite old recording of Michele Campanella's dizzying fingers play Liszt's *Opera Paraphrases,* and letting his mind go blank. He was hoping this restorative effort would mean that when he entered the office in the morning, he would be struck by brilliant insights. It didn't work. He was as baffled as ever. With his door firmly closed, he fingered the reports, stared at the erase board, and struggled for answers. Then the door cracked open and Edith's head appeared; Garrett cursed.

"Not again, Edith! Can't you help me get just five minutes of peace?" Something about her face stopped him. She was smiling, pleased, but not the usual grin she flashed for office banter.

"These guests are very special, Sheriff. You're going to be happy to welcome them." She pushed the door fully open to admit a young man wearing a casual tee, Bermuda shorts, and sneakers without socks above which were tanned legs covered heavily in red hair; with him was a small woman in jeans, a bright red shirt, and sandals. Garrett didn't recognize either of them, and Edith simply ducked out the door, saying, "I'll get Mac and Asa."

Before Garrett could collect himself, the man stepped forward, held out his hand, and said, "Good morning, Sheriff.

It's good to meet you. I'm Noah Bridger, of Bridger Law Offices, P.C., based in Denver. And you may recognize this lady? Camilia Romero, from up by Croysant?" Camilia, too, shook hands.

Whoa! As Garrett went frantically into 'absorb this information' mode and greeted Bridger and Camilia, Mac and Hobbs entered, their faces thick with curiosity. Introductions were made, invitations to sit extended, and Edith miraculously appeared with a generous amount of donuts and coffee. Then Hobbs couldn't wait any longer.

"Where in the world have you been, Camilia? We've been looking everywhere for you. There has been a lot of concern here about your possibly being kidnapped."

Camilia smiled shyly and said, "I'm sure you know that an ICE agent came to our house. Eddy and I were so worried. We decided I should go to Denver and talk to somebody who could help. You see, my friend, Flor, had recommended Mr. Bridger to me, so I went there."

Hobbs frowned. "But how did you get to Denver? None of the vehicles you had access to have been taken. I've had people watching train stations, airlines, Uber, and so-on. Did you get a friend to drive you? But who?" Hobbs was annoyed with himself. This was a small area, and he felt that he should have been able to cover it.

Bridger laughed. Garrett noted that the freckled face had laugh lines beaten into it. This was a happy man. He said, "She didn't have time for all that, airplanes and so-on. And look what happened—she was afraid someone could track her, and she was right. You would have done it. No, she ran. She just ran right over to Denver and got me."

"Oh, come on. That's impossible!" Hobbs exploded. "You're not only talking 300 miles, but you're talking summer heat and Colorado's high mountain ranges. Camilia is a little woman ..."

McCracken, however, had begun to lose it. An expression of awe was creeping across her face. "OMG! Oh my god! Camilia, you ran! You aren't just any Mexican. You are a Tarahumara!"

Before Camilia could reply, the optimistic attorney said, "Well, Deputy, Camilia is, after all, not ashamed of being Mexican. But she would prefer that you refer to her as Raramuri.

Hidden Treasure (or) Where is Jesus?

'Tarahumara' is the name the Spanish colonialists gave her people. But," he concluded cheerfully, "You're right. Camilia is one of the running people."

This information left McCracken slack-jawed, sending her into a state of abject hero worship. Camilia nodded modestly, and Garrett was looking from person to person, trying to keep up. Fortunately, Hobbs's eidetic memory had kicked in, and he was ready to bring it into play. "Now I've got it!" he exclaimed. "Your people are the greatest runners in the entire world. They can outrun horses! Every Raramuri can run—men, women, little kids ..."

An embarrassed blush was creeping into Camilia's cheeks, but Hobbs and McCracken were on a roll. McCracken said, "That's right. The Tara ... uh, the Raramuri just run for fun. They live way back in the Sierra Madre, and they run from village to village to communicate. There've been big races even here, in Colorado, around Leadville and Telluride, and the Raramuri ran in those and amazed people because they win without even getting winded. At the end of the race all those trained runners, people like me, are bent over, sucking for breath and holding their sides, and the Raramuri winners are all just standing around, chatting and joking, like maybe they ran a lap in some gym."

Hobbs was fishing the statistics out of his own teeming brain now. "Garrett, Raramuri have been known to run 400 miles in 50 hours without stopping. A Raramuri whose name was Arnulfo Quimare ran the Boston Marathon in 3:38. I think that was in the nineties. As I understand it, the only thing that holds them back is that they are country people who don't much like traffic and so-on, and they prefer to run for fun rather than to compete."

"I'd give anything to run like you, Ms. Romero," McCracken babbled. "I've heard that when you run, your blood pressure goes down and your heart rate hits 130 at most. Do you have a special diet or anything?"

Camilia had given up. "Maybe you mix me, personally, up with what you call 'my people.' I pretty much eat American food, maybe some Mexican, like anyone else that likes their heritage. Anyhow, when I was raised in the Sierra Madres, we ate a lot of corn and beans. We had goats, and I remember lime trees. I heard that drought and climate change are making it hard to live there, now. Many of my family have told me that they don't always have enough to eat at all."

McCracken lowered her eyes. "I'm sorry. I didn't mean to be rude."

Smiling, Camilia said, "It's okay. You weren't rude. You just seem to admire 'my people' a lot. You look like an athlete yourself. Anyhow, we don't eat special stuff, just what we can grow and get." Glancing slyly at the sheriff, she said, "And we use a lot of peyote. A lot."

Still catching up, Garrett said, "Well, there you go. That must help, uh, keep you running." The others giggled.

Now feeling some pride, Camilia pointed at her sandals and said, "We run barefoot, you know, or in homemade huaraches. See? I made these. The straps are leather, and the bottoms, the soles, are tire rubber. When Raramuri run in America, they won't wear commercial running shoes. They bring their own huaraches."

Bridger was beaming. "Tell them about your Uncle Luis and the deer."

Camila shrugged. "Oh, that's just ... well, you know, Raramuri are said to hunt by outrunning their quarry. I don't remember that very much; I was little when I left the mountains. But I remember Uncle Luis when I was a little girl. We teased him because he bragged so much about the deer he outran. He bragged that he could always catch our dinner."

Like Mac, Hobbs was filled with awe. He said, "I read that when you watch a Raramuri run, they seem to move with the ground. What a phrase. To move with the ground."

McCracken breathed, "If I could just watch you run," to which Camilia responded, "No problem. Maybe we can run together some time. If we get to stay in America, that is."

"Camilia, I'm relieved you're safe," Garrett said. "But you're right. What about the immigration difficulties now?"

Bridger picked it up. "There is too much political upheaval around immigration law right now to make safe predictions. Our law firm can help; that's what we specialize in, you know, and we do a lot of work pro bono or financed through NGOs. Our company credo is that immigrants are America's hidden treasure; believe me, it's a hard principle to stand up for in the current political climate. Our first advice to the Romeros will be, of course, to keep a low profile for now. We're hoping your office can work with us."

McCracken said, "Did you know that the ICE agent that raided the Romeros was found murdered on a nearby ranch? We're up to our assholes in alligators here already."

This tickled Bridger. He laughed, then said, "We have been keeping tabs on events here as well as we can."

Garrett said, "I didn't report him to Immigration yet, but I'll have to do that before much longer. We're not sure of a name."

"We need to talk about that," Bridger said. "Camilia made it to Denver Saturday night, but she didn't contact me then because she didn't want to bother me on the weekend. Raramuri are famously courteous. Then I was in court Monday morning, so it was Monday afternoon before we could talk. After that, we took two days to do research. We worked our tails off, but I think you'll appreciate what we found out. It should help a little with Deputy McCracken's alligators."

Hobbs's curiosity was definitely piqued. "What you got, then?"

"The ICE agent had business cards with him when he busted into Romeros'. Camilia got one of them, and they give the guy's name as Roy Plover. I've got contacts at Immigration and Customs, so we followed that up. They're very good. They thoroughly checked files for me, found out who works there. No Roy Plover."

"You're shitting me!" The three law officers were gobstopped.

"On my word. You people got no ICE agent. Roy Plover was a fake. Fake agent, fake name, fake human. Period. Here's the deal. We know that this is a fairly common racket. There are a number of men who get hold of an official looking uniform, maybe even sew on the letters 'ICE' or 'POLICE' or both, and go to the homes of people who may not have all their immigration papers in order. It has so far been done most commonly in New York City, but it looks like it may have spread to the West. These bad actors bang on the door or burst into the house and act tough and threaten the family. Then they tell them they can 'fix' the problem for just a small sum of money. Usually the people from whom they are extorting will pay them as much as they can, out of fear. It can make a tidy income for the criminal."

"Well, I'll be go to hell," Garrett exclaimed.

Camilia, always soft-spoken, said, "That's what happened to us, except Toño walloped that guy with his safe and we got away."

"His *safe*?" This was developing into a series of eureka revelations. Garrett asked, "How could Toño wallop the guy with his safe?"

"It's okay," Bridger advised Camilia. "Just tell him what happened, Ms. Romero."

"Well, you know, our Toño doesn't just run well because he's Raramuri. He's an all around athlete. He's got an accurate, strong pitching arm. And he's smart, too! I'm sure that, from the minute that man opened his mouth, Toño spotted him as a crook." Camilia proceeded to tell the whole story of their terrifying night, and finished by saying, "So now Mr. Bridger is going to drive me on up to Croysant to finish sorting things out and get back with my men."

"She and her family should be safe?" Bridger asked, raising a questioning eyebrow at Garrett, and Garrett, getting the implication, nodded.

"Right now, Mr. Bridger, it appears I'll be dealing with my new problem. Just who the hell is that guy that we found in the culvert?"

38

Tess and Gus Tell Their Story

"She must know where Jesus is," McCracken commented after the cordial goodbyes.

Garrett and Hobbs did a double take. It hadn't occurred to them that the child wasn't with Camilia. Hobbs said, "I didn't think about the kid—I usually trust somebody else to look after the kids."

"Well, he wasn't with her, and we sure don't know where he is," Mac worried.

Garrett's phone rang. "Garrett here," and then, "You what?!" A long, long interlude. Mac and Hobbs refilled their coffee, ate donuts, and waited. Finally Garrett said, "We'll be up. Yeah, Mac and me. We'll go tend to it."

Deliberating, staring at the dry erase board which had remained nearly empty, Garrett pocketed his phone. He said, "That was Jenny. Asa, you still got Mr. Percy Bush in your sights?"

"Yes, sir, we do."

"Well, I think you'd better arrange to bring him in. We're going to have a few questions for him. And Mac, ask Edith to bring me that missing person report that the 'Perp' filled out. I need another look at it. Then I need you to go to evidence and bring us that knife we found at the scene. You and I are going to return it to Ms. Westberg."

Hobbs hesitated at the door. "Want to tell me what's going on, Boss?"

"Not yet, Asa. Just let me get my ducks in a row. I don't have the full picture, so we won't waste our precious time on speculation."

As expected, Tess met Mac and Garrett at the door. "I told Gus you were coming. He's irrigatin' up by the oak stand, but he agreed to wait and talk to you before he goes back out." She brought them through the large kitchen/dining area and settled them in the parlor. The inevitable cookies were on a large wooden coffee table made from a tree stump, and as they sat she went for iced tea. Gus appeared in the door, pushing a duckbill hat back on his sweaty head. "Darned hot," he commented. "Cooler here in the living room." He sat down in a brown vinyl recliner, passed the cookies, then stretched out his feet with a grunt of comfort.

Mac and Garrett agreed about the summer heat and took a cookie. Everyone waited for Tess. Mac was uncomfortable with the silence, but Gus appeared unperturbed. Only when Tess appeared with the frosty mugs of tea did he say, "Now, quit your fussing, Tess, and sit down. These people didn't come here to eat. They just want to follow up on what you told the Sheriff's girl." Tess sat.

Leaning toward her, Garrett said, "Mrs. Westberg, we hate to bother you, but things are coming to light, and we need to resolve this case."

Tess nodded. "Right. The man-in-the-culvert case. I understand, Sheriff."

Fishing in his pocket, Garrett produced the knife. "We think this is yours?" It was a question.

"Oh! Yes, it is! Thank you! That was my father's knife and I lost it when … I lost it just before … well, you must have found it down there by the culvert." She put the knife in her left jeans pocket, looking relieved. "I couldn't believe it was gone."

"Yes, we found it at the crime scene. Which brings me to the one very simple, but very important, question that I need to have answered today. That wasn't an ICE agent in that culvert, Mrs. Westberg. We know that now, and we believe you knew it, too, when you first saw the corpse. So who was that man, Mrs.

Hidden Treasure (or) Where is Jesus?

Westberg? The one you found in the culvert?"

Without wavering, Tess said, "It was Paul Frickleson."

This was news to McCracken. She shot a surprised glance toward the sheriff. He was saying, "So let me confirm this from what Jenny told me. You found Paul Frickleson dead in a culvert on your ranch, and you thought your husband had killed him, so to protect Gus, you tried to hide the corpse, and didn't report the death."

Tess had set her jaw and McCracken could imagine that she resembled the old settler stock from which she had arisen. This was now a woman who saw what had to be done, and she was determined to do it. She had considered the consequences and located within herself the power to endure them. You could see her upright stance, thinking that in the end, one must do what is right. Her answer for Garrett was direct. "Yes, Sheriff. That would be correct. Although I didn't tell Jenny who it was."

Garrett, however, had been watching not Tess, but Gus. The startled old man looked nonplussed. "Tess! You did what?"

"I did what the sheriff just said. I covered that horrible man with rocks and hoped that no one would ever find him or find out who he was. I mashed his face. He deserved it."

Quietly, Garrett asked, "And, Mrs. Westberg, why would you think your husband would kill Paul Frickleson?"

"I thought that because I know Gus has a powerful ability to recognize true evil, and he would not abide it. He has endured the Fricklesons all his life, and he would have reached a decision that the one thing he could do for this world would be to eliminate at least one of their kind."

Tess was making her case, but Gus had covered his face with his hands. He said, "Oh, lord. Here we go." Garrett said, "All his life, Tess?"

"All his life. Let me tell you. I wanted Gus from the first, from grade school, but in high school a girl called Joyce told him she was pregnant and that it was his baby, so he had to marry her. It couldn't have been his baby. They never even had … uh … relations. He told her that, and you wouldn't believe what she said! She said, 'Oh, I thought we did. Boys come and go, so who could know?' Oh, Mr. Garrett, this is so embarrassing! I can't imagine it, but that's what she said, isn't it, Gus? And she told him she would tell people the baby was his, no matter what he said, so no one would believe him."

Gus had dropped his hands from his face; he looked resigned. "Tess, honey, you didn't need to go so far back." Turning to the sheriff, he said, "She's right. It couldn't have been my baby. My father kept a tight rein on me then. Joyce was manipulative. She told me it might not literally be my baby, but if I would accept it and marry her, it would have a decent life, and otherwise not. I just couldn't do that, but I always felt guilty about the way it came out."

Tess said angrily, "She aborted that baby, that's how it came out! She aborted it, and blamed Gus. Could you believe that? Then she disappeared from around here for several years and when she came back she was married. Guess who she married."

Indicating they had no idea, Garrett and McCracken waited. Tess said, "She brought a racist, anti-Semitic, white supremacist here into our good valley. His name was John Paul Frickleson. He was a trouble maker."

Garrett and McCracken looked at each other, trying to do the math. Tess said, "Oh, not the one you are dealing with. Not the younger man that ended up stuffed in the culvert. That's the son. The one who came here with Joyce was his father. And Joyce and the older John Paul filled their son with anger and lies from the day he was born. Unfortunately, their evil seeds of hatred fell on fertile ground."

Gus said, "Well, eventually they moved away again. We were relieved. Tess is right. They led a debauched life. It killed them both at an early age."

"We were relieved," Tess continued, "But only for a while. A few years ago, the son, the young Frickleson, moved back here. He decided he had a vendetta against Gus. He accused him of killing his brother, the aborted baby. He would show up where Gus was trying to irrigate and accuse him of thinking he was too good to marry his mother, Joyce. Gus loves to irrigate. Moving that water and bringing it to the thirsty fields, that soothes his soul. But it got so he could barely leave the house without running into Paul Frickleson, and that man's mouth just seethed with racist and anti-Semitic filth."

Gus gave an odd chuckle. "The man was like so many racists; his ideology was devoid of logic. One minute he would accuse me of being an anti-American Nazi, and the next he would say I was a 'dirty Jew.' I tried to reason with him. I explained that I was *mischlinge*, meaning mixed race. My mom was Jewish, and my dad was a pure Aryan who hated Hitler. This was just grist for the mill of someone like Frickleson; after that, whenever he saw me, he'd say, "Oh, there goes the Nazi Jew.

"So, anyhow, Tess, I'm not sure you should have told the sheriff all of this. You're a stubborn woman with a big mouth." He smiled innocently at Garrett, but the look he then fixed on Tess was one of well-seasoned enchantment.

The room fell silent. Finally, Garrett said, "Well, Gus, did you in fact kill Paul Frickleson?"

Good humoredly, Gus shook his head. "Of course not. I wouldn't repay evil with evil."

Garrett was smiling. "I didn't think you did. I'm just happy we could clear this all up."

As McCracken and Garrett stood to go, Gus laughed. "But we do need to be honest about one thing. I am real glad he's dead."

39

A Wager is Made and Won

Back in the car, McCracken said quietly, "But you know, don't you, Chief? I can tell that you already know who did it."

"Yeah, I think maybe I do." Garrett slowed the car to pull onto Highway 46. Both he and Mac stared at Frickleson's house as they passed, still appalled by what had been found there.

Mac said, "Well, I guess the murderer wasn't Mr. John Paul Frickleson."

Garrett sighed. "No, you might say he was a little indisposed at the time." Mac snorted, then Garrett continued. "I think you better get a land line. Have Red and Louie pick up Nola Rippe and bring her in. Asa may have picked up 'Percy Bush' already, so let the deputies know that we don't want any contact between Bush and Rippe." Looking at the car clock, the sheriff said, "It's two-thirty now. You want to give me some odds as to what time you think we'll have a confession?"

Throwing him her shit-eating grin, Mac said, "Now, Sheriff. Law officers don't gamble. I just figure Red and me will be eating supper by six. Six, I say! And the food will no doubt cost ten bucks."

"See you that and raise you to a 5:30 at twenty bucks." Before Mac could say "sure," he'd hit the gas pedal and put on the flashers. Thrown back against her seat, Mac laughed and said, "Cheater."

For the rest of the way, Garrett was silent, weighing possible approaches to the task ahead. He knew where "Percy Bush" fit in, which meant he could use that knowledge to threaten Rippe or tempt her with a plea bargain. Truth was, he didn't want to bargain with this woman. He didn't want to flatter her, either, but from what he'd learned about her so far, he thought flattery might work. Flattery was what his deputies teased him about, calling it one of the sheriff's "most notorious enhanced interrogation techniques." Well, at least it wasn't water boarding, and this time it might work. By the time they got her into the interview room, he'd convinced himself that flattery was the way to go. Besides, he had the other tools for back-up.

The woman was pale, showing all the signs of opioid withdrawal. She kept yawning, her eyes tearing, her nose running. She wiped it on her shirt tail; like father, like daughter. The discomfort should help bring her around. Mac, Louie, and Red were in the room, leaning against the wall by the door. Garrett didn't want so much police presence, but they were stoney-faced and silent. He understood that they needed the emotional release of hearing this woman say what she had done. The public defender arrived and sat beside Nola.

Garrett, across the table from Nola Rippe and the P.D., pushed the button on the recorder and led with, "Well, you are one amazing woman. I can't imagine how you pulled all that off."

Nola Rippe offered a sickly smile and a shrug. Garrett continued, "Of course, as a law officer, one of the things I noticed first was the gun. That wasn't your own gun, and it was an unusual gun, too. Two barrels, one a .45 and one a shotgun, each with only one shot. You must really know your guns, to be able to figure it out so fast."

The P.D. raised her eyebrows, but before she could intercede, Nola, believing Garrett was as incompetent as he claimed to be, answered him. "Oh, Christ, Sheriff. Any good marksman knows that little gun. The Bond Arms Cowboy Defender? Look it up. Your deputies over there know it. Just look it up. Shooters love it. It wasn't that hard to use it, anyhow. That was Frick's gun. I'd used it for target practice a dozen times over at his place."

Still keeping his admiring tone, Garrett said, "But even so,, you shot Frankie Belle dead on from over twenty feet away. And in a public place!"

The P.D. flinched and her mouth shot open, but Rippe was faster. "I sure did, didn't I? And I had on surgical gloves, too, for fingerprints, those clear ones that people wouldn't notice." She sniffled. "Well planned, I say, and all by me, alone." The P.D. subsided back into her chair, her hands opened out in a gesture of resignation.

Garrett nodded and said, "Oh, Deputy McCracken, I'm not sure of the time. What time is it? Could you make a note?"

"It's 5:17, Chief," she responded, but she shot a knowing look at him, thinking, 'You sly dog, you. You're making sure that I'm aware I just lost twenty bucks.'

"Okay, thank you then, Deputy. Now, Ms. Rippe, you didn't just shoot those people. Somehow you got Paul Frickleson feet first into Westbergs' culvert. You shot him at the old school house, right? The community club house now. But why a culvert? And why Westbergs'? And then … well, it's just amazing. How did you do all that? Did you have his gun with you already and …" he paused, genuinely curious. "… and what next?"

Nola Rippe jumped up, knocking over her chair. "No, Jesus Christ! That's not how it happened. You tell it right, damn it. Give me some credit." She began to pace, wringing her hands. The deputies stiffened, wary. They knew, as did Garrett, that she was exhibiting the agitation associated with opioid withdrawal, and that she could rapidly turn violent.

Garrett said soothingly, "But that's the point. We do want to know the truth. You need to tell us what happened." He restored the chair to its place.

Sitting again, she turned to the sheriff, knees jerking and hands flipping restlessly against the table surface. "You're right. People don't appreciate me. They think irrigators are dumb. I've been hired to irrigate just damn near every ranch in that valley, and I know things. How to get the water where it belongs, but more than that. Last Thursday I got done late, and I was headed over to Gallenas's to get those stupid little bastards, Syd and Spook. I saw Frick's car parked at the community house, which was unusual, since why wouldn't he just park at his own place across the road? It didn't look like he was around, so I stopped to have a look. And there was the gun, right on the front seat, all loaded and ready for business."

Her hands had stopped twitching and she leaned toward Garrett, her voice heavy with confidentiality. "I'd been wondering for some time what I need Frick for, anyhow. There were the two businesses, the kids and the drugs. Old Papa Powder — he probably called himself Percy Bush to you guys. He has a real name somewhere, but that's not it. Anyhow, him and his people get the opioids in Denver, sometimes other places, for us to distribute here. We take pictures of the girls, then we trade. Of course, he gets a kickback, too. He's got a lot of clients who deal in naked little girl pictures, but he said ours are some of the better ones. And he thinks the girls have good career potential as they grow. He sells pictures everywhere — on the street, over the Internet, you know."

A muffled gagging sound was coming from where the deputies stood, but Nola didn't notice. "The important thing was, you see, was that there was no point in Frickleson. He was trying to cut me out. Him and Frankie Belle. He had old Frankie on the hook with the drugs. She was his puppet. Between him and that soft old bastard, Mickey, they convinced Frankie to turn me into Social Services."

Rippe was getting worked up again. Garrett considered the implication that the 'old bastard' was her own father, but he kept quiet. "Frick even filed for custody the other day. They were going to take those girls, those dirty, scheming assholes. He claimed to be the father. Fat chance. And they were going to claim I wasn't a fit mother because of drugs. Now, how does that sit with you for irony, huh? Anyhow, those are my girls. I own them, and I wasn't going to let anybody get hold of them now that they might turn into real money makers. For sure not Frick, the prick."

She was back up, pacing. "So when I saw that loaded gun, I thought, 'now's my chance. We'll see who cuts who out.' I waited, and when he came waltzing along and pulled open the car door, I pushed him back. Then I shot him. Shot him dead. Right there in the old school yard. Then I did Frankie Belle in on Saturday because, you know, why the hell not?"

She followed this last statement with a high, hysterical giggle, then a fit of violent retching. Louie stepped forward with a plastic basin. Later, Mac asked her why she had brought the basin, and Louie laughed. "Ah, shit, Mac, police work mixed with motherhood. See, when you got six kids and an epidemic of stomach flu hits the neighborhood, you know ahead to put your kids to bed at night with puke pails all over the place. And when you arrested enough addicts, you come prepared for them, too."

After Nola Rippe had emptied an already fairly empty stomach, her P.D. made another attempt to stand up for her. "I think Ms. Rippe has had enough stress for this evening, Sheriff," to which an ungrateful Nola responded violently.

"Shut up, you old bat! These people want to know how I got the nasty bastard into that culvert."

Garrett, feeling more relaxed now, said, "Well, that we do. That we do."

On fire with her craving for the drugs she could no longer have, Nola Rippe couldn't sit. She faced the cluster of law officers who had grouped themselves near the table and became an orator, illustrating her descriptions with violent motions indicating lifting the weight of the corpse, and wild gestures showing the process involved in its disposal. "See," she expounded, "I was on my ATV, had my shovel and all with me. Like I said, I know all the irrigation systems up there, and I knew that culvert of Westbergs' was the nearest one that would be even close enough to the right size to fit old Frick into. A summer storm was raising hell with my work, but I got him wrapped in some plastic, that thick stuff I use to make dams with. I figured the storm and plastic would help to control the blood. Then I got the dirty bastard up on the back of the four-wheeler." This was acted out and easily imagined, as Nola Rippe was a husky woman.

"Awkward," she continued. "He was floppy and awkward. I had to use five bungee cords to get him tied down, but I finally got him. When I got to Westbergs', the old farts had their lights out, probably in bed, so I just went right on down to the culvert. I had to hurry then, because the storm was building up again over to the southeast.

"I got him off the four-wheeler and laid him feet first at the top of the pipe and tied his feet together with baling twine. Then I tied a stick to some more twine and floated the stick through the culvert. You know, how kids do with toy boats? That was the hardest part. The stick kept hanging up inside the culvert. It was like a nightmare fishing trip, where your line keeps getting tangled in the rocks at the bottom of the creek." All this was accompanied by tugs and flourishes to illustrate the stubbornness of the line.

"Once I finally got it through, though, I could drive the ATV on down to the pipe outlet and tie that twine to the lead on the winch. I used a good square knot and was thankful for the miracle of baling twine. It's good, strong shit. Oh, yeah, and of course, I'd tied the upper end of my twine to the twine I used to bind Frick's feet together."

Suddenly, Nola played out. She dropped like a stone back into her chair. "Then I just did it. Got on my ATV, started up the winch, and winched him through." She was gasping for air. "I winched the asshole right on into the pipe, and he should have been clear inside it. Then you assholes wouldn't have found him so damn fast, and maybe I could've made it out of the country. But my knot wasn't as good as it should have been, up by the feet. It slipped and got untied. It came off. Too much hurry, hurry. Plus the pipe was a little narrower than I remembered. He kind of hung up at the shoulders. Anyhow, I had to leave his head out. I couldn't do more. It was starting to really fire up another round of lightning, and the storm was threatening with a come-to-Jesus attitude. I had to gather up my stuff and leave." She sighed, holding her head. "It was kind of good, in a way. I figured the storm helped with the tracks and the blood. All I had left to do was pull his car over to his place so it wouldn't look suspicious, and go pick up the little shits."

She seemed to have finished. Garrett said, "Thank you, Ms. Rippe. That was an amazing story."

As he clicked off the recorder, Nola said, "I know you got my buddy here, Mr. Papa Powder. Wish I could have seen him before you caught him. You people fucked me up royally when you started swarmin' over Frick's house this week. I ran out of stuff, you know, and I truly feel like shit right now. I could have got some relief from the stuff Papa Powder brought if my plan had went right." She got up to be escorted out by her P.D.

Tired of treating her with any respect, Garrett gave a curt nod. "Yes, I'm sure you could." The deputies were clustered by the door, talking quietly as Garrett gathered himself up. At that point, the door opened. It was Edith.

"Good grief, Edith!" the sheriff burst out. "You poor woman—don't you ever go home? I suppose this is another emergency."

"It most certainly is, Boss." Edith looked worried. "No one can find Jesus."

40

Finding Jesus

Garrett was depleted. He went to the Cowpath first, in search of a burger and of Jenny. He needed to replenish both his tummy and his soul. Jenny met him at the door, wringing her hands. "It's my fault, Patrick. Lew Harris told me he had a little boy in his car, and I just shrugged it off. I just thought it was more of 'crazy old Lew' talking, and forgot all about it. That was last Thursday! Jesus has been gone a week!"

His arms went around her and he allowed himself one long breath, his nose buried in the fragrant dark hair, then he had to move it along. Jenny brought the burger and coffee and watched him eat while she talked. "Here's how I understand it. Camilia's lawyer dropped her off at Clarys' and went on back to the motel in Peaseford. He said he could use a night's sleep, and apparently he thought that since the Romeros were together and temporarily safe from immigration cops, they could get the rest sorted out themselves.

"So Eddie and Cammy went over to Westbergs' and got Toño, then to Lew's. That's where Eduardo thought Jesus was supposed to be. Of course, when they got to Lew's, he told them a garbled story about how he thought Eddie wanted him to keep the two little girls, instead. That would have been Rippe's daughters."

Around a mouthful of burger, Garrett mumbled, "Not anymore."

Awful events need to find humor to ease the pain. Jenny

answered Garrett's comment with, "Well, I guess it's just too bad, then. The girls have lost their mother and the ranchers have lost the best irrigator they ever had."

Garrett just looked up with a weak smile and shook his head. "Oh, Jenny."

"Okay, sorry. Well, anyhow, somewhere, somehow, Lew got those kids mixed up. He has no idea what became of Jesus. The Romeros went to Nancy Jane's and to Alma's, neither place with any success. No Nancy Jane there, either. Now there's less than an hour of daylight left and the search parties are out everywhere and getting frantic."

Were they ever! Even his deputies. Garrett had told his deputies that they'd done great with Bush and Rippe, and that they were done for the day, but they ignored him and headed to Croysant. The deputies wanted to go back to Lew Harris's to see what they could turn up. Garrett had spotted the teen squad all over the hills just outside the Cowpath, and Tiffany, Larry's mom, was parked with the advanced life support unit in the Cowpath lot, taking radio traffic and coordinating search efforts.

Since Larry and Pewter had taken Syd and Spook from Lew's house, Garrett asked Jenny if she knew where the little girls were now that the Gallenases were preoccupied with this search, and she beamed, happy to give him one good report. "The Fouriers have them right now. Patrick, I think the Fouriers are going to try to adopt those little girls. Honey and Garfield have wanted to have children for years, and that big pushover, Garfield, fell in love with those girls when he met them. Honey seems thrilled, and of course, Larry and Pewter will still be in place as head baby sitters. They're all good people."

This information made Garrett much happier. He was ready to join the search for Jesus. He'd just finished his coffee when Noah Bridger appeared in the doorway, his normally cheerful face sober. "Sheriff. I heard you were here. They tell me Camilia didn't find her boy?"

"That's right." Garrett introduced the lawyer to Jenny, then said, "Jenny was just catching me up to spin. Apparently we have a lot of neighborhood search parties that have formed."

Jenny wiped her hands on a bar towel. "I think the main ones are where they think he disappeared. The teen squad has spread out here near the Cowpath; the deputies and the official Search and Rescue groups are combing over every bush and twig, as well as the pond, over at Lew Harris's place; and a random bunch of people are searching up at Nancy Jane Barnswallowper's."

The attorney was horrified. "Good lord, they think he may be lost outside? He may have been gone for a week! And there's that big Croysant Reservoir just over there."

Garrett felt his stomach tighten. 'Happy hour' was definitely over. He didn't want to think about implications yet. To Bridger's comment he said, "I know." Jenny twisted the bar towel while Garrett worked his mustache. "Yeah," he repeated. "I know. All not good. But let's try ... um, let's try to get more information before we go off half cocked. Jen, what would you think of calling Duz and Carmen, or maybe Gritty, or both, and see if they'd meet us at their mom's place. Maybe we can get farther with her than Romeros did if we get her family there." To Bridger, he said, "You should come with us. You don't know this country well enough to search without getting lost yourself. Alma is this very old lady just up the road here. Her memory is shot, but sometimes she knows things she doesn't think she knows, if that makes any sense. She will just need us to listen carefully and decode."

Bridger nodded, confused but willing to cooperate, and Jenny said, "Well, I think Alma is pretty sharp, if you want to know the truth." She closed her phone. "Duz and Carmen have been searching along Oozle, but they're on their way. Gritty is already there. Mr. Bridger, as I understand it, last week when they fled from the ICE agent, Eddie and Cammy left little Chucho at Alma's for Lew to pick up. So that will be a good place to start, if you want to help us out."

For some reason, Bridger had imagined Alma's children to be young people. When they arrived, he found them to be in their sixties. The one in the wheelchair, introduced as Gritty, was brisk. She hustled them into a room crowded with furniture that had seen better days. She pointed to a chair near Alma's recliner for the sheriff, then just as everyone else was finding a place, Toño and Gordy arrived. "Sheriff, we heard you were here.

Any news?" Garrett thought that Toño's demeanor was far too strained for that of any teenaged kid.

Alma, meanwhile, was patting Garrett's hand. "This is so nice of you to visit, Lyle. I know your mother, you know. Does she still have that beautiful garden?"

They had been down this road before. Garrett had given up on explaining to Alma that he was not Lyle, his handsome brother. She knew who he was, anyhow; she just had the names switched. He also did not want to go into the fact that his mother had been deceased for many years. Instead, he said kindly, "Yes, her garden is always beautiful."

Looking around at the half dozen people seated near her, Alma was very excited. She wasn't sure that she knew all these people or why they had come, but she loved to be in the middle of important activity. She said, "Lyle, Gritty says you are here because you've lost a child."

Duz started to clarify for her, beginning, "Mom, the child…" but Alma interrupted. "Oh, I'm sorry. Gritty, these people need cookies. Could you and Carmen bring iced tea and cookies?" Then she addressed Garrett again. "I can't stand iced tea myself, but everyone else seems to need it. Now Duz, over there. You know Duz, right, Lyle? Duz just loves candy. Has ever since he was a little boy." She indicated a full candy dish on the dresser across from her. "Duz, you must share your candy. Pass it around. Don't be selfish. Now, what were we discussing?"

Patiently, Duz sent the candy dish around the room, but Toño had reached the end of his tether. His voice cracking, he said, "Mrs. Weinant, do you know where Jesus is?"

Toño had given his brother's name its English pronunciation. He now had Alma's full attention. "Oh! You boys finally came back for your paper. I thought it was the other boys that brought it, but you know, sometimes I get confused. Of course, I know where your Jesus is. That bad man took it. Remember, Duz, when I called you about the bad man here in the house? He said he was police, but you could tell he wasn't."

Garrett and Jenny were exchanging looks. Ah, yes, the figurine in Frickleson's pocket! But Alma wasn't done. Her heavy old voice continued, as coherent as a young woman's. "But lucky for your father, I put his important paper in a different Jesus. There might be something about it being Jesus, but I had a funny feeling it shouldn't be just sitting out there in plain sight, so after you boys left I moved it to the Jesus that Doreen Van Doren brought me from Rio. She said the Jesus she brought is made after a big statue they have in Brazil called Christ the Redeemer. She is very Catholic, which is okay, so she brought it as a souvenir from her vacation." As she talked, Alma was fishing clumsily in her cardigan pocket. "Here it is. I thought your paper would be safer with this Jesus guarding it instead of the other one." She handed the figurine to Toño, who was so stunned, he fumbled and almost dropped it.

Noah Bridger held out his hand and took the statue, then poked around with his finger at the hollow middle. He removed the lottery ticket. Holding it out to Toño, he said, "Okay, Toño, that's the ticket, all right, your father's lottery ticket that your mother told me about. Boy, is he going to be happy to see that — it's a scratch ticket worth $20,000! Like I told Camilia, he can cash it without being identified as an illegal immigrant because there are ways to get his winnings that involve setting up a trust." The joy had returned to Bridger's friendly, freckled face. "From what your mother told me, this will go a long way toward that college education you deserve."

Toño fingered the ticket and stared uncomprehendingly at the lawyer. Gordy spoke for him. "Mr. Bridger, you understand that if we can't find Jesus, Toño can't care about winning the lottery."

Gordy had given the name the Spanish pronunciation, and Alma's head shot up, her face excited and alert. "Oh, 'hay-soos'! Is that the boy you lost? Why, just the other day Lew picked him up right here. Eduardo and Camilia left him here for Lew, and Lew picked him up. Lew and I had a long conversation about whether to call him 'Jesus,' since he is in America, or 'hay-soos.' Jesus is probably correct, but I've thought it over, and I think a child should be called by the name a mother gives him."

Greta Amelia, a.k.a. Gritty, and Douglas Ulysses Zane, a.k.a. Duz, may have missed the irony of that statement, although Carmen was looking at her mother-in-law with the high degree of insight that she had gained over the years from having lived with this family. Garrett said cautiously, "So your old friend, Lew Harris, picked 'Hay-soos' up here at your house?"

"Or Jesus. You can call him Jesus, if you want. I love children, no matter what you call them."

Jenny could attest to that. Alma had a comforting way with children that was almost magical, but sadly, this conversational direction didn't seem to be getting them very far. What had Lew done with Jesus after he picked him up here? Was he really in the car by the time Lew arrived at the Cowpath that night, leaving him to supposedly be guarded by Lucky?"

Alma was tiring. She said sleepily, "Did I ever tell you, Jenny, about my sister Elaine? When she got older, she just repeated herself and repeated herself."

For some reason, this made Jenny weepy again. Gritty shared a crooked smile with her. "You did, Mom. You told us that. Now maybe it's time for all these nice people to leave, and we'll get you tucked in for the night."

Alma wasn't done talking, however. She added, as if Gritty hadn't spoken, "You know, I just love Lew, but he's getting older now, too. He's getting addled, like my sister, Elaine. I think maybe that's why he decided he was just too old to take care of a little guy like Jesus."

Everyone in the room had been standing to go, and the whole group stopped dead in their tracks. Duz spoke first. "So didn't Lew keep Jesus?"

Alma said, "Oh, no, of course not. You remember. He took him to Patch. I don't know why he decided on Patch. That man is darned near as old as Lew, but then, you know how it is between Patch and Hallie Flute's saucy little niece. The whole community knows they have a thing going on. Lew probably figured that with Nancy Jane to help him, Patch would do okay. You know, that Barnswallowper girl is very capable."

Duz had knelt at his mother's knee. "Mom, Patch? Are you sure?"

"I'm tired, Duz. Can't you remember? Patch and Nancy Jane came by just the other day for children's books for little Jesus, and while he was here, he found a stuffed rabbit. He hugged it

Hidden Treasure (or) Where is Jesus?

so hard that we agreed he should take that, too."

The boys were already out the door as Jenny and Bridger were saying polite thank-you's for the cookies, but Garrett hung back. Alma was drifting, almost asleep. The sheriff, occasionally known as Lyle, couldn't resist. He put an affectionate hand on her forehead and leaned down to give her a gentle kiss. Her eyes came open and she looked up at him blearily. "It's true, isn't it? You can look, but you can't always find Jesus where you expect to find him."

Nancy Jane Barnswallowper knew when she was surrounded. It would do no good to reach for her gun, because these were her neighbors; she couldn't shoot her neighbors, and they just kept coming. The Fowlers, the Clarys, the Harrises, the Browns and Johnsons, those nosy teenagers, and, unfortunately, there was the sheriff and his woman and some of his deputies. She turned to Patch. "What can we do?"

"We gotta stand our ground. We ain't gonna let 'em take the kid. Here, cover him up with my coat. I'll try to talk to 'em." Nancy Jane reached in the back to throw the coat over Jesus, sitting in his car seat, but he was having none of it. He felt he was too old for a peek-a-boo game, especially one that hampered his breathing, and he vigorously kicked the coat to the floor of the truck. The sheriff was knocking on the passenger window, so Nancy Jane had to give up on her futile effort to hide Jesus. She rolled down her window.

"Ms. Barnswallowper, where on earth have you been?"

"Sheriff, I'll be honest with you. I had to hide out up at Outlaw's Roost, you know, above my place up K-4 road. You drive up there quite a ways, then take that loggin' road left …" She noticed the impatient look on Garrett's face. "Anyhow, we had to come back for mi … uh …" She had started to say 'milk', but thought this might mean he had caught her red handed. Instead, she finished, "We came back for supplies. Don't you worry about us; we can get out of your way in just a minute."

"But why were you hiding?"

"Well, Sheriff, you should know. Your deputy should have told you. I got in trouble with the law. I went into Frickleson's place and stumbled onto some drugs. I smelled 'em to see what they was. Now I suppose you have to run me in for sniffin' drugs. Your deputies saw me, but I didn't intend to do it. Will that help my case, Sheriff? I guess I gotta go with you, but now Patch is different. He has been with me, but there isn't any way he is a, uh, what you call them people? An accessory. He ain't no accessory to my crimes, so you should let him go right now."

Garrett peered past her into the back seat. "But you have little Jesus Romero there in back. What are you doing with him?" Then, it having been a long day, the sheriff couldn't resist. "Are you trying to kidnap him?"

Her jig was up. This was worse than she had thought. Nancy Jane decided to throw herself on the mercy of the law. "Oh, Mr. Garrett, I am going to come clean and pray that you will help us. There is a federal agent on the loose, and he's trying to arrest the Romeros. They didn't do a single thing, but they're Mexicans. I'm afraid they won't get a fair shake in court. They got away last week, but then Patch went in for soda pop and he found little Jesus wandering around outside Lew Harris's car. Jesus was tryin' to find Lucky; he said Lucky got out of the car. We don't know what happened to the rest of the Romeros, but we are going to keep Jesus safe as long as we have to."

Jim Patchit, sitting in the driver's seat, had the deepest, most rumbling, troll-like voice of anyone in Riversmet County, and he used it now. "Sheriff, I tell you, ain't nobody gonna hurt this kid." The roar of the man's vocal cords made Garrett jump and people come to gather around the pickup.

Looking up at the approaching crowd, Garrett began to smile. "Well, Mr. Patchit, we couldn't agree with you more. All these people you see coming up here want to help you keep Jesus safe. You two aren't in trouble. We just think it's time now for him to join the rest of his family. Look over there. Can you see, in the light from your headlamps?"

As Patch and Nancy Jane leaned forward to peer into the darkness, Garrett quietly reached into the back seat and unbuckled the car seat. Jesus said, "Bye, bye, *mis abuelos*," and scrambled from the seat. The old couple didn't hear him. They had spotted the Romeros, running up the hill toward them. The *chabochi* had moved to the roadside, making space for them to run, and everyone was clapping. Toño and Camilia were far ahead of Eduardo, but all of their faces glowed with relief and joy.

Toño felt his body move with the ground as he surged past his mother to reach for the little brother who was dashing toward him, his tiny bare feet effortlessly skimming along the gravel road.

A Thank-You

You wouldn't be reading this book if a lot of good people hadn't read, edited, advised, and encouraged me while it was coming together. I'm talking about Erin M. Gallob, Douglas J. Gallob, Judy Elliott-Gallob, Sara Ferguson, Tanya Applegate, Joe Applegate, David A.C. Gallob, Diana Matus, Rita Clagett, Cheyenne and Matt Weedman, and David G. Gallob. But enough about these people. I wanted to start with the Fed Ex guy.

To the best of my knowledge, this man, who works, yes, for Fed Ex, never thought of himself as an immigrant at all. He is, though. He wasn't born in America, and throughout his life he has encountered many of the difficulties that besiege an immigrant: language barriers, prejudice, and, at first, the confusion of finding yourself somewhere totally different from your place of birth. When he first came to America, at age three, Dave and I used to wake up in the middle of the night to find him standing beside our bed, looking at us with an expression that said, "Who the hell are you people?"

That was then. This is now. Now, Miles peacefully goes about his normal American life with his beautiful wife, Shashawna (Irish/Cherokee extraction) and our exceptional granddaughters, Torriayn and Mahlia. Miles came to us from Vietnam, and because he did, all our lives have been immeasurably enriched. Because of him, I have a deeper understanding of what it takes to be a part of this country. Special thanks, then, to our son, Miles David Gallob.

Next, I want to thank Tim Carpenter, our grandson-in-law, who is with the state department and works on border logistics. Right now he is in Portugal, but as I was writing this book he was stationed in Juarez. He gave me much valuable information about border crossings from Mexico, the perils and the legalities. Thank you, Tim, for helping out! And, of course, thanks to Roxanne, his wife, our granddaughter, and the necessary link in the information chain that leads to Tim.

Hidden Treasure (or) Where is Jesus?

I'm particularly grateful to the Ramirez family, who so warmly welcomed Dave, Erin, and I into their home. They shared their experiences as immigrants to this country. They also shared delicious flan and salmon! Learning from them provided me with clarity, information, and the inspiration to create the immigration story you find in this book.

I am always grateful to my publisher and editor, she who owns Earth Star Publications, Ann Miller. She is utterly reliable when it comes to producing a beautiful, well-formatted book that I can be proud of.

Sincere thanks, also, to Jerry and Alice Zeldenthuis, who helped with the research critical to this book.

Now, back to the incredible friends and family I named at the first of this section. I want to thank them all from the bottom of my heart. I want to thank them for introducing me to Necrosearch. I want to thank them for fixing ellipses. I want to thank them for correct spellings, such as 'clench,' not 'clinch,' and 'winch,' not 'wench.' I want to thank them for the advice I didn't follow, such as details about defendant interviews, because I couldn't make it fit the narrative. I want to thank them for spotting problems with bullet vs. shotgun shell wound descriptions. And for advice about Fortnite and TeenSpeak. And for saying it was the best Garrett mystery so far. And for so many other things that the list would make a whole new book, so I'll stop here, and just trust that these people know how much I appreciate them.

And what, you might be asking, about this David G. Gallob person I mentioned earlier? Well, duh. That man is indispensable. He is the love of my life.

About the Author

Karen Weinant Gallob, a rancher, writer, anthropologist, and the matriarch of a big, bulky, sprawling family, publishes articles, reviews, stories, poetry, and novels. She's interested in the relationships among language, culture, and human perceptions of reality. Her work is deeply informed by her unique — occasionally somewhat warped :-) — understanding of this North Fork Valley community into which she was born. Some of her neighbors are EMT's who like to learn about Flight for Life transport. This apparently pleases her.

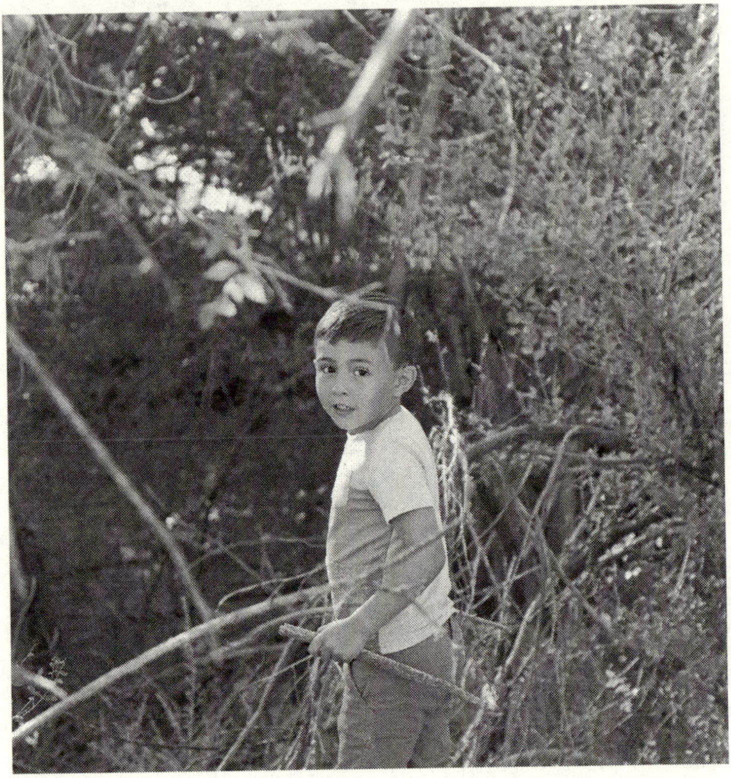

Made in the USA
San Bernardino, CA
05 November 2018